Praise for Skye Taylor

"Time to pack up and head to Florida where revenge makes for a bloody summer for Detective Jesse Quinn. Don't miss **Bullseye**, a sensational kick-off to a fresh new mystery series." ~ C. Hope Clark, author of the award-winning Edisto Island Mysteries and The Carolina Slade Mysteries. www.chopeclark.com

"Skye Taylor's **Worry Stone** is a deeply emotional tale. Authentic and evocative, this love story between a veteran and a one-time war protester makes us appreciate the healing power of love. I loved it!" ~ Eve Gaddy, National Bestselling author of Trouble in Texas

"Falling for Zoe is a deftly plotted and delightful story of family, of real life, and love, and trying to do the right thing. **Falling for Zoe** is a romantic gem." ~ Cheryl Reavis, Best selling, award-winning author

"Bravo Zulu for **Healing a Hero**, filled with turmoil, tenderness, and painful secrets from the past. Will Gunnery Sergeant Philip Cameron have to choose between the Corps and the woman he loves?" ~ Heather Ashby, author of the Love in the Fleet series

BULLSEYE
A Jesse Quinn Mystery

Dan Hoffman's wife is dead. His fingerprints are on the glass prism she was bludgeoned with, and powerful people want him in cuffs. But Detective Jesse Quinn has a history with Dan and she believes he's innocent.

A man on the run claims the murder is tied to a long-ago cover-up over an incident in Afghanistan. Four people are dead, and two attempts have been made. A rival in the Sheriff's office wants to take over the investigation and time is running out.

Will Jesse be able to put all the pieces together before she is sidelined and Dan arrested for his wife's murder?

The Jesse Quinn Mysteries
Bullseye
Framed (coming in 2021)

The Camerons of Tide's Way Novels
Contemporary Romance
Falling for Zoe
Loving Meg
Trusting Will
Healing a Hero
Keeping His Promise
Worry Stone
Loving Ben (Short Story)
Mike's Wager (Short Story)

Also by Skye Taylor
Time Travel Romance
Iain's Plaid

Political suspense
The Candidate

DEDICATION

To my kids – Lori, Alex, Rebecca, Bobbi and Jeff

I can't imagine my life without you. Without the love, the challenges, and the rewards of being a parent and watching you become the smart, wonderful, giving adults all of you grew up to be. Thanks for always being there for me, and for cheering me on in whatever new adventure I take on, from jumping out of perfectly good airplanes, to jumping into the whole new career of becoming a published author.

BULLSEYE

A Jesse Quinn Mystery

Skye Taylor

SandCastleBooks.net

SandCastleBooks
Print ISBN: 978-1-7322287-7-1

Published in the United States of America

Skye Taylor enjoys hearing from her readers.
Visit her at: www.Skye-writer.com

Cover design by Carrie Richter –The Monkey Factory
Interior layout by Capri Porter

CHAPTER 1

I WHISTLED AS I PULLED INTO MY DRIVEWAY. My next-door neighbor perched on a stool before an easel painting yet another picture of the dunes and the sea beyond. At least that's what she appeared to be studying so intently before daubing the canvas with her brush. I waved as I skirted Seth Cameron's fire-engine red Dodge Ram. Seemed like my son's former tutor, now friend and mentor spent more time here helping Mike with the all-consuming task of rebuilding an old Camaro than he did at his own place high in the dunes just two miles down the road. Maybe because he only got to spend time with his twin boys on the weekend and didn't enjoy rattling around in his house alone. Or was it because he hadn't given up trying to get something going with me?

His interest wasn't one-sided, but life as a single mom with a demanding career made me wary of adding to my emotional commitments. I enjoyed his company, but right now, after an exhausting day dealing with an abused wife and her drunk husband, I looked forward to the peace and comfort of a glass of wine with my feet up on the railing of my deck.

My whistling stopped the second my mother's car came into view hiding behind Seth's pickup. I hurried up the stairs to my kitchen. Savory smells emanated from my oven, and Mother sat in the old rocker by the big window. Mother never just dropped by. She most assuredly had nothing to do with the mouth-watering aroma.

Evelyn Chandler Quinn ran a manicured hand over my cat's

back. *My* cat who never deigned to sit in my lap.

Normally, I would remove my service weapon immediately on entering the house and lock it in the safe, but just because it bothered Mother to see me wearing it, I kept it on and removed my jacket to make the Glock even more obvious. "Why are you here?" So much for tact. I really should be less confrontational, but Mother brings out the worst in me. Especially when I'm tired.

Her brows rose along with her nose. "Really, Jessalyn. You can't have forgotten opening night."

Shit! Memory flooded back. The Lamplight Theater season opening night. An event Mother annually purchased tickets for, expecting me to attend whether I cared to or not.

Jacqui, my twelve going on twenty-one daughter strutted into the kitchen wearing a body-hugging dress I'd never seen and an overabundance of makeup.

Mother rose to her feet, dumping the cat onto the floor. "Jacqueline, my little princess, you look marvelous. Doesn't she look marvelous? I knew that dress would be perfect for tonight."

The cat arched his back and hissed. I clamped my mouth shut before I said crap I couldn't take back. The thoughts going through my head would hurt Jacqui and do further damage to our already strained relationship.

Nothing in my closet was even remotely appropriate for the gala. Except maybe last year's dress, which would be an even worse sin. Not that I was going. It didn't matter what the performance was, the whole scene just wasn't my thing.

Jacqui twirled while sliding her hands over the shimmery material and her burgeoning curves, then lifted her chin. "Oma bought it for me." She was a younger version of her grandmother, haughty and condescending; so much so that I wanted to rip the dress off her and send her to her room. In addition to being inappropriate for a girl barely into her teens, it showed off a body I would have died to have when I was her age. Jealousy didn't become me.

Footsteps thumped up the stairs from the enclosed garage below. Mike tended to take them three at a time. He popped into the kitchen, jerked to a stop and gawked. "Wow, Sis. You look . . . older."

Yeah, she looked like bait for a child, sex-ring sting. Sarcasm didn't become me either so I bit my tongue on the observation.

Seth followed Mike into the kitchen, took one glance at Jacqui and frowned. A high school math teacher, Seth had tutored Mike after he almost flunked his freshman year of high school, and then slipped easily into the role of friend, filling gaps Mike's father didn't care enough to fill, and stirring up desire in me I wasn't sure I wanted stirred up.

Jacqui ignored me and continued to preen, perhaps hoping for a glance of male approval from Seth. Unmoved by the unfolding drama, Mike headed to the kitchen sink to wash his hands.

Our half-grown rescue puppy pranced in on Seth's heels and sat panting at my feet. I gave Murphy the hand signal for down, and the eager golden retriever plopped obediently just as the phone on my belt vibrated. At least one being in my life obeyed without question.

I pulled the phone out, ignoring Mother's pout of disapproval at the interruption, or maybe the gun on my hip or the whole cop thing. Who knew?

"Quinn." The conversation brief, terse and almost welcome. I slid the phone back into its holster and grabbed my jacket off the chair. "Sorry, Mother, duty calls." So, no wine. No feet on the deck railing. No peace and rest for the already weary. And fortunately, no gala for me.

"Mom, how can you not go to the play?" Jacqui whined.

Mother sniffed. "She has better things to do. Come, Princess. We can't be late." She filed out without further comment, and Jacqui sashayed behind without even saying goodbye.

I watched the door click shut. I'd grown accustomed to Mother's disapproval, but Jacqui's distain stung. Where had the easy relationship my daughter and I once shared gone? It was bad enough Jacqui's father's young new girlfriend was way cooler than good old mom, but even her grandmother had come between us, and that hurt.

"Seth showed me how to make lasagna," Mike said drying his hands. "You're going to miss my masterpiece." He rummaged in the fridge and dumped salad makings on the table.

"I gotta go," I repeated to the men preparing to put dinner on the table.

"It's okay, Mom," Mike said and stopped long enough to give me a brief but energetic hug.

Seth paused in the process of slicing a loaf of Italian bread. "Maybe you can take a to-go bag? I'll fix one if you want." His coffee-colored eyes offered sympathy and understanding.

"Better not. It'll be cold before I have a chance to eat it. But thanks for the offer." Regret stirred. Anything other than the theater with my mother would be better than what I was sure to face when I left here, but spending time with Mike and Seth, over a meal they had prepared would have been so welcome.

Should've told Lieutenant Ward to send someone else. But I'd been so eager to thwart my mother's plans that I hadn't. Now I had to rush out to a beach house filled with guilty memories, and carry on cool and professional, as if I didn't have a history with Dan Hoffman no one needed to know about.

Suck it up, I told myself as I headed for the door.

STILL STRUGGLING WITH THE FACT that a piece of my past was now a possible crime scene, I eased my unmarked cruiser around a clutch of gawking neighbors, and pulled in behind a patrol car with its lights still strobing. In our usually peaceful Northeast Florida town of St. Augustine violent deaths usually involved vehicles and alcohol. If this turned into homicide, the sheriff, and the media would be all over it. And all over me.

The tang of salty air filled my senses as I gazed up at the familiar, sprawling mansion where I'd spent so much of my youth. Hanging out with my ex's sister and being courted by Elliott the Rat while the house still belonged to the Edwards family.

Then there was that intense fling I wasn't so proud of. The one with Dan Hoffman, current owner of the property.

Dan had called 911 when he arrived home from work and found his wife Laney unconscious. According to Lt. Ward, Dan had desperately demanded an ambulance, but when the EMT rig rolled in the wife was already dead.

I searched the cluster of vehicles, hoping to see my partner's Jeep. I suspected he'd been surfing on his day off, but he'd answered his cell and promised to meet me here. No sign of him yet.

I ducked under the yellow crime scene tape stretched across the cobblestone drive, and strode toward the house. At the top of the wide, stone staircase a handsome black rookie stepped into my path.

"Ma'am? This is a crime scene. No one is—"

I shoved the front of my suit jacket aside. As he gawked at the badge hanging on a lanyard around my neck, I held out my ID folder.

He accepted the black folder. "Jessalyn Quinn." He frowned, then his head jerked up and his eyes met mine. "You're Jesse Quinn? *The* Jesse Quinn?"

"That would be me." I tried to add a jaunty grin.

"But you're . . . I mean—"

I made the *tsking* sound Mother never missed an opportunity to scold me for. "Too short? Too female? Looks can be deceiving. Didn't they teach you that at the academy?"

Nothing about my diminutive, tailored appearance matches the reputation of an impetuous rookie barely off probation who had taken out three armed thieves at a convenience store my first week alone on the job. I'd been far too hasty back then and way overconfident. However, having prevailed in spite of taking a round in my thigh, the incident had gained me creds. Big time. No one had ever questioned my ability to handle myself since if you didn't count the testosterone-laden ribbing dished out on a regular basis.

"Sorry, Detective Quinn. No disrespect meant." The young deputy started poking at the electronic tablet he held, logging my information and the time I'd arrived.

"None taken." I slipped my ID back into my pocket. "Were you first on the scene?"

He nodded. "I was just a couple blocks away. Got here before the EMTs."

"Deputy—" I glanced at his name tag. "MacKenzie. I'll catch up with you later."

"Just ask for Mac," he replied, nodding.

"Mac," I repeated as I stepped past him and into the cool

interior of the beautiful old house. Another deputy with a phone pressed to her ear nodded in acknowledgement of my arrival and pointed to the left, toward a ballroom-sized living room.

When I'd stepped out of my cruiser, the tidal wave of déjà vu had been strong, but inside, the clash of history, of memories good and bad, swelled in my chest. I did my best to ignore the tightness and inspect my surroundings impartially.

Laney Hoffman's taste leaned decidedly modern. The living room, all white leather and too much glass, appeared undisturbed. My sturdy, leather-soled shoes clicked loudly on the bare, hardwood floor that had once been covered with a luxurious Oriental carpet. A carpet that had tickled my bare backside on more than one occasion. Another wave of shame burned through me as I hurried through to the next room.

The old family room hit me even harder. I clenched my teeth and forced the memories back into the box where they belonged.

Floor to ceiling bookshelves had replaced the casual furniture designed for comfort, and a beautiful mahogany desk now squatted catty-corner in the middle, half facing a set of sliders opening onto a rear deck. The place held a faint odor of lemon wax. And death.

The still form of a tall, slender woman lay crumpled in front of the desk

Blood matted the dead woman's blond hair and pooled under her head, staining the area carpet beneath. Her blue eyes stared sightlessly up at the ceiling. In spite of all the bodies I'd seen, my insides went skittish. Whatever the woman had been hit with had crushed her skull just above and forward of her right ear. Death, or at least unconsciousness, had probably come quickly.

I slipped on paper booties and gloves, then pulled out my phone and took a series of photos. The evidence tech would document thoroughly, but these were for me, to keep this moment alone with the dead woman fresh in my mind.

I crouched next to the still form, studying the nasty wounds, wondering what had done so much damage.

"Yo, Quinn!"

I twisted around to face Sandeep Kabati. He didn't look old enough to be out of high school, never mind hold a doctorate and run the medical examiner's department, but he excelled at what he did. Deceptive appearances, like I'd told Mac outside. Sandeep's quick professional rise was well-earned.

"You ready for me?" he asked.

As ready as I'd ever be, I nodded and stood.

"Most likely somewhere between four and six this afternoon," Sandeep answered my unasked question several minutes later. And that—" He pointed to a heavy glass object lying just under the edge of the desk. "Is the probable murder weapon."

How had I missed it? I slipped my phone out and took a few shots of an irregular shaped chunk of glass covered in blood lying just under the edge of the desk. "What is it?"

"Replica of an antique deck prism," Sandeep answered. "Sometimes called a bullseye. Kind of ironic, huh?"

"What's a deck prism?"

Sandeep rocked back on his heels. "Before electricity, they were installed in the decks of sailing ships to let light into the hold below." He aimed the end of his pen toward the tapered point of the prism. "Instead of a beam of light going straight down and only shining in a small circle, this shape diffused the light outward. The museum over at the lighthouse has an exhibit explaining all about it. Things weigh several pounds."

The heavy glass 'bullseye', flat on one end, hexagonal in shape and tapered to a point on the other end. A lethal point, as it turned out. Ironic name. I turned back to the victim and studied the unmistakable imprints of the prism's pointed shape on the woman's temple and face. Explained the crushed skull. I *tsked* again in sympathy. My head hurt just thinking about it.

"How hard would someone have to hit her to do that much damage?" I guesstimated the perp was considerably taller than the victim or she'd been seated when struck. Laney was above average height, but her husband was well over six feet, and he'd be the first one questioned.

The thought made me ill. The Dan Hoffman I knew couldn't have done this. He was a gentle man. Caring. Considerate. Loving. My chest hurt as my head rejected the notion.

"Depends on momentum." Sandeep answered as he continued his examination. "Raised high enough, and swung down quickly enough, it wouldn't take a lot of force. But—" he wagged his head, "more than one blow. Definitely not an accident."

"A weapon of opportunity, then. Not premeditated. And with passion." *Please don't let it have been Dan.*

Leaving Sandeep to finish his preliminary work, I studied the room again, an urgency to find details pushing me, prodding me. Other than the glass prism on the floor and the apparent result of its use, I spotted no sign of struggle. That worried me more. A half-dozen file folders, neatly stacked on one corner of the desk beneath a few pieces of mail remained undisturbed. Pens rested in an upright mug sporting the University of Florida logo. Nothing appeared out of place.

A credenza matching the desk prominently displayed several family photos. One of Dan and his bride on the day of their wedding in one half of a gilded dual frame. The other photo taken on a tropical beach might have been from their honeymoon. The older man in an ornate silver frame was Laney's well-known father from several years earlier judging by the amount of carefully groomed hair on man's head. There were school photos of two dark-haired little girls, but Laney and Dan were childless. Maybe his nieces? I hadn't seen Dan's sister in years and didn't spend time on Facebook keeping up with old friends and their offspring. The last frame, an eleven by fourteen with a plain wood finish, appeared totally at odds with the rest of the decor. Her blond locks tucked up under a shallow-brimmed hat and dressed in camouflage fatigues, Laney Hoffman grinned broadly in the center of a group of jovial, similarly clad men. I took shots of the photo lineup.

"You didn't happen to see my partner on your way in, did you?" I asked the still-squatting ME when the silence stopped speaking to me.

"Rafe? No. But Sergeant Broussard is out in the courtyard with the husband."

My pulse jolted, then settled into a heavy beating rhythm. I shoved my phone back into my pocket and headed toward the door that opened into the walled courtyard, sheltered from both the street and the ocean. Broussard's presence meant Lieutenant Ward hadn't completely trusted Rafe and me to handle the scene on our own. I resented the implication. Broussard would be looking hard at Dan.

I stepped out into the humid air and paused, trying to put my game face back on. If my sergeant got even a whiff of something less than professional between Dan and me, I'd be off the case faster than a car spinning out at the Indy 500.

Broussard sat across a painted, concrete table from Dan with his serious interrogation face on. I crossed the cobbled courtyard and joined them, surprised Dan was speaking to a detective at all. As a defense attorney, his advice to a client would have been to say nothing to anyone without a lawyer present. Maybe shock had rattled him into unguarded speech.

His face ashen, his hands trembled. I'd never seen Dan look so shaken. Nothing like the confident football jock I'd admired in high school, the skilled defense attorney I'd sparred with in court or the gallant lover I'd had a brief fling with a few years earlier. My heart ached for him and what he would face in the coming days.

Broussard addressed me formally. "Corporal Quinn. Nice of you to join us."

I nodded in return. "Sergeant Broussard."

Although I hadn't expected to see my mentor, it was an election year. Everyone up the chain would like this case closed by the time the eleven o'clock news aired tonight. And the deceased's father was the sheriff's biggest contributor, so it stood to reason the lieutenant would call in a bigger gun to back up Rafe and me.

On the other hand, perhaps Ward figured the more bodies he threw at the problem, the quicker it would go away. Like that was going to happen! He could put the entire Criminal Investigations Division on the case and it still had the potential to become a political nightmare. It was already Dan's nightmare.

Everyone knew that Lawrence Upshaw thought his son-in-law Dan Hoffman, born in poverty to a slut who couldn't name the baby's father, lacked the breeding for his society daughter. And Upshaw pulled a lot of weight.

"I didn't do it," Dan blurted even though no one had suggested he had. "Laney forgets to lock the doors. I should've told her to be more careful. Anyone could have walked in. It's my fault. I—"

I started to put a hand on Dan's wrist to halt the flow of self-recrimination and stopped myself. Statements like that could get him convicted, and he should know better. "You're the husband, Dan. They always suspect the spouse. You should know that better than anyone. We'll get this sorted out."

Broussard shot me a warning look, then rose to his feet. "I'm going to escort Mr. Hoffman down to CID."

I stood with him. "Call your attorney, Dan. Don't say another word."

Broussard glared at me. He was doing his job. I wasn't. Dan Hoffman couldn't have killed his wife, but in my opinion, if he had in a wild moment of insanity smashed her over the head with that hideous object, he'd have been prepared for Broussard's questions. He wouldn't look shell-shocked.

With a shaking hand Dan extracted his cell phone from a holster on his belt and punched in a number. His gaze met mine. "Please. You have to believe—"

His call was answered, and he didn't finish what he'd started to say, but I knew what he asked. Believe in his innocence and do everything in my power to prove it. With my sergeant standing right there, I could say nothing, and only hoped my eyes conveyed my trust and support.

One of Dan's partners showed up ten minutes later and accompanied him to the sheriff's office with Broussard. Rafe joined me in the courtyard with profuse apologies about how long it had taken to hustle home, stow his surfboard, throw on suitable clothes and get on the road in what passed for rush-hour traffic in St Augustine Beach.

Rafe tipped his head, a question in the action. "Are you okay?"

Did my distress show that much? Rafe was an observant

man and a good partner to work with, but our pairing was pretty recent. He didn't know me all that well.

I shrugged off his concern and sought to distract him. "Have you been inside? It's not pretty."

Rafe glanced back at the house and nodded. "Sandeep gave me a few minutes before he zipped up the body bag. What'd I miss?"

After filling Rafe in on what I'd learned so far – what anyone knew so far, we took young Mac aside and asked him to replay what he'd come upon when he first rolled on the scene, while two other deputies were dispatched to canvas the neighborhood looking for possible witnesses.

"Mr. Hoffman was pretty shook up," Mac said, looking a little shaken himself. "He begged me to make her wake up. I could see it was useless, but I checked for a pulse so he wouldn't think I didn't care. After the rescue rig rolled up, I took him out to the courtyard. I hope that was the right thing do to, but he was getting in the way. I didn't want him to mess up the crime scene any more than he already had."

"You did the right thing," I assured him.

Mac gave me a half smile and pointed to the house next door. "Neighbor lady was hanging over the hedge. She wanted to talk to me, but I told her a detective would be by later. Maybe she saw something."

"Was anyone else around when you first arrived?" Rafe asked.

Mac shook his head. "Didn't see anyone else. Street was pretty dead. Not even anyone walking a dog."

"Well, if you remember anything else, call me." I handed him my card with my personal cell number on it.

Mac took the card and tucked it into his pocket. "Yes, Ma'am."

After the other deputies had reported back, Rafe and I split the list of neighbors to question a second time that night.

I headed toward the neighbor Mac had pointed out. Probably should've sent Rafe to interview that particular neighbor, but I'd gone out of my way during that wild, crazy few months to avoid being seen so I just prayed she either hadn't lived here then or wouldn't remember.

As I cleared the top step a shadow slipped past behind the sheer curtain stretched across the tall window bordering the front door. The door opened before I knocked. A diminutive older woman looked up at me with faded blue eyes glittering with curiosity.

I produced my badge. "I'm Detective Jesse Quinn, ma'am. May I ask you a few questions?" Without a glance at my creds, she ushered me into a foyer with a high ceiling where a large fan with blades shaped like palm fronds gently stirred the air.

"Come in," the woman invited as she led me through to a living room that matched the foyer in old fashioned grandness as different from Laney's glass and leather as it could possibly be.

The woman stuck out her hand. "Jenny Harker. Please, have a seat." No recognition on her face. A blessing. I relaxed a tad. She gestured toward a couch with flowered chintz upholstery protected with clear plastic like my grandmother used to have.

"Have you been home all afternoon, Mrs. Harker?" I pulled out my notebook. "You don't mind if I take notes?"

The woman made a motion dismissing my concerns and launched into animated recital. "I'm always home in the afternoon. Sometimes I go out in the morning to the hairdresser, or the grocery store, you know. Or sometimes to the doctor, but that's always in the morning, unless I just can't get a morning appointment. I like to be home before two. That's when my programs come on, and I don't like to miss them."

The woman was a chatterbox, but I let her run on.

"Today was different, though. All the goings on over at the Hoffman's. What on earth happened? Nothing good I'm thinking. Who did they cart out on that stretcher? Oh!" She pressed three fingers to her lips. "Was that Laney on that stretcher? What happened to her?"

She paused for breath.

"When was the last time you saw Mrs. Hoffman?" I asked not answering any of the busy-body's questions.

Her eyes grew wide. "She's dead, isn't she?"

I sighed. She'd know soon enough. "I'm afraid she is. Do you recall when you last saw her alive?"

Mrs. Harker's eyes went round. "Maybe her lover did it."

A lover? Dan and Laney Hoffman hadn't even been married a year. "How do you know Mrs. Hoffman had a lover?" Poor Dan.

Mrs. Harker leaned forward, eager to be the bearer of such juicy gossip. "There was a man here just the other day, hugging and kissing her right there by the front door where the whole world could watch. She's not a good wife."

Mrs. Harker wagged her head. "She shouted and poked at poor Dan. Always angry with him. And he was so in love with her. He just let her walk all over him." Amped up with all the drama and excitement, Mrs. Harker's voice rose as her words spilled. She twisted a lacy handkerchief as the story poured out.

Clearly the honeymoon was over in the Hoffman household. If there ever had been one to start with. This man had been nothing but kind to me at my worst moments, and now I was going to be forced to treat him as a potential murderer. Maybe there was a side of Dan I'd never seen. Laney Hoffman, I didn't really know. Although we'd grown up in the same well-off circles, Laney was almost a half a generation younger and we'd never crossed paths.

I glanced up from my notebook. "Did Mr. Hoffman ever shout back at his wife? Or abuse her physically?" If Laney had been cheating on him that might have been sufficient motive.

Mrs. Harker shook her silver-blond curls vigorously. "Oh my, no. Dan would never do a thing like that. He just let her go on until she wound herself down. He is such a nice man." The woman held a soft spot for her neighbor.

But every man had a breaking point. Perhaps Dan had just discovered his wife's infidelity, and as Sandeep had pointed out, the weapon was one of opportunity, there to grab when passion flew, even if Dan hadn't meant to kill her. Which could account for the shocked expression on his face. And the angry blows to Laney's head.

Desperate to look for other answers, I turned the page. "Tell me about this man you saw Mrs. Hoffman kissing."

Jenny Harker squinted her eyes as if retrieving the details from memory.

"He was handsome. What I could see of him, of course. Brown hair, average height. Drove a dark blue SUV. With big tires. He parked up the street. I watched him walk up and drive off in it. He was inside the house with her for a while before they came out and he started kissing her so indecent-like on the front stoop."

I scribbled fast. A wife who railed at her husband. A husband who apparently didn't fight back. And a possible lover the husband didn't know about . . . or did. Lots of motive. I swallowed uncomfortably at the conclusion Broussard would likely jump to.

"He wasn't there long enough to get in bed with her," the woman rattled on. "I don't think. Well, maybe. Young folk these days – you just never can tell about things like that. It's all about sex and no romance. But she was a married woman." Mrs. Harker harrumphed.

"Have you ever seen this man before two days ago?"

Mrs. Harker shook her head, the silvery curls bouncing again.

"Have you seen anyone else at the house in the last couple days?"

"I saw a green car parked in the street I didn't recognize. That was earlier today. Didn't see who was driving it, though."

I kept the questions coming. "Anyone calling on Mrs. Hoffman? A delivery person? Another neighbor? Anyone at all? Any unusual activity out front of the house or on the beach?" For the most part the beach behind these homes was not populated with anyone other than the owners because trekking gear from the car park four miles north or three miles south wasn't worth it. So any activity there could be significant.

Again, the emphatic shake of the head.

"Is there anything else you can think of?"

Mrs. Harker pointed toward the row of windows overlooking the ocean. "They were fighting out there by the beach yesterday but I couldn't hear what they were saying. Only saw Laney pounding on Dan's chest and screaming her stupid head off."

"And what did Mr. Hoffman do about that?"

"Nothing. He just kept his hands in his pockets and kind of rocked back on his feet a little. She stormed into the house and a few minutes later she backed her car out of the garage and tore off down the street. He just sat down on that little bench on the dune looking lonely and sad."

My eyes stung. A good man. My friend and one-time lover had married a shrew. He deserved so much better than either of us.

I blinked back the sudden emotion. "Was yesterday morning the last time you saw Mrs. Hoffman alive?"

Mrs. Harker pressed a finger to her lower lip and frowned. "I think so. No! Wait! I did see her again. This morning, coming home. Around lunchtime. She opened the garage, drove her car inside and shut the door. I didn't see her after that."

"But you're sure it was Mrs. Hoffman driving?"

"Why yes. She drives a convertible. I could not mistake who was driving."

"Did you see Mr. Hoffman arrive home this evening?"

Mrs. Harker nodded slowly. "I saw him pull in when I went to the kitchen to fix my afternoon tea."

"And what time would that have been?" Dispatch could pinpoint the time he called to report her unconscious. But how much time would have been between his arrival home and that 911 call?

"I-I'm not really sure."

Or not willing to tell?

"But then I heard the sirens."

Time enough for a disillusioned husband to lose his cool, do his wife in, and *then* call 911 pretending he'd come home and found her like that?

CHAPTER 2

THE SLIVER OF A YOUNG MOON hung low in the sky, doing nothing to banish the gloom of night when I reached the sheriff's office. Before I was even out of my cruiser, Scotty Parker, determined local newshound, nabbed me, digging for intel.

I pushed past him. "No comment." Reporters I could do without. They rarely published anything without bias and could screw up an investigation.

Not to be deterred, Scotty hustled after me. "Did Hoffman do it?"

I rounded on him. "What part of no comment don't you get, Parker?" He damned well knew I couldn't and wouldn't comment on an ongoing investigation. I prayed to God Dan hadn't offed his wife, and if he hadn't, I owed him everything I had to get him exonerated . . . which also meant doing my best to keep the press from dragging his name through the mud.

At a time when I doubted everything about myself, Dan had been there for me. With his friendship, he'd supported my decision to follow in my dad's footsteps and become a cop. Something Elliott scoffed at and Mother thought was beneath me. As a man, he'd restored my tattered sense of self-worth, showed me I was desirable and worth loving. I hadn't loved him the way he deserved to be loved, but I'd taken what he offered.

"Upshaw will be out for his son-in-law's blood," Scotty said as he chased after me. "Must be why so many people are on this thing. Bet the sheriff is breathing down your neck."

The relish in his voice set my teeth on edge. Rafe's battered Jeep crunched into the lot before I could tear into the smart-assed reporter. Parker glanced toward the sound, and I grabbed the opportunity to let myself into the building and leave his annoying presence outside for Rafe to deal with. I headed to the ladies' room before my bladder gave out. I took my time freshening up. My night was just beginning and home but a distant wish.

"Where did you disappear to?" Rafe asked as I entered the detectives' small conference room.

"How did you manage to avoid Scotty?" I asked, ignoring his question.

Rafe's eyes sparkled in deviltry. "I didn't. Just flipped him the bird and kept walking,"

I shook my head. "I felt like slapping him."

Rafe snorted. "I'd like to see that." He threw himself into a chair and dropped his tablet on the table. "I didn't find out much. No one saw anything. Lots of opinion. Not much fact. How about you?"

"More than I'd like. Not as much as I'd hoped." I hung my jacket over the back of the chair opposite him. "That next-door neighbor Mac gave me the heads-up on, one Jenny Harker, seems to have noticed a lot of the comings and goings of the Hoffman household."

Nosey as she was, good thing her memory didn't go back four years.

"She doesn't believe Dan Hoffman would kill his wife in a rage or in cold blood. Unfortunately, most of what she told me amounts to a lot of motive." I proceeded to recount the details.

"The woman wasn't well liked," Rafe agreed. "But the neighbors I spoke to couldn't say enough good about Dan

Hoffman. Pretty much everyone seemed shocked that we'd even consider him for it."

I wasn't considering him for it, but I kept that thought to myself. "Where's Broussard?"

"He's got Hoffman in the box. He's waiting on us to join him."

I shot to my feet, anxious to assist, afraid of what was about to happen. "Let's go."

Moments later I tapped on the window of the door to the interview room.

Broussard got to his feet, nodded to the two men sitting opposite him and came out into the hall, shutting the door behind him. "We might as well let him go. He's lawyered up and isn't talking.

"Let me talk to him." I peered at Dan through the glass. He still appeared very much in shock. Not waiting for my sergeant's reply, I turned and let myself into the small room.

Every womanly instinct in me wanted to rush to the other side of the table and wrap my arms about this man who'd just lost his wife and had every right to grieve. But I stifled that urge and took Broussard's empty chair.

"I'm sorry for your loss." The words were never adequate and sounded even more stilted in light of our past.

"Martin Kelly," the second man at the table said, half rising from his seat and extending his right hand.

I shook it briefly and let go. "I know who you are, Mr. Kelly." I'd seen him in the courtroom a few times and respected the reputation. He was a decent lawyer. Sharp, but fair.

Kelly nodded but didn't sit back down. "I've advised Mr. Hoffman to say nothing, and I see no reason to keep him here any longer. He'll be staying in the firm's suite at the Fairfield, but I would appreciate a call first, if you have more questions."

"Dan," I ignored the lawyer and turned to Hoffman. "Can you think of anyone you've opposed in court who might want revenge?" I needed a few leads to give Broussard and Rafe - someone else to focus on besides Dan.

Dan thought for a moment, then shook his head.

"How about someone your wife might have gotten into a disagreement with? One of your neighbors saw a man leaving your home two days ago. Have you any idea who it might have been?"

Dan sat up straighter, tried to pull himself together, but failed.

Kelly lifted a hand. "I object to—"

"Are you sure you don't know who might have visited your wife two days ago?" If Dan didn't already know, sooner or later he was going to find out his wife was cheating on him, but I wasn't going to air that dirty laundry with Broussard listening in.

Dan stared at his hands and failed to meet my gaze as he shook his head again.

Watching the play of emotions on Dan's face, a gut-deep certainty grew that he was innocent. Hurt, angry even. But innocent. He might know about the lover and was embarrassed by the knowledge at least as much as he was hurt by the infidelity.

"How well did you know your wife's friends from before your marriage?"

"I d—"

His lawyer touched Dan's sleeve. Dan glanced up at Kelly, then slumped back into his seat.

Try another tack. "Has your wife ever been physically or verbally abusive toward you?"

"I think we're done here," Kelly cut in. "Unless you're

holding my client with a formal arrest, we're leaving." Kelly started for the door and Dan followed suit. Back at his home, he'd looked pretty much the same as the last time I'd seen him in court, sharply dressed, an imposing presence of a man, with the exception of his hair that stood at angles as if he'd been pulling at it with anxious hands. Now he just looked beaten and somehow smaller. His eyes pleaded with me, sending a silent message. I needed to find a way to speak with him alone. In private and off the record . . . as a friend.

I watched them go. We were a long way from having enough evidence or cause to charge Dan, but there was enough probable cause to get a search warrant for the house, his car and possibly his office, phone and computer.

This would be a long night for everyone.

I grabbed my phone, glanced through the photos I'd taken of the crime scene, then clicked over to contacts and texted my son, seeking solace in the normalcy of checking in on my kid.

How was the lasagna?

Mike: Better than yours. Coming home soon?

Me: Not likely. Sorry.

Mike: What's up?

I gave up texting and dialed. "Hey, Mikey Mike. I'm not going to make it home tonight. I've caught a murder investigation and there's too much to do. You mind?"

"If you were saddling me with Jacqui, I might," Mike answered.

"Your grandmother will keep her overnight. I'll send her a text." No need to listen to another lecture about my job and my duties to my kids.

"Will you be okay on your own tonight?"

"Mom, stop worrying. Go do your thing."

"Love you,"

"Back at ya." He clicked off.

Broussard leaned against the wall watching me. "Checking on the kids?"

I sighed. "Yeah." I hurriedly sent a text to Jacqui and another to Mother.

"Rafe's waiting for us in the conference room. I sent a deputy to the judge for a warrant. Let's sit down and compare notes." The sergeant headed toward the conference room without waiting to see if I followed.

I hesitated in the doorway while Broussard detoured to the coffee maker. "Does Lawrence Upshaw know yet?"

"Lieutenant Ward went to do the notification." Broussard said without turning around. "Keeping Upshaw under control will be *his* priority while we work toward the indictment of the unfortunate, unfavored son-in-law."

Resentment rose hot in my throat. Or figure out who really did it. I strode to the table, grabbed a chair and sat. "I don't think he did it."

Rafe glanced over at me. "And where is that assurance coming from?"

Broussard returned to the table and narrowed his eyes at me.

This must be how a parent felt when the school principle calls them into his office to accuse their child of cheating or bullying. Not my child! Never! Not Dan! I know him and he couldn't have done this.

"It's in his eyes," I finally said.

"We go where the facts lead us," Broussard said sternly as he set a chipped mug of steaming coffee on the table and took a seat. "I suggest we order food and get to work."

"Already done," Rafe said. "Hazel went out to Panera's."

Hazel Bonney was a civilian employee who did anything anyone asked of her. Widowed and childless, she mothered everyone in the squad and spent more time in the building than anyone else.

Broussard crossed his feet at the ankles and leaned back in his chair, hands behind his head. He gave me another uncomfortable stare. "So, what else did you two dig up?"

Jesse waved at Rafe to go first.

Rafe mashed a hand across his eyes as if trying to wipe away the weariness of a day surfing followed by a callout to a death scene. "I feel like the Dan Hoffman we know from court is an entirely different man from the one his neighbors socialize with. According to everyone I spoke to, he's an easy-going guy who's friendly and quick to help out, unlike his wife who thinks she's better than everyone else. One guy actually called Hoffman a pussy. Said he gives in to every whim his spoiled little wife ever has. I expect there might be quite a few people out there with a good reason to dislike the woman.

Broussard tapped the eraser end of his pencil on his notebook. "No facts though."

Rafe tipped his head in acknowledgement. "We don't have a lot to go on, and from what I'm hearing from Ward, the sheriff will be coming down hard on us to wrap this up quickly before Upshaw comes breathing down everybody's necks. Did Hoffman say anything when you two first got there?" Rafe tapped away on his tablet, making notes for himself. He was all about technology, while the Sergeant and I still clung to our little paper notebooks and pens.

I deferred to Broussard who'd talked to Dan first. Before the lawyer showed up.

"Not much," Broussard said. "At first he seemed in denial that she was dead. Then he insisted he wasn't home when it happened."

Because he didn't do it. I kept the comment to myself. "By morning Molly and Kyle will have their preliminary evidence report which should give us more to go on than we have now." My head pounded. Exhaustion weighed me down like a sopping wet blanket. I wanted to go home and down a couple Tylenol and think about something else.

Rafe dropped the tablet and stylus on the table. "What do you think, Sarge? Hoffman do it?"

Before Broussard could answer, Hazel appeared bearing a cardboard container and a smile. She set the box down and retreated.

For a few moments none of us spoke as the men dove into their dinner. Not as hungry as either of them, I swallowed a small bite of my sandwich and shoved the paper tray aside. "So where do we begin?"

Broussard flipped the cover of his notebook open, and set a legal sized pad of paper on the table. He'd already begun his pro and con list with the heading at the top reading, Did Dan Hoffman Murder his Wife? There were a number of entries on the Pro side. None on the Con.

I shook my head. "I have a gut feeling on this one, Sarge. Lots of reasons why he might want to slap her at times, but I don't see him coshing her over the head with that deck prism. I don't see him being violent with her or any woman, for any reason."

Rafe snorted. "You and your hunches."

Broussard just pursed his lips.

"None of his neighbors thought he was capable of violence either. Besides, I'm usually right." My intuition often latched onto the right trail. It was my strength as a cop. Impulsively running with the bit between my teeth, however, was my downfall. But I had more invested in this case than I cared to share.

Broussard tapped his pen on the empty half of the page. "So, give me something to put on the con side."

Dan's pleading look wasn't proof of anything. "I can't . . . yet," I admitted reluctantly. I then relayed my conversation with Mrs. Harker and one other neighbor. Rafe repeated some of the comments made by people he'd spoken to that tended toward sharp dislike of the woman. Broussard scribbled away.

"Is there anyone Hoffman faced in court that might want revenge?" Rafe asked.

I shook my head. "I asked him that and he didn't think so."

"Against his wife?" Broussard jerked his head in a negative. "That would have been premeditated. The choice of murder weapon doesn't lend itself to that kind of killing."

The image of Laney Hoffman's bashed in skull churned my gut. Whoever had killed Laney had been angry. Vindictive, maybe, but angry and very emotional. And the prism had been a weapon of opportunity. Not a gun, or anything else brought with murder in mind. Broussard made a valid point.

Rafe set his tablet aside. "We're spinning our wheels. I don't know about you guys, but I'm about to fall asleep. All that sun and fun." He glanced at his watch. "Almost four am and we still don't have that warrant." He got to his feet.

"You play too hard on your day off, that's your problem." Broussard, twenty years our senior, got to his feet looking perkier than either us. I felt, as my grandmother used to say, as if someone had dragged me ass-backward through a knothole. "I'm headed home for a few. I'm going to leave the house search to the two of you. I'll attend the autopsy." Broussard nodded at us.

"Thanks, Sarge." And thank heaven I'm relieved of that duty this time around. Autopsies were one thing I hated about this job. When it's my turn, I go. And I refuse to hide behind the window, but rather stand at the ME's side where I can answer any questions he might have. But I don't enjoy watching a person's insides being pulled out, weighed and catalogued like someone taking inventory at a produce market. "What time did Sandeep say he'd be cutting?"

"Eight sharp." Broussard pulled on his jacket and headed for the door. "So, unless something comes up between now and then, I'll see you as soon as the autopsy's done."

Rafe followed Broussard to the door. "I'm going to crash on the couch in Broussard's office until that warrant comes back."

I smiled for the first time in what felt like hours at the image of Rafe's nearly six feet draped over the inadequate length of Broussard's very short couch.

Too wired to think about a nap, I stayed where I was and ran through the events another time. Dan's pleading eyes haunted me, and Lawrence Upshaw showing up demanding answers before we had anything to go on wouldn't be easy either. I thought briefly about my kids and wondered if Mike had remembered to feed the animals and take Murphy for a walk. Turning off my brain wasn't happening, but I folded my arms on the table in front of me and rested my head on them.

"Jesse."

Jerked awake, I blinked up at Rafe.

He held the signed search warrant in his hand. "Let's go."

Still groggy from the unexpected nap and stiff from the position in which I'd gotten it, I pushed myself to my feet and rubbed the sleep out of my eyes. I peered at my watch as I grabbed my suit jacket.

Before we got to the door, Broussard strode in, rumpled and unshaven. Clearly, he'd never made it to his bed.

"Dan Huffman shot himself."

CHAPTER 3

I GASPED. THE WALLS OF THE SMALL conference room seemed to close in on me for a claustrophobic moment. "Dan shot himself?" Ice sliced through me. Not possible. Just not. He wouldn't. He detested firearms and never touched them, even when presenting them as evidence in court. I pictured him pinching the corner of the evidence bag as if it contained a deadly virus.

"Yeah, and if his aim was to end his life, he missed," Broussard said, sarcasm heavy in his voice. "He's in surgery. No idea if he'll make it."

No way the Dan Hoffman I knew would take his own life. I fought to steady my voice. "I can't believe it."

Rafe's keen green eyes studied my face, all too discerning. "You okay?"

Gut-punched, I struggled not to show it. I nodded. "Sure, just . . . But why?"

Broussard shrugged. "The why should be obvious. He threw a fit, bashed his wife's head in, then got scared and wanted out."

"He wouldn't do that!" A fiery need to defend a friend swept in with a force all its own. "He's never been a coward. Besides, he hates guns."

Broussard frowned "Just how friendly were you and Dan?" Already with the past tense.

My pulse pounded so rapidly I wondered if Rafe and Broussard could see it.

Rafe's eyes narrowed. "What am I missing?"

I grabbed the warrant from his hand. "Shouldn't we be moving on this?" I had to do something. Had to move. Had to pretend I wasn't in shock.

Ignoring me, Rafe pressed. "How do you know what Hoffman would or wouldn't do?"

"I've known Dan Hoffman since we were at Trinity."

"Trinity High School?" Rafe's brows rose. "I thought Dan grew up dirt poor."

Rafe hadn't grown up in St. Augustine and didn't know the players. How to help Rafe understand the kind of man Dan was without giving myself away? What he'd overcome to become the man he was. The man I knew and owed so much to.

"Dan didn't know who his birth father was, but after his mother met Joe Alford in AA and had an affair with him, Alford became a father figure to Dan. Alford was already married with two little kids and eventually he went back to his wife, but when Dan's mother was killed in a hit and run, and Dan ended up in the system, Alford stepped up and sent him to Trinity. He paid for college, and law school too."

Rafe nodded. "Well that explains Trinity, but not why you're convinced he didn't kill his wife."

Broussard stared hard. "Sounds like you know a little too much about this guy, Detective. We need to talk."

Rafe turned slightly, as if to put himself between me and the sergeant. My partner, looking out for me, even if he didn't know what needed looking out for.

"Dan's sister was my friend, and he was always fiercely protective of her. Of his mom. Of anyone he loved." Of me. Was this nightmare just going to keep getting worse? I struggled to get a grip on the emotions that wanted to swallow me whole.

Broussard's phone rang, and he jerked it to his ear. He nodded as if his caller could see him, then clicked it off. "Hoffman's out of surgery. He's still critical, and we can't talk to him yet." He studied his phone a moment. "I've got an autopsy in a half hour. You two go execute that warrant. Get Ben or Molly to meet you there." He turned to me. "Afterwards, you and I need to talk. That clear?"

"Yes, sir."

Rafe saluted without comment. He'd hit me with questions soon enough. Our partnership was barely three months old, and we were still growing accustomed to each other, but he recognized enough to get that this case was hitting me hard.

"Give me ten minutes to grab a shower and find some fresh clothes," I said as we headed out of the conference room. Maybe the break would short circuit the questions I could see in his eyes.

Rafe glanced down at his rumpled shirt. "Good idea. Think I'll do the same. See you in ten at my Jeep."

It was more like twenty before he arrived. I'd showered fast and scrubbed hard, skipped the makeup, and grabbed the only clean blouse in my locker. Rafe had clearly taken more time with his appearance than I had.

"Sure you don't want to take my unmarked?" I asked as he scooped his gear off the passenger seat. Rafe's official vehicle was in the shop, but he liked to drive, and I was happy to let him most of the time.

"I'm sure," he answered hiking himself up into his seat. "*We* need to talk, too, and I don't want you distracted."

Questions still hovered in his eyes. Great. How much should I tell him? How much could I get away with not telling him?

He drove out of the lot, and we cruised in silence until we crossed the bridge onto the island. Rafe glanced briefly at me.

"What's Broussard worked up about?"

"Don't worry about it."

Rafe drummed his thumbs on the steering wheel. "I get the feeling Dan Hoffman is more than just a high school friend, which is probably what's got Broussard's back up, too. Maybe you should take yourself off the case. Or at least level with me so I can have your back." He kept his eyes forward, but his attention was all on me.

I bit my lip trying to decide how much to confess. Glimpses of the beach flew past Rafe's profile while he waited for my reply. He was my partner now. I needed to learn how to trust him. Up to now, he'd proven to be an unusually thoughtful man, but would he understand this?

I looked back at my hands in my lap. "We had a relationship."

"In high school?"

"After my marriage broke up. He was . . ." The words died in my throat.

"He was . . ." Rafe prompted.

"I think he was in love with me." Hell, I knew damned well Dan had been in love with me. I just hadn't been in love with him. I'd used him to layer salve on my mangled self-confidence and prove I was still a desirable woman.

"But you didn't feel the same way." Rafe's words were soft and laced with a compassion that surprised me. "Is it over?"

"It's been over for years."

Rafe nodded. "What are you going to tell Broussard?"

"Nothing."

Rafe snorted. "You think you'll get away with that?"

"He doesn't have a need to know." He hadn't known about it when it happened, and he didn't need to know about it now. My history wasn't stopping me from pursuing this investigation thoroughly. It might even push me to investigate *more* thoroughly.

"Promise me one thing," Rafe said as he stopped at a red light and looked directly at me. "If you can't be objective, take yourself off the case." His expression was gentle but set. More serious than I'd ever seen on him.

Noting my hesitation, he pushed. "Promise me, Jess."

I swallowed. "Promise."

He studied me a little longer. "Okay, then." The light switched to green and he turned back to his driving.

I watched him drive, digesting his reaction to my confession, and the fragile new bond that had formed.

My phone vibrated. Happy to be distracted, I pulled the phone from its holster and tapped to read the text that had just come in. "Well, that's interesting."

An impatient driver swerved around and passed us. "Jackass. I should pull him over," Rafe muttered.

"Forget him." I tapped a rapid reply then rested the phone on my thigh. "The report came back on the prints already. Dan's, not surprising. But another print turns out to be a guy who worked for Arlington Security, a firm that does base security for the Army in Afghanistan and Iraq among other things. His name is Victor Moretti. And one other print, not in the system."

"Whoa! They have a photo of the guy?"

"Just asked for it."

Rafe pulled off A1A and cruised behind the row of pricey homes perched on the dune overlooking the Atlantic Ocean. I inhaled the briny scent of the sea. As we pulled into the Hoffman driveway, my phone vibrated again.

"Holy shite!" I'd seen that face before. On the credenza in Dan Hoffman's home office.

Rafe turned the engine off and turned to face me. "What?"

"I think we need to take a few minutes to visit Mrs. Harker before we tackle the search." I held my phone out for Rafe to see. "Wanna bet she's seen this guy?"

He studied the face on the tiny screen. "Not betting against it considering your description of the lady."

I drew the phone back and pulled up the photos I'd taken the day before, found the one of a group of men with Laney in the unusual frame, and thrust it back in Rafe's direction.

"Damn! Same guy. Where did you get this photo from?"

"On the credenza in Dan Hoffman's office."

Rafe's brows rose dramatically. "She's looking pretty chummy with the guy. They must have had a falling out if he's our perp, but that would account for his prints being on that damned thing she got coshed with. What's it called? A Bullet?"

"Bullseye. Or deck prism. Ask Sandeep. He seems to know all about them." I slid out of the Jeep and headed across the lawn to the Harker house with Rafe right behind me. Laney Hoffman was the sort of woman who would have a housekeeper, and that might account for the unidentified print, but at the moment, Vic Moretti was looking like the hottest lead. Other than Dan. I shuddered.

Jenny Harker stood in her open doorway.

"Detective Quinn. And who is this handsome gentleman?" She smiled at Rafe with interest.

"My partner. Detective Rafe Morgan." I held out my phone. "We wondered if you've ever seen this man?"

Mrs. Harker put her hand to her mouth as her eyes widened. "Oh, My! That's the lover I told you about. The man who was kissing Laney Hoffman on her veranda."

From lover to killer in less than forty-eight hours? "You're sure?"

"Oh, yes. Very sure. I don't forget a handsome man." She glanced at Rafe again, this time her eyes roving. Clearly, she wasn't planning to forget Rafe either.

I ignored the flirty look Rafe gave the older woman. "Do you happen to know if the Hoffmans employed anyone to work in or around the house?" There was that other unidentified print to nail down still.

"Yes. Yes, they did. Dan did his own yard work, but Laney had a cleaning woman. Same woman as …" Mrs. Harker broke off clamping her mouth shut.

"Same woman as you?" I guessed.

She opened her mouth and shut it, clearly flustered.

"Look, ma'am." Rafe smiled engagingly. "We're just ruling out people who had business in the Hoffman house and might have left fingerprints behind. We don't want to get anyone in trouble. If your cleaning lady isn't quite legal, we aren't here to jam her up. We just need to talk to her. See if she heard or saw anything out of the ordinary."

The older woman looked from Rafe to me and back, biting her lip. Probably trying to make up her mind about how much to reveal. Or not. "M-maria," she finally admitted. "Her name's Maria. She's a good girl. Please don't make trouble for her."

Not making any promises, I asked, "Does she have a last name? And an address?"

Mrs. Harker glanced at Rafe. "You promise she won't be in trouble?"

"Not as long as she didn't have anything to do with Laney Hoffman's death," Rafe assured her. Not that either of them could promise Maria wouldn't be in trouble down the line if she was working in the US illegally.

Mrs. Harker gasped. "Maria would never—She's a sweet

girl."

"Name and address," I repeated.

"Torres. Maria Torres. She lives with her aunt on Magnolia Drive. On the corner of Busam. I don't know what I'd do without her." Mrs. Harker made her case again.

"And you shouldn't have to," Rafe replied soothingly.

Mrs. Harker looked relieved.

I handed the woman another of my cards. "Well, thank you, Mrs. Harker. You've been very helpful. If you think of anything else, just call." I turned away. "Come on Detective Morgan. We're on the clock."

As soon as we were out of earshot, I added, "She's old enough to be your grandmother, for Pete's sake."

Rafe smirked. "The ladies love me. Doesn't matter how old they are." Then he got serious. "So, now we get to hunt down Maria Torres and chase a guy named Victor Moretti. Do we do the search first, see if Torres is home, or head back to central to look up current intel on Moretti?"

"We've got the warrant, let's get the search done. I'll ask Anna Santos to get the low-down on Moretti and Maria's likely cleaning someone's house and won't be home until later."

I prayed nothing incriminating Dan would surface. I still didn't believe he killed his wife in spite of the inexplicable suicide attempt. Maria's fingerprints were likely all over the house, as were Dan's, but we still needed to dot our i's and cross our t's. And one never knew what one might find on a computer. Anna, another detective in our department was a genius on a computer and didn't seem to mind being asked to dig into things for anyone else on the squad.

Rafe lifted the yellow crime scene tape for me to duck under and followed me into the foyer. "I'll start downstairs. You head up?" I nodded and started up the wide curving staircase. My footsteps sounded hollow and slowed at the top. I forced myself to keep going. The guest rooms first. I hadn't been in any of them since Dan bought the house from Elliott's parents when they moved to Arizona, although I'd slept there plenty when I hung out with Elliott's sister.

The guest rooms turned up nothing. The master suite, at the end of the hall would be the most promising and hold the most memories. I reluctantly stepped into the room.

New furnishings, new carpeting and a different color on the walls did little to squash images of me and Dan and the passion we'd secretly shared in this place. My breathing came unevenly. I closed my eyes searching for calm. Then I pulled my shoulders back, opened my eyes and took a deep breath. *I can do this.*

I nudged a stray curl off my forehead with the back of my latex covered hand and reached for Dan's top dresser drawer. I riffled quickly through his underwear. I tried the left-hand drawer. He was tidier about his things than I remembered. Ties neatly rolled and lined to one side. Next to them, two stacks of white folded men's handkerchiefs – who carried handkerchiefs anymore? And two jeweler's boxes.

The first held a collection of tie-tacks and cufflinks. The second contained a stunning gold locket encrusted with emeralds and matching earrings. Definitely not Dan's. Then I noticed the card slid endwise at the side of the drawer. An anniversary card. Unsigned. They'd been married in November. Unlike Elliot, Dan apparently had remembered the day and been prepared well ahead of time. It wasn't evidence, so I tucked it back in the drawer and moved on.

Twenty minutes later, I moved back into the hall, relieved to be out of the room. Relieved that nothing had turned up in closets or dressers. Nothing in the medicine cabinet of interest. Nothing one wouldn't expect to find in the master suite. Even the hamper had been emptied. Maria was an efficient lady if Laney and her lover had been up here just two days ago. I headed back to the stairs.

I found Rafe sitting at the impressive desk thumbing through the pages of a slender pink journal. The area rug had been removed and all signs of yesterday's grisly discovery cleaned up. I stepped into the room. "Anything?"

He looked up with a grin.

"A diary of sorts. Hidden in a bigger book meant to look like one of a set of classic novels. Laney was definitely having an affair. No mention of Vic, Moretti or even VM, but pages and pages about someone she had the hots for with the initials KW. And a comment about the need to tell KW about her little problem."

Who the hell was KW? And how much did Dan know about him?

CHAPTER 4

RAFE AND I WERE BACK AT CENTRAL going over the evidence, and creating our murder board while my egg sandwich from the drive-thru sat like a lump in my stomach. I picked up Laney's pink journal.

Rafe nodded at my carton still overflowing with fries. "You gonna eat them?" He'd wolfed down his food as if he hadn't eaten for a week. I pushed my untouched fries across the table.

Rafe munched down a few, then echoed the first thought that had come into my head when I'd found him reading the journal in the Hoffmans' study. "Who the hell is KW?" He drew an empty box, wrote KW in the center of it, then a big question mark next to it.

Neither Laney's flowery desk calendar, nor the one on her unlocked cell phone made any reference to KW. Vic Moretti was in her contact list, but the phone records showed no incoming or outgoing calls or texts to him.

I brought up the group shot of the cami-clad crew I'd seen on the Hoffman's credenza again and handed my phone to Rafe. "Suppose KW is one of these guys?"

Rafe studied the photo, then pointed to the man with his arm draped around Laney's shoulders. "That's Vic Moretti. Matches the ID photo we got from Arlington. I wonder if they'd be willing to give up the names of the rest of the men in this group?"

I took my phone back and tapped speed dial for Anna Santos. "Hey Anna. Did you get any more info from Arlington on who

Vic Moretti might have been in contact with since he left the company?"

When the answer came, I shook my head for Rafe's sake. "Can you get back with them and see if they'll give you the names of the men Moretti worked with while he was in Afghanistan at the time Laney Hoffman was there? Her last name would have been Upshaw at the time. Thanks." I hung up, then sent the photo to the printer.

Sergeant Broussard appeared on the threshold and crooked a finger at me. His come-to-Jesus expression made my gut clench.

Reluctantly, I got to my feet and started to grab my phone, but Rafe stopped me. With his back to the sergeant, he whispered. "Just stick to the present and don't focus on what you think you owe Hoffman." He slid my phone out of my fingers and spoke louder. "Want to review your pics from yesterday."

I hadn't wanted to share my past, but now that I'd confided some of it with my partner, I felt relieved. Something about shared burdens, my grandmother would have said. Rafe wasn't sharing my guilt and probably not even my views about Dan, but I didn't feel as alone as I had that morning.

I followed Broussard down the hall, past the array of photos of deputies lost in the line of duty. Past my father's portrait. Oddly, Sergeant Beau Broussard looked a lot like daddy, and he'd been my mentor, but I couldn't tell him about Dan. I wouldn't have been able to tell Daddy either. I needed to keep my past out of the investigation, and my friendship with Dan separate. I might owe him, but I also owed the job.

Broussard stepped into his office, waited for me to follow and shut the door behind us. He moved to the other side of the desk and lowered himself into his chair, gesturing for me to take the one opposite.

He began without preamble. "Is there something going on between you and the deceased's husband?"

Great way to word that question. "No." I didn't have to lie.

Broussard rubbed his temples with his fingertips as if I gave him a headache. A habit of his when he wasn't pleased. Did he do it just for me or maybe anyone he had to call into his office for a confrontation. "That wasn't the vibe I got from you earlier this morning. Or yesterday out at his house, either."

"I told you. He's a friend. I was concerned because he looked so shaken up. Not like himself." All of which was true.

Broussard stared at me, his face unreadable. "You're a good detective. I've watched you find your way in an area mostly dominated by men, and I've watched you approach every investigation with impartiality. But you're different this time. Should I should pull you off this case?

He was giving me an out. No one would hold it against me if I turned this investigation over to someone else. But then I thought of Dan, unconscious in a hospital bed and unable to defend himself. Was I the only one who thought him innocent?

I shook my head and kept eye contact, letting Rafe's words of encouragement run through me. "Sometimes I get a hunch about someone. Not that I always know why, but I just feel like I know they're innocent, or they're guilty. Sure, I know Dan, but that just makes that hunch stronger. Doesn't mean I can't be impartial."

I hadn't done anything so far to warrant being hauled off the investigation and had no plans to.

Broussard studied me a moment longer, then leaned back in his chair. "Well, here's a fact you can add to your hunch. Unless Hoffman's ambidextrous, he probably didn't try to take his own life."

I knew it. I stiffened my shoulders lest my relief show. "He's a lefty. And he supposedly shot himself with his right hand?" A man who refused to touch a gun, even an unloaded one in an evidence bag.

"That's the surgeon's opinion. Dr. Wells apparently played football in high school with Hoffman and says he even threw southpaw as a quarterback."

I glanced down at my own left hand and pictured Dan on the football field. He had thrown lefty. "So, two killers out there."

"Maybe," Broussard said. "Whoever tried to make it look like a suicide didn't know Hoffman, but it could still be the same person who killed his wife."

I considered that possibility, then came back to two suspects. "His father-in-law has motive to go after Dan, but he definitely didn't kill his own daughter. Maybe we need to find out where Lawrence Upshaw was in the wee hours of this morning."

Broussard nodded. "I'll add that to my list for this afternoon. What did you turn up at the Hoffman home?"

I told him about the pink journal.

He sighed heavily. "And no idea who KW is."

I shook my head.

Broussard did the temple thing again. It wasn't just me. "We've got our work cut out for us then. I've got a meeting with the Under Sheriff to bring him up to speed. And—" he grimaced, "he wants me present for a press conference. The last thing we need is to give those damned newsies nothing but hypotheses. Crap." He hunted around on his desk for something, then picked up a pink message slip. "Here. Anna said you asked for this."

The slip held a list of names, but no heading. I frowned and looked at Broussard.

"The Arlington crew you asked about."

"That was fast work." I rapidly scanned the list looking for KW. Nothing. "This is getting complicated."

"Too complicated!" He picked up his pen and turned to a clean page on his notepad. "Go collect Morgan and see if you can chase down Moretti. And any leads that might turn up on this KW guy."

I'd been dismissed. Careful not to show my relief that the interview was over, I left my mentor's office and headed back to find Rafe.

RAFE DROVE AGAIN AND I RODE SHOTGUN. He hadn't asked how it went with Broussard, and I didn't complain about the lack of air conditioning or the wind blasting in the open sides of his Jeep.

Rafe popped his tie free and tossed it on the dash where the loose end flopped like a fish out of water.

"Did you know it's only twenty-two degrees on the top of Mount Washington?" I asked as he unbuttoned his collar.

Rafe glanced at me with one brow raised. "And that's supposed to make me thankful it's eighty-six here?"

"It was supposed to make you feel cooler." My dad had been a fan of following weather in far-away places, and I'd adopted the quirk after he'd died. Rafe usually just shook his head at my random announcements.

He glanced at his phone mounted in a dash cradle. "How do you want to approach this?"

"Ask Moretti if he's had any contact with Laney Hoffman since leaving Afghanistan, to start with. We already know the answer, and we'll know if he's lying. And hopefully find out what if any relationship he had with her there or since. If Laney had been hooking up with the guy even after her marriage to Dan, maybe KW was a nickname she gave him."

"Nickname?" Rafe snickered.

"Like Kinky Warrior? Or maybe Killer Whiz?"

The snickering grew more pronounced. "Not sure where you get this stuff."

"But it's possible." And also possible Laney broke off their relationship, he got angry and conked her over the head with the nearest object, and we could wrap this whole investigation up before supper so I could go home and be a mother for a few hours.

When Rafe's phone announced we'd reached our destination, he slowed and pulled to the curb in front of a modest-sized stucco home with an orange tiled roof, rubber-stamp identical to the other homes in the development. Unlike more expensive, often gated communities, this development appeared to have hired one architect with one drawing and an assortment of front door colors. A handful had a garage at the end of the short driveway. The development was so close to the river, I'd bet the lawns flooded every time it rained hard and a ripe river smell overpowered any salt air that made it this far in from the beach.

The Moretti driveway was empty, the garage door open and nothing parked inside. Didn't look like Victor Moretti was home. My hope for a quick resolution faltered.

Rafe peered past me at the house. "Doesn't look promising."

"Won't know until we knock." I opened the door and stepped onto the narrow grass strip between the sidewalk and the curb. Rafe joined me and we strode up the paver-stone path. A minute or two after Rafe's knock the door opened and a woman stepped out pulling the door closed behind her.

Toned and muscular in workout clothes, she topped me by several inches. Her face set and unwelcoming. "I don't need saving and I'm not buying anything."

"Detective Morgan," Rafe the lady-charmer said with his best smile as he proffered his badge. "And Detective Quinn. We're with the St. Johns County Sheriff's department. We're here to speak to Victor Moretti."

The woman's belligerent expression crumbled. "I don't know where my husband is. He didn't come home last night. I wanted to file a missing person's report, but they told me it was too soon. Is . . . is that why you're here?"

I stepped closer. "May we come in? We'd like to ask you a few questions and I'm sure you'd rather not answer them standing out here."

She backed through her door and held it open for us, her body language suddenly more conciliatory.

The AC was a welcome relief from the suffocating heat outside. October couldn't come soon enough. Mrs. Moretti led us through an archway into a family room with an enormous flat-screen television taking up half of the wall opposite an oversized recliner and a matching couch. Rafe sank into the recliner leaving me to share the couch with Mrs. Moretti.

"Please tell me you're not here because Vic is in trouble." She bit her lip. "He's . . . he hasn't been in an accident, has he?"

Rafe flashed me a warning glance, his thoughts probably mirroring mine. "No accident, Mrs. Moretti," Rafe rushed to assure her. "We just want to speak with him about a case we're working on."

"Well, he's not here," she repeated. "And I'm getting worried." She plucked a tissue from a box on the end table and dabbed at the corners of her eyes.

"When was the last time you saw him?" *Please God, don't let this turn into another dead body.*

I asked the question, but Mrs. Moretti directed her answers to Rafe with another sniff. "When he left for work yesterday morning. After breakfast. I always fix his breakfast before he leaves."

I tried to gain her attention again. "Where does your husband work?"

She still didn't look my way. "At the feed store. The one on 208."

I asked for the name of her husband's supervisor, and she finally turned to me. Extracting a smart phone out of her sport bra, she tapped it a few times and rattled off a name and a phone number.

"I like to unwind at the end of my day before going home," Rafe suggested in a deceptively conversational tone. "Is there any possibility he met friends after work?"

Mrs. Moretti dabbed her eyes again. "He would have told me if he was going to a friend's house."

Not if that friend was a female.

A soft snickering sounded from Rafe. He must have had the same thought I had. "Does Mr. Moretti ever go out after work, perhaps to a bar or a club, alone or with friends? Has he ever stayed out all night before this?"

"Yes and no." Mrs. Moretti stopped patting imaginary tears and picked at an unseen flaw on her skin-tight leggings. "He goes out more than he should, but he's never stayed away all night."

Rafe glanced at me. "Maybe you could give us the names and phone numbers of any friends you know he hangs out with?"

Again, the woman tapped her phone and rattled off two

names. I jotted them in my notebook.

"He wasn't with either of them." Mrs. Moretti frowned as she tucked her phone back into her sport bra. "Not last night anyway, or else they're lying to cover up for him. I already called them." Sounded like Victor Moretti was kept firmly in line by this woman. Maybe that explained a possible affair with someone softer and less controlling. Or maybe he liked his women that way, considering the descriptions neighbors had given of Laney Hoffman.

But if Moretti was on the run, where was he likely to go if not to friends he could trust? "Is there anywhere you can think of that your husband might have spent last night?" Maybe he had a fishing camp on the river.

Mrs. Moretti got to her feet, the queen signaling the end of the interview. "Mostly, he hangs out at Finnegan's. Now, please go find him and bring him home."

Rafe and I stood and followed her out of the room.

"We'll be in touch, Mrs. Moretti," Rafe said at the front door. "He's probably at some friend's house sleeping off a drunk he didn't want you to know about."

I *tsked* out of Mrs. Moretti's hearing. *Or sleeping in some other woman's bed.* There was something hard and unlikable about this woman that had my hackles up.

"So, where to next, Jess?" Rafe asked as we buckled ourselves back into his Jeep.

"The feed store's the closest. Then let's hit that coffee shop at the plaza. I need some caffeine."

Rafe cranked the Jeep to life and put it into gear. I glanced back at the house. Mrs. Moretti watched us from her front window, her phone pressed to her ear.

"Sure wish I knew who she's calling," I muttered as Rafe

pulled away from the curb. "Don't know about you, but I didn't believe all that drama, and the crocodile tears were a little over the top."

Rafe pulled away from the curb. "Ya think?"

I tapped my palm on my knee. "Maybe she's calling her husband to warn him we're on his tail."

CHAPTER 5

WHILE RAFE HUNG OUTSIDE chatting with two employees he'd seen grabbing a cigarette break beside the building, I went in to find the boss.

A hulking man in a plaid flannel shirt in spite of the heat admitted to being the manager.

"I'm sorry deputy. I wish I could help you, but I ain't seen Vic in two days. Strange because he's a guy you can count on, ya know? I don't think anyone's seen him, but you can ask around if you want. I tried calling him yesterday, but it went straight to voice mail."

I handed him my card. "Thanks for your time. Call if he shows up, okay?"

"Sure thing." The man pocketed my card and went back to counting packets of fishing lures hanging on a pegboard.

Rafe was just climbing into the Jeep when I stepped back into the sweltering heat. "What'd he say?" Rafe asked as I hiked my butt into the Jeep.

"Hasn't seen him in two days. Hasn't had a call to explain his absence which the manager claims isn't like him. How about his coworkers?"

Rafe turned the key. "Ditto. Kind of makes him look like a serious person of interest, doesn't it?"

Since the question was rhetorical, I didn't reply. My mind churned with the possible connections between Laney Hoffman's murder, the attack on Dan Hoffman and Victor Moretti's unexplained absence from both home and work when the fat tires on Rafe's Jeep crunched into the empty parking lot in front of Finnegan's Irish Pub.

"Kinda early for a drink," I commented as we drove down one side of the building and circled around the rear.

"Bartender might've been here," Rafe muttered as he completed the circuit and ended up back at the street. "The Mrs. said Moretti hung out here a lot. I figured it might save time coming back out this way later."

I didn't want to think about how much later we'd still be at this. "Maybe. But the chance of catching the guy who closes up is slim. He's probably still in bed."

"Or her." Rafe smirked. "There's a hot babe serving up drinks in this place. Or so I've heard."

I smirked back.

"Okay. Seen. She's stacked like a . . . well, just say she's easy on the eyes. Raven hair and fair-skinned. A true Irish lass. So, we'll check back later." He caught a break in the traffic and headed for the coffee shop.

Two minutes later, Rafe wedged the Jeep into a narrow slot in front of the coffee shop, grabbed his travel mug and headed inside, leaving me to check for messages from Santos or Broussard.

"Here," Rafe said returning to the Jeep a few minutes later. He handed me a reusable container bearing the logo of the coffee shop.

I dropped my phone in my lap and reached for the mug. "I have at least a dozen coffee mugs. You didn't have to buy a new one."

Rafe climbed back into the driver's seat. "But you didn't have one in my Jeep. Now you do." He nestled his battered cup in one half of the holder between the seats.

I muttered my thanks and took a healthy swig of the strong, amaretto flavored iced coffee. My favorite. Rafe already had my number. He was a thoughtful and generous man and I was lucky to have drawn him as partner in spite of his being a chick-magnet, and reveling in the attention his good looks drew.

"They get it right?" he nodded at my cup.

"Yeah." I took another sip.

"On the off chance he knew Vic and maybe had seen him recently I asked the guy at the counter about him. He said he hasn't seen him since the day before yesterday."

"Anything out of the usual then?"

Rafe shook his head. "Nope. He comes in from time to time, orders the same thing, some frufru whipped thing with flavoring, and always two cream-filled donuts. Same as two days ago."

Rafe put his hand on the key, ready to restart the Jeep. "Wanna see if we can surprise Laney's best friend at home?"

I nodded.

One of the details Broussard had pried out of Dan Hoffman was the name and address of his wife's best friend, maid of honor at her wedding, and hopefully, confidant.

There would be no surprising the woman as we discovered fifteen minutes later. The house set so far back from the road it couldn't be seen from the gate which only opened after Rafe pressed the intercom button and held their credentials up to the little camera set next to the intercom.

A man in black with a white dress shirt stood between the tall columns flanking the front entrance as we rumbled up the gracefully curving drive surrounded by an ocean of carefully manicured lawn and artfully arranged clusters of palms. I thought butlers were a dead or dying breed. Even my mother didn't have one and she sure would have enjoyed the prestige.

"Deputies," the man said nodding slightly at our approach. "Please come in. Mrs. Collins will see you in the solarium." He turned, obviously expecting us to follow.

The dimensions of this mansion completely outclassed those of the Hoffman house, but it wasn't overbearing, just expansive. With Rafe behind me, we followed the butler, secretary or whatever he was, down a long corridor past a cathedral-ceilinged living room, a dining room that could seat two dozen guests with space to spare, an office that could have serviced a senator and his entire staff, and a library resembling something from Masterpiece Theater. Sun streamed in across the hall floor as we arrived at the solarium, what I would have called a lanai had it been a quarter the size and attached to my house.

Amidst a semi-circle of lacquered-iron lawn chairs and matching table amid a highly scented array of blossoming plants, Rachel Collins sat, poised with a book on her lap and a pot of tea on a tray with delicate china cups. She didn't stand.

"Detectives Jessalyn Quinn and Rafael Morgan of the St. Johns County Sheriff's Department, ma'am." The black-clad man had clearly taken his time inspecting our credentials before allowing us access to the grounds.

"We are sorry to bother you at a time like this," I began, expecting a best friend in mourning.

Mrs. Collins gestured to the empty chairs opposite hers. "Please, have a seat. Would you like some tea?"

I shook my head.

Mrs. Collins nodded prompting her man to leave. "How may I help you?" she asked.

With no easy way to begin the conversation, I fell back on the standard. "We understand that you are—were close friends with Laney Upshaw Hoffman, and we're sorry for your loss."

Mrs. Collins patted the corner of her eye with a wisp of lacy handkerchief that appeared out of nowhere.

"So tragic." Mrs. Collins patted the other eye. "But I'm not sure how I can help you. We were close in high school and stayed close afterward for a while, but then Laney got involved with that congressman and finessed her way onto the oversight committee that went to Afghanistan for a couple months. She was different after that."

I turned to a fresh page in my notebook. "How was she different?" More than likely, something to do with the missing Victor Moretti.

Mrs. Collins ran a carefully manicured fingertip around the lip of her china teacup, a distant look on her face. She shrugged delicately. "It's hard to explain. She was engaged to a very sweet man we knew from college when she left, but she broke it off right after she got home. She must have met someone else while she was out of the country, but never said anything about him. I don't think she forgave me for taking Greg's side over the broken engagement. In any case, if there had been someone else, he was no longer a part of her life because next thing any of us knew, she was engaged to Dan Hoffman and . . ." She trailed off.

"And?" I prompted.

Rafe sat with his hands splayed across his thighs letting me carry the interview.

"She was spending her time with a different sort of people. And her politics had changed." The expression on Mrs. Collin's face mirrored the one my mother used when she disapproved of my life choices.

"Do you know any of those people? Any names?"

Mrs. Collins shook her head, the fashionably coifed hair brushing prominent cheekbones. "I don't. I'd like to be of some help, but I'm afraid I can't. I haven't seen Laney since—" She frowned as if reviewing her calendar. "Since the fund raiser her father hosted two months ago in support of Sheriff Kennedy. Dan was not with her, and she spent most of the evening with a lady companion. I think the lady's name was Marissa, but I wasn't introduced to her." She wrinkled her nose as if sniffing something unpleasant. "Tall, slender, and walked like a model. She had blonde hair, but it wasn't her natural color. Very pretty."

When she'd clearly finished with her recollections, I asked, "Have you ever met Victor Moretti?"

Mrs. Collins pursed her lips. "That name does not sound familiar. I'm sure I haven't."

"Perhaps someone with the initials KW?"

Another elegant shrug.

I fished a card out of my pocket and handed it across the table. "Thank you for your time, Mrs. Collins. If you think of anything, please give us a call."

She studied the card, set it on her tray and nodded. Our permission to leave.

"Well, that's how well hubby knew her," Rafe muttered as we returned to his Jeep that looked so out of place in the graceful drive.

"I'll give Broussard a call and see if he's heard anything about a friend named Marissa." I climbed back into the Jeep. "That medically induced coma they're keeping Dan in, isn't helping." The word coma, even medically induced and presumably within the doctor's control, sent a shiver down my spine. How many people never awoke from them?

My back hurt and my head throbbed. I sagged against the

hot vinyl seats, soaking up the heat, wishing the warmth would make the exhaustion and ache go away. The day was slipping away far too quickly, and we'd hit nothing but dead ends so far.

"At least Finnegan's will be open now," Rafe said over the rumble of his Jeep on the fancy driveway cobbles.

Finnegan's Irish lass fit the picture Rafe's description had conjured up in my imagination. Raven hair falling in voluptuous waves past her shoulders and stopping just above an equally voluptuous cleavage. Rafe winked at me as the woman plopped a bowl of pretzels on the bar and left to fill our drink order.

"Do either Barbie Doll or Ms. Ambition know you flirt with sexy barmaids when you're not with them?"

Rafe loved the ladies and they sure loved him. How he managed to date two different women with neither having caught on that they weren't his one and only was a mystery to me. I'd met neither, but Rafe had talked about them enough that I felt like I knew them. Barbie Doll was his plaything. Ms. Ambition the woman who might be able to tame his bachelor ways, if he ever got serious. They had real names, but Rafe always smiled when I used the nicknames I'd assigned, so I kept it up.

"They should," he said, his grin splitting his handsome face. "I flirt when I'm out with them. Hell, I flirt with all the ladies. Except you, of course." Even his wink had undeniable charm to it.

Rafe possessed the kind of charisma that could navigate today's politically correct world without getting anyone's panties in a wad. I considered it a mark of trust between us that he treated me as he would a male partner.

Rafe set his phone on the bar and began reading over his notes while I turned on my stool and surveyed the room. Except for the flag of Ireland tacked to the ceiling above our heads and a preponderance of Irish beer and liquor signs, the place was typical of any neighborhood bar. A scattering of tables and chairs, eight flat screen televisions mounted where they could be seen from anywhere in the room and a twelve-foot bar with a lineup of alcohol arranged in tiers in front of a mirror that made keeping an eye on patrons possible even with one's back to the room.

"Here ya go, handsome," the Irish lass said as she pushed a foaming glass of Guinness across the scared surface toward Rafe. "And sweet tea for the lady cop." She plunked a coaster and a glass clinking with ice in front of me. "Anything else I can get you?"

Rafe winked at her. "Maybe you wouldn't mind answering a couple questions."

"Depends on the questions." She winked back and leaned into Rafe's space. "Do they have anything to do with how I'm spending my time when this place closes?"

I stifled a snicker. "Do you know this man?" I handed Irish a photo of Victor Moretti.

She nodded. "Vic's a regular, but I haven't seen him in a few days. More than that, actually. More like a week. Why?"

I handed her the photo of Laney we took from her driver's license. "How about this lady?"

Irish studied the photo briefly, then handed it back. "Nope. Can't say I've ever seen her."

"How about any of these gentlemen?" I tried again with a printout of the group photo I'd found in Dan Hoffman's study.

This time the woman turned and held the photo closer to the light, squinting at each face. She shook her head. "None of 'em, except for Vic. Kinda wish I did. They look like an interesting bunch. Soldiers? And friends of that lady?" She pointed to the photo of Laney.

My turn to shrug.

"Wait!" Irish's eyes widened. "That's the woman that got offed yesterday. Vic didn't have anything to do with that. He's one of the good guys."

"We haven't been able to locate him," Rafe said. "We were hoping to catch up with him here. Or find out where we could."

Irish leaned forward, her formidable cleavage on display, her eyes on Rafe to see if he noticed. Which he clearly had and was enjoying the show. I prodded him in the ribs to stay on task.

"Ouch." He gave me a sideways glance.

"Vic's good people." She crossed her arms over her chest, her expression a little cooler. "If I hear anything, I'll let you know."

Rafe handed her his card, which she kissed before slipping it into her shirt to nestle between her gals. Then two sandwiches appeared on the open counter through to the kitchen as someone unseen called her name. Irish grabbed the order and ducked under the end of the bar to deliver it to a table in the corner.

"Another dead end," I muttered tipping down the last of my sweet tea.

"But a delightful view, for all that." Rafe watched the bartender's hips as she swayed across the floor.

We slid off our stools to leave. As we passed a table occupied by a lone customer, the man reached out and tagged Rafe. Rafe spun toward the guy so rapidly the man cowered back in his chair.

"That lady you were asking about?" the man said, still wary. "I've seen her places."

Rafe grabbed a chair and sat straddling the back. I remained standing, but handed Rafe Laney Hoffman's photo.

Rafe placed the photo on the table, planted his fingers on it and turned it to face the man. "Is this the woman you're talking about?"

"Yeah, that's her," the man said, his head bobbing.

"Where have you seen her?" Rafe asked.

The man relaxed some. "Places. Other bars. She gets around."

A bar-hopping socialite? Not exactly the picture either Lawrence Upshaw or Dan Hoffman painted of their deceased loved-one, but it fit with the description Rachel Collins had given of her former friend.

The man chewed on the inside of his cheek. "I don't know if it's her favorite place or not, but I've seen her at The Black Parrot a lot. Sometimes she's with a tall lady with dyed-blond hair. And sometimes with a dark-haired man. Average height."

I leaned my hands on the table and added the group shot to the one of Laney Hoffman. "Do you know any of these?"

The man shook his head. "Except the dead lady. Don't know her exactly, just of her and I've heard people call the guy she's been hanging with Kyle, but that's all I know."

KW! My heart skipped a beat.

"You mind giving us your name?"

The man jerked back in his chair looking alarmed. "I'm just trying to be a good citizen. I heard you asking after her, but I don't want to get involved."

"Just for our notes, that's all," Rafe assured him. "You're not involved."

The guy hesitated for a moment, then gave us his name and mobile number.

Rafe stood, twirled the chair back into place and pushed it in. "Thanks, buddy."

I followed Rafe out into the heat and glare of the late afternoon sun.

"Next stop, The Black Parrot," I directed as we piled back into Rafe's Jeep.

Minus the flag and the flashing Bailey's Irish Cream Liquor sign, The Black Parrot was a repeat of Finnegan's. A few more customers here, and we had to wait for the bartender's attention.

"What can I do for St. Johns County's finest?" The sandy-haired bartender with a neatly trimmed beard had finally found his way to our end of the bar. "Who's the lady, Rafe?"

"My partner, Detective Jesse Quinn."

"Nice to meet you, Detective." He reached across the bar to shake my hand. "Name's Gibbs."

I handed over Moretti's photo. "We're looking for this man."

The bartender took the photo, then shook his head. "Not anyone I recognize. Sorry, Detective."

"How about her?"

"Well, of course, I know Laney. She's a regular."

Laney had been leading a double life Dan knew nothing about. He might be an ace in the courtroom, but he was too trusting and too blind when it came to his own love life. "When was the last time you saw her?"

The man scratched his beard. "Two nights ago? No, three. Three nights ago. She was here with a guy named Kyle. Actually, she wasn't technically here with him. She was here first, and he came in later. I think it was arranged, but they had an argument and he left."

"Do you have a last name?" Rafe jumped into the interview.

"Her girlfriend might know. Laney Hoffman hangs out—" He swallowed. "Used to hang out with Marissa. Nasty business."

"Hey, Gibbs! We need another round over here."

Before we lost his attention, I raised my voice and asked. "Do you have the girlfriend's last name?"

Gibbs circled a finger above his head without looking at the voice demanding attention. "Marissa Tate. She covers for me sometimes when I'm short-handed. Wait a sec."

He ducked into a back room, then came back with a slip of paper with both a phone number and an address.

"Describe this Marissa Tate for us." Rafe said.

"Tall. Blond. Lousy dye job, legs that never end. She's a looker, if you like the type."

"And what type would that be?" Rafe asked.

The man wagged his head. "Not your type, Rafe. Smokes like a house afire. Loud, thinks a little too well of herself. She calls herself a model because she got a gig once, but she's an okay bartender. Available when I need her, most of the time."

I dug out another card and handed it to the man. "Call one of us if you see the first guy we showed you. Or if you think of anything else." I was getting tired of the call us routine, but you never knew when someone just might think of something after we walked away.

"Sure thing, ma'am." He tossed me a mocking salute and hustled away to assemble another round for the table by the dance floor.

"Do you know every bartender in town on a first name basis?" I asked my partner as we exited the bar and headed for his Jeep.

"Most of 'em." He wagged his eyebrows at me. Barbie Doll introduces me. All except Irish. Her I met all on my own."

A snort escaped me that would have horrified my mother. "I'm interested to see what kind of woman isn't your type."

Rafe plugged the new address into his phone. "You're not

my type. No offense."

"Good thing. You aren't my type either."

Although, as I studied him while he navigated through the late afternoon traffic, I wondered why not. He was smart, thoughtful and funny. Tall and handsome, even with the tumble of red curls that defied whatever cut his barber was going for. He sported a fashionable scruff, and he dressed like he could have walked off the pages of GQ. In fact, he possessed a lot of the characteristics that made Seth Cameron so attractive. The comparison made me wonder if Rafe could cook, or if he'd ever gotten grease under his fingernails fixing up old cars. What would he be like with teenage boys?

"What are you looking at?"

"You," I answered honestly. "I was just wondering why you aren't my type."

Rafe's green eyes danced and he suppressed a grin. "Are you rethinking that?"

I laughed. "Not even. You already have too many women falling all over themselves when you're around. You need me to keep you grounded."

Abruptly the laugher left me. Dan was still in a coma. Victor Moretti was still in the wind and we had no idea who KW was, except that his first name was likely Kyle and he'd been seen arguing with Laney Hoffman the night before she was murdered.

CHAPTER 6

THE SUN HAD JUST BEGUN to fill the western sky with a colorful array of orange and pink as Rafe turned into the trailer park located behind a short strip of stores that included a pizza shop, a laundromat, a nail salon and a beach cottage rental office. He navigated his way past the pick-up lane for the pizzeria, just as my phone rang.

"Pull over, Rafe. It's our micromanaging lieutenant."

Damn.

Rafe swerved into a patch of beaten down dirt in front of a row of mailboxes. As I hit speaker Fletcher Ward's voice blasted through the Jeep.

"Where are you on tracking down Moretti?"

I grimaced. "He's in the wind, Lieutenant. His wife hasn't seen him since yesterday morning and has no idea where to find him. He's not at work, nor at the hangout she suggested. We're tracking down leads."

"Kennedy's breathing down our neck," Ward growled. "Upshaw wants Hoffman cuffed to his hospital bed, and we need something to tell the news people."

Rafe leaned over to ask. "Deputy Morgan here, sir. Have you talked to Broussard? He was checking out Hoffman's alibies for the time between leaving work and finding his wife's body."

"And came up with exactly nothing," Ward snorted. "Nothing to corroborate Hoffman's narrative, that is."

"But nothing to refute it either. Right?" I prayed so anyway. We could hear Ward breathing.

"Look, I'm not trying to be the heavy here, but I need something to give Kennedy so he can keep Upshaw from going off the deep end."

Ward didn't know how to be anything but heavy and oblivious to the obstacles deputies in the field ran into. Made the rest of us wonder if he'd ever spent a day in a fruitless chase.

I bit my tongue on a snarky comment. "We are a minute away from catching up to a woman who we've been told is a recent friend of the deceased. Maybe she can give us something. Any news on Dan Hoffman's condition?"

Ignoring my question, Ward spit out, "Don't plan to go home tonight." Then clicked off.

"We didn't go home last night," I complained. I thought of my kids and prayed they weren't planning anything in my absence I wouldn't approve of.

Rafe muttered as he put the Jeep back in gear. "Gonna be another long night, probably without anything worth staying up for."

"No nookie for you, two nights in a row."

Rafe pouted. Even his pout was charming.

"My kids are going to disown me." At least Jacqui would. Mike was more forgiving and supportive, but that didn't stop the guilt trip my mother laid on me, or that I laid on myself. Rafe however, juggled two women and I'd bet he'd enjoy two nights of missed sleep that didn't involve chasing down murderers.

Moments later we arrived at 106 Seashell Lane. As mobile homes go, it wasn't awful. The park seemed a little run down, but not totally gone to seed and most of the trailers were confined in neatly fenced yards. Some even had grass.

Latticework in desperate need of paint skirted the base of Marissa Tate's trailer and a small deck jutted off one side. Flower boxes lined the railing, but whatever had been planted in them had given up the ghost a long time ago.

We stepped out of the Jeep and climbed the two steps to the deck. Rafe rapped on the door. After a long minute with no response, he rapped again harder, and spoke to the door in a firm, carrying voice.

"Marissa Tate? We're with the St. Johns County Sheriff's office. We need to ask you a few questions."

The door flew open.

"Hush!" a very pretty woman with a half-grown-out dye job hissed. "You want my neighbors to think I'm a criminal or something? What'd'ya want?"

"If you're Marissa Tate we'd like to ask you about your friend Laney Hoffman." Rafe stepped forward placing his foot just far enough over the threshold that she wouldn't be able to shut the door.

I wasn't expecting trouble, but I kept my hand close to the butt of my weapon. Rafe and I produced our ID folders.

The woman looked past us at Rafe's Jeep.

"I'm Marissa Tate, but it's a good thing you didn't come here in a cruiser, or I'd tell you to get lost." Her voice had the rasp of a life-long smoker.

I stepped closer. "May we come in?"

Her eyes took on a suspicious sheen. "What for?"

Gibbs had labeled her a good bartender and that required being sociable. Her suspicion, however, hinted at something to hide.

"We'd like to ask you about Laney Hoffman," Rafe repeated with more patience than I had.

Ms. Tate took her time stepping back to let us enter. The overpowering stench of stale cigarette smoke hit me. I *tsked.*

My suit would have to go to the cleaners before I could wear it again.

Our reluctant hostess gestured to a grouping of tired gray-blue furnishings that more or less matched the faded denim curtains. A scarred and cluttered coffee table held a shell that served as an ashtray and several empty beer cans.

"Have a seat." No offer of refreshment. None of the refinement of the Collins home. Laney Hoffman's taste in friends and surroundings had definitely taken a seriously different direction if Marissa Tate was any example.

I perched gingerly on the edge of the couch and Rafe settled onto a chair opposite me. Ms. Tate took the other chair and crossed her endlessly-long legs showing ample thigh. Without asking if we minded, she pinched her lips around a fresh cigarette from one of two half-used packs on the table and lit up, wreathing her head with a cloud of smoke that quickly spread to the rest of the living room.

Rafe coughed once. He might be a hopeless flirt, but he was definitely not impressed with this woman.

Ms. Tate took the cigarette from her mouth. "This is about her being killed. Isn't it?"

"I'm sorry for your loss," I said, pulling out my notebook. "We are investigating her death, yes."

"Laney was a terrific person. I can't imagine why anyone would want to kill her." Another vigorous round of puffing renewed the miasma of cigarette smoke. "She was just so pretty and full of life."

Rafe cleared his throat as if the smoke had clogged it. "How long have you known Mrs. Hoffman?"

Ms. Tate pursed her lips as if the question required considerable thought. "About a year. She started coming into the

Black Parrot around then, and we got to be friendly. I wouldn't say we were BFFs or anything, but she shared a lot. You know how it is, being a bartender. Everyone shares their miseries like we're father confessors or something."

I asked, "Do you know if she was unhappy in her marriage?" The wedding hadn't been all that long ago, but Dan must have suspected something of Laney's discontent considering Mrs. Harker's recital of their recent argument. Maybe she'd shared more with her sometimes friend.

Ms. Tate pulled another cigarette from the pack and lit it from the first one. "She was over the moon about Dan, and she was thrilled to become Mrs. Hoffman. But I guess she never considered what kind of hours he might work, and it wasn't long before some of that shine wore off."

"What exactly wore the shine off?" Rafe asked using her words. "Was it just long hours, or was it something else?"

Kyle Somebody-or-other had to be accounted for.

"She wanted a baby and Dan wasn't getting the job done," the woman said.

Rafe's brows rose. Newly married and not getting it on? I could almost read Rafe's thought process.

"They fucked like rabbits according to Laney," Tate continued. "When he was home, anyway. Not using any protection, she kept thinking it'd happen. She was getting kind of frustrated and wanted him to see a doctor, but he said he was too busy. That's when she started hanging out at the Parrot, and talking to me."

"They argue about it?"

"Probably." Ms. Tate glanced at Rafe, then back at me. "She never said. Do you think Dan Hoffman killed her because he found out she was sleeping around and another man got her pregnant?"

Crap! More motive to bury Dan with.

Rafe flicked a glance at me, brows lifted. I shared his surprise. Broussard hadn't mentioned any pregnancy in his summary of the autopsy.

Marissa flicked ashes into the overflowing shell. "Laney was pretty drunk the night she told me that bit of news. Claimed it was Kyle's baby and not Dan's. I told her it didn't matter whose kid it was, she needed to stop drinking. Alcohol isn't good for babies."

Rafe jumped on the name. "Who is this guy, Kyle?"

"Kyle Wallace. She took up with him four, maybe five months or so back. She was frustrated. Her husband had some big case going that took him back and forth to Atlanta quite a bit. Kyle came onto her one night and she left with him. They were a number for a while. He's a good-looking guy. Not the brightest bulb in the box, but still. Maybe she was only sleeping with him to get pregnant."

Then possibly fell for him? Complicating everything, considering the mushy crap in her journal. I wondered why she'd never mentioned the pregnancy in the privacy of those pages, though. Maybe writing the words down was too scary. Maybe she feared Dan's reaction. Or Kyle's.

Rafe tapped something into his tablet. "Mrs. Hoffman and a man who might have been Kyle Wallace were seen arguing a few nights ago. Any idea what they might have been arguing about?"

Ms. Tate jerked her head back in surprise. "I didn't even know they were still seeing each other."

My mind ran through the possibilities. If Dan wasn't the father, maybe he had threatened divorce. Maybe that's what had provoked her screaming at him out front of their home the morning of her death. And if Kyle was a married man, refused to leave his wife or even acknowledge his paternity, that could explain the argument at the bar.

"Do you know where we can find Kyle Wallace?" Rafe asked.

"Sure. He lives out on the island. In one of those little complexes near the Winn-Dixie."

Rafe tapped rapidly. "How about where he works?"

"He's a real estate guy. Owns a bunch of rental properties so no telling where you'd find him. You could call his office and they might be able to tell you where he is. He's part of that Caffey Group. They do a lot of weekly rentals along the beach."

This was beginning to feel like a scavenger hunt. Rafe handed Ms. Tate his card and asked her to contact us if she thought of anything else, then got to his feet. I joined him and sucked in a deep breath of fresh air as soon as we stepped out onto her deck.

In the Jeep, I Googled for a phone number for The Caffey Group. I called and identified myself, asking if Kyle Wallace was working and where.

"420 E Street," I told Rafe as he turned out of the trailer park and back onto Route 1. "Apparently he's installing a new washer for one of his tenants."

"I shouldn't be surprised at the mess people make of their lives by now, but this takes the cake," Rafe said as he headed for the bridge to the island. "She's married to a successful attorney who everyone seems to think is crazy about her. She's got a mansion of a house on the beach, and more money than she can spend. And she takes up with some guy she meets in a bar just to get pregnant. Didn't she ever hear of IVF?"

Pregnancy! That sure added a ton of motive on a man I could've sworn was as innocent as they come

CHAPTER 7

THE LAST TWENTY-FOUR HOURS played through my head as we headed back toward the beach. The vibration of the Jeep's big tires added to the disconnected weariness taking over my body and my brain, but with Dan's guilt hanging out there and the first clue to Laney's secret life dangling in front of us, I had to stay focused. When he pulled to a stop, I sighed audibly.

Even Rafe, six years younger and in far better shape slumped as he shut the engine off and sat there for a minute, until I slid from the Jeep and squared my shoulders.

Rafe joined at me. "This better be the last stop of the day. The Lieutenant's plan for us to work all night be damned."

A battered Dodge Durango with a carry platform attached to the back sat in front of the house on E Street, one of eight modest homes on a street four blocks off the beach. The tag matched that on record for Kyle Wallace, and presumably, he'd transported the washing machine he was replacing on that rack, but neither he nor the washer were in sight.

No one answered the front door when we knocked so we circled around to the back of the house where we found a small shed built onto the rear wall. A man on his knees had his head thrust into the narrow space between the wall and the washing machine.

"Mr. Wallace?" I guessed. Who else could it be?

When the bent figure didn't respond, Rafe prodded the sole of the man's sneaker with his shoe.

The man backed out of the space and looked up. "Yeah? I'm

Wallace. What can I do for you?"

I flipped open my ID case. "We'd like to ask you a few questions."

Wallace scrambled to his feet. "Yes, ma'am. What's the trouble?"

"You know Laney Hoffman?"

Wallace swallowed, his eyes shifting down to the left. "Am I in trouble?"

"Depends." Rafe shrugged. "Do you have an alibi for yesterday between three in the afternoon and six pm?"

Wallace's eyes widened. "I didn't do whatever you think I've done."

Maybe he had a good reason to look alarmed. "What were you doing during that time period?" I repeated Rafe's question. "Can anyone vouch for you?"

"I was up in Fernandina Beach." He seemed to relax a bit.

Damn. Please don't let this be another dead end. "What time was that?"

Wallace pulled a kerchief out of his back pocket and moped his brow. "All afternoon. You can ask my wife. I was with her. This is about Laney getting offed, isn't it?"

So, he knew she was dead and his first thought was to ask if he was in trouble?

I explained. "You aren't in trouble unless you're lying about your whereabouts, but we'd like you to come down to Central for an interview. We're trying to put the last few days of Mrs. Hoffman's life together so we can figure out what happened to her."

Wallace glanced quickly between Rafe and me, then swallowed. "I didn't kill her."

"We're not saying you did. We'd just like your help finding

out who did."

His Adam's apple bobbed twice more. "I don't know nothing about it. You can't arrest me."

"You're not being arrested," Rafe said more patiently than I would have.

I wanted to grab the jerk by the filthy shirt covering his bulging beer gut and tell him we were tired and didn't have time for his shit. Except we needed his cooperation and at the moment we had no basis for an arrest.

Wallace nodded in capitulation. "I've just got a couple more minutes here and I'm done. Can I meet you there?"

"We'll wait," I said. No way was I letting this man out of my sight. Then I stalked back toward the street.

"Why drag him in?" Rafe asked as we stopped beside his Jeep.

"I want him off balance and out of his own element."

"Good thought. I hope this doesn't take long. I'm starving."

IN A CRAMPED INTERVIEW ROOM back at Central, I crossed my ankles and leaned against the wall, letting Rafe take the lead on questioning Kyle Wallace. If the man was where he said he was, then he wasn't our guy, but a lead is a lead, and the more people we talked to the more we knew about Laney and her lifestyle, and hopefully that would ultimately lead us to her killer. And take Dan off the short list.

"How well do you know Laney Hoffman?" Rafe asked leaning back in his chair all casual and unconfrontational. Something he was good at. I tended to get into a person's space.

"Everyone knew Laney Hoffman," Kyle replied lifting his hands, palms up. She was a spoiled little society bitch. Besides, we graduated high school together. We dated a little."

Rafe tipped his head. "But not recently?"

"I've seen her around."

"Just around?" Rafe sounded bored. He sat forward in his chair and began doodling on a yellow pad of paper as if nothing Kyle said was all that important. It was an affectation Rafe liked in order to look busy, when in reality he took notes on his tablet or his phone.

Kyle shrugged again. "Just around."

Rafe started sketching a parrot. "You were seen talking with her at The Black Parrot recently. That's not exactly just around."

"Yeah, I saw her. And we talked."

Rafe added detail to the parrot's feathers. He was a pretty good artist. "According to witnesses, it looked more like you were arguing. And that your meeting wasn't accidental."

I stuck my hands in my pockets, another habit my mother would have chastised me for, and slouched while I waited for Rafe to spring his trap.

Wallace sputtered, "Okay, so it wasn't accidental. She called me and asked me to meet her there. When she came onto me, I told her I was a married man and whatever we had going in high school was over ages ago, so stop chasing me. She got angry."

"If it was over ages ago, why would you agree to meet her there in the first place?" Rafe drew a perch under the parrot's feet. Then the perch grew teeth. Like an animal trap.

Wallace hissed. "Because she asked me to. She said she knew a guy who had a house he wanted to flip. When you work for yourself, contacts are important. You take what you can get from wherever it comes. Ya know?"

Rafe nodded as if he understood, but a new edge entered his voice that I recognized. "And that's all it was? A meeting to pass on a business prospect?"

"Yeah."

"What was the argument about?"

"No argument. I don't know what someone told you, but we didn't argue about anything. I bought her a beer. She gave me a lead. We went our separate ways."

Rafe looked Wallace in the eye. "And that's the only contact you've had with her since high school?"

Wallace's nod was jerky and eager. His eyes didn't meet Rafe's.

"What would you say if I told you that at the time of her death, Laney Hoffman was pregnant, and she told a friend of hers that the baby was yours?" Rafe's pencil dug into the paper and the teeth on the trap closed around the parrot's feet.

Kyle's jaw dropped. "N—no way! I used protection. Every time."

Rafe tore his sketch from the pad and crumpled it into a ball. Bagged!

I moved to the table and placed my palms flat as I got into Kyle's face. "So, you admit there was more to your recent relationship than just a real estate lead. You were screwing her."

Wallace's eyes went wide, a lot of white and narrowed pupil. "Y—you c—can't tell my wife. She'll kick me out of the house. My own house." Kyle pleaded. "It was just a couple times. A few times," he corrected. "But it wasn't serious. She was married, too. It was just—sex. You know. A good fuck and nothing more. And I always used condoms. The kid's probably Hoffman's."

I shook my head. "Don't lie to us, Mr. Wallace."

Like any cornered perp, Kyle glanced around the room seeking an escape.

I violated his space a little deeper. "Is that what you were arguing about? The pregnancy? And you denied responsibility."

He wilted in his chair. "Yeah. But I didn't kill her."

"About this trip to Fernandina Beach?" Rafe tapped rapidly on his tablet with a silver stylus, redirecting Wallace's attention. "Where you claim to have been during the time Laney Hoffman met her maker. Were you lying about that, too?"

Kyle shook his head vigorously. "I lied about sleeping with her, but I didn't kill her. It's the God's honest truth."

My elation at the ease with which Rafe had trapped Kyle into admitting his affair with Laney ebbed.

Wallace hurried to cement his alibi. "I was in Fernandina Beach, like I said. My wife is into crafts and there was a sidewalk craft festival. I drove her up early so she could get a good table, and I helped set it up. Maybe around one o'clock I think. I stayed the whole time and we didn't get home until after eleven."

"So, your wife can verify you were with her?" Rafe paused, his stylus poised over his tablet.

I remained where I was, hands planted on the table my face in Kyle's space, waiting for his response.

Sweat beaded on Wallace's forehead. I could smell the nervous fear radiating off him. "You can't ask my wife. She can't know about Laney. Please?" His eyes pleaded with me.

Rafe stopped taping and held his stylus poised over the tablet. "Can anyone else verify you were in Fernandina Beach the whole time?"

A wave of relief flowed over Kyle's features. "Yeah. The guy who asked me to help set up for some big evening event. His name is Steve something. He's the manager of that little hotel in downtown Fernandina. He asked me to help set up chairs and tables. Then there were about a hundred vases he wanted real flowers stuck into, with water. And then we had dozens of little lanterns that needed to be checked for fuel. It took forever because the waiters who were supposed to help were late. I finally told him I had to go around seven. I'm diabetic and I'd missed my dinner and needed to eat."

Wallace grimaced, eager to be cleared without his wife being involved.

I stepped back and tapped Rafe on the shoulder to let him know I was going to step into the hall. Kyle wasn't our guy.

A quick search brought up the hotel number. I dialed and when a young female voice answered, I asked for Steve.

"Which Steve?" she asked.

"The one who set up the area for the evening entertainment after the craft festival."

"Wait a sec." The phone clattered to a hard surface.

A pleasant baritone came on the line. "Steve Mason."

I identified myself and asked the man if he had been the one setting up for the entertainment, then if he'd solicited the help of Kyle Wallace. He didn't recall the helper's last name, but his description fit the man sitting in our interview room. He agreed for me to send a local law enforcement officer over with a photo for him to verify.

Kyle and Rafe glanced up at me expectantly as I stepped back into the room.

"His alibi checks out."

Kyle sagged with relief.

"I can go?" Kyle was already on his feet.

I handed him my card. "Thank you for coming in, Mr. Wallace. We'll let you know if there's anything else we need. And please call us if there's anything you think of that might help us find Laney Hoffman's killer.

"Yeah. Yeah, sure. Sure thing." Kyle backed out of the door and sent a brief salute our way before bolting toward the exit.

Rafe tucked the silver stylus back into his pocket. "Lieutenant

Ward is going to ream us a new one when we report in on today's goose chase."

"I thought we were onto something when we got Kyle's name." I plopped into the chair so recently occupied by our only real lead of the day. "Now what?"

CHAPTER 8

LIKE A SUDOKU PUZZLE you think you've got all figured out until the last few numbers don't fit, KW had been such a promising possibility. But he didn't fit.

"With Moretti still in the wind, I vote we get some rest," Rafe said as he got to his feet and headed back to the tiny office we shared.

The BOLO had not unearthed Victor Moretti or his SUV, Dan remained in a coma, and my son flew solo on a Friday night when teenagers wander into God-only-knows-what trouble. I felt as rumpled as my suit jacket. Rafe was right. I sagged into my chair, too tired to think.

Lieutenant Ward was not going to be happy when he arrived at his desk in the morning and discovered we were no closer to making an arrest and had nothing to show for a day's efforts, but we'd barked up every tree we could find. It would give Ward and Upshaw all that much more fuel to argue their case against Dan.

Rafe dropped his tablet on his desk, glanced at his watch, then at me, but didn't sit down. "No use hanging out here tonight."

"You got a hot date or something?" I asked.

He made a growling sound in his throat. "Or something."

"Ms. Ambition or Barbie Doll?"

He winked, suddenly appearing not as tired as he had just moments ago. "Barbie."

I shook my head. "One of these days your double life will catch up with you."

Rafe opened his desk drawer and slid the tablet inside. "But not tonight." He made a suggestive gesture hinting at what was going to happen in his world tonight.

"Doesn't the possibility that these two ladies might run into each other and start comparing notes worry you?"

He snagged the jacket off his chair and draped it over one shoulder. "They move in totally different circles."

"It would worry me," I said. "Those fireworks would light up all of St Augustine."

Rafe made a dismissive gesture with his hand. "You worry too much. Lighten up. See you bright and early, before Ward gets here."

"Bright and early," I agreed as he turned on his heel to leave the room. At the door he spoke over his shoulder. "You need to get laid, Jess. Makes days like this easier to cope with."

He winked and disappeared around the corner.

Seth Cameron's sparkling brown eyes flitted through my mind. I hadn't been with a man since I turned my back on Dan Hoffman four years ago. In truth, I'd been so focused on making good in my new career I hadn't missed either the intimacy or the stress of having a man in my life. At least, until Seth showed up in the principal's office at Mike's school.

I still don't need a guy. At least that's what I keep telling myself. I especially don't need a distraction in the middle of what might be the most important case of my career to date.

With movie star looks and charm to go with it, Seth Cameron would make any woman's blood run hot, and back when he first made it plain he was as interested in me as in helping Mike, I had reminded myself that a personal involvement with the man bordered on a conflict of interest. Or at least a complication. And I'd thought once Mike was back on track Seth would be gone and no longer the temptation I didn't need.

Except Seth wasn't gone. And he hadn't given up tempting me.

I collected my jacket and notebook and headed for the door. Hungry and aching with exhaustion, I still had one more stop to make before heading home.

THE HOSPITAL HAD THAT AFTER-HOURS hush that descended when visiting hours were over. Dimmed lights and the occasional squeak of a nurse's shoes surrounded me as I found Dan's room and nodded at the deputy on duty. An attempt had been made on Dan's life and whoever was responsible remained out there.

The deputy stood. "Mind if I take a quick break if you're going to be here for a few?"

"Sure," I said, and stepped into the room.

So heartbreakingly still, Dan lay hooked up to several monitors with flowing patterns of colored lights. He sported a two-day scruff and his cheeks were almost as pale as the pillowcase. This was ICU – with no chairs for visitors, and no privacy from the watchful eyes at the nurses' station, either. I moved to Dan's side and slid my hand into his unresponsive one.

"I'm so sorry, Dan. We're doing everything we can to find out who did this."

A sudden wave of guilt washed over me. If I had loved Dan the way he'd cared for me, he wouldn't be here now. I wasn't responsible, but the guilt stuck. If he hadn't married Laney, he wouldn't be struggling to hang onto life. I was sure of it, even if I didn't have a clue who murdered the woman or if the same person came after Dan.

I bent closer. "I'm going to prove you're innocent. You

deserve that much from me, and I promise—" but I couldn't promise anything. I hadn't been able to promise to love him when that's all he'd asked of me. Now the stakes were even higher. I squeezed his hand and bowed my head to offer up a prayer. Only God could promise miracles.

"Ma'am?" The deputy had returned. He glanced at our linked hands without comment. I dropped Dan's hand as if holding it was a sin.

I put on my game face and headed for the door. I mumbled something about praying, thanked the guard and strode down the hall without looking back.

Halfway across the parking lot my phone rang.

Caller ID perked me up. "Hey, Mikey-Mike. What's up?"

"Jacqui's here and she's pouting because I told her the boyfriend had to go home. She says I'm not the boss of her."

Boyfriend! What boyfriend? And what happened to Mother keeping her for the weekend?

"I'm on my way. I'll deal with it when I get there."

"Good, 'cause I've got my stuff to do. Oh, and I ordered her a pizza when she complained there was nothing to eat." Usually easy-going, Mike's voice held an unfamiliar edge. "And this kid she brought home is not someone you want her hanging with. Trust me."

The vision of a teenager covered in tattoos with piercings in too many places crossed my mind. I slid into my cruiser and cranked the engine. "I'll be home in ten minutes. Maybe a couple more. Hang in there."

"I'll be in the garage," he said before clicking off. He was probably afraid I'd tell him to stay inside to babysit.

Twelve minutes later, as I swung into my driveway my headlights swept across the rear end of Seth's pickup truck.

Mike hadn't mentioned Seth being present. Seemed odd Seth hadn't sent the boy packing if he was as objectionable as Mike suggested.

The house was uncommonly quiet when I entered. The cat blinked at me solemnly from his sphynx-like pose on the rocker in the corner of the kitchen. No sign of Jacqui, the unsavory boyfriend, Mike, Seth or the exuberant puppy who usually met me at the door, tail wagging furiously.

Assuming Mike and Seth were down in the garage with Murphy tagging along, I strode toward the living room, girding myself to evict the boyfriend and face Jacqui's anger.

The living room was empty. Uneasy, I checked the deck beyond it. Still no sign of my daughter. She wouldn't! I seethed as I stormed down the hall to Jacqui's bedroom.

A dim sliver of light leaked out underneath the bedroom door. Without knocking, I shoved it open. My pre-teen daughter leaped off the lap of the boy lounging against her headboard.

The boy wasn't covered in tats, but he wasn't wearing a shirt either. He was breathing hard, and his tented shorts gave away his state of mind.

"Mother!" Jacqui's imperious tone, so like her grandmother. "You have no right to—"

"This is *my* home and I have every right." I jerked my thumb at the young man. "Out."

He snatched his shirt and flipflops off the floor and scrambled past me without saying a goodbye to either of us.

My heart throbbed and my stomach clenched. Mike and I had discussed house rules, but it hadn't occurred to me that Jacqui was old enough for me to worry about boys in her bedroom.

Far too angry to listen to excuses, I spun on my heel to leave. "We'll talk about this later."

Was this my fault for trying to have a career and be a parent? Having gotten Mike straightened out, albeit with Seth's help, I should have had at least a couple easy years before Jacqui turned into a teenage vamp.

I needed to find Mike, but first I needed to calm down. I slipped out onto the front deck and stood at the edge listening to the rote of the sea. Moonlight glinted off the sliver of ocean visible from our house, second in from the dune. The sound and scent of the sea usually brought me a sense of peace. Couldn't say I'd found much peace, but when my breathing returned to normal and the thudding of my heart subsided, I headed back through the house and down the stairs to the garage.

Mike had slaved to earn the money for the broken-down Mustang convertible he claimed would be road-ready by the time he had his license. An event not far off since he already had his learners permit.

Two jean-clad butts hung over the fender, heads out of sight under the hood of the Mustang. A drop light dangled above them. Murphy had been curled up on an old blanket, but now headed my way. There's nothing like a pooch to make one feel welcome, no matter how awful one's day. I bent and scratched behind the dog's ears, let her lick my chin and then straightened. Neither of the jean-clad butts had moved.

I tugged at Mike's back pocket.

He jerked up, whacking his head on the light and cursing. "Jesus! Mom!"

"Hey, Jesse." Seth straightened more cautiously, saw me and smiled . . . a slow sexy smile that made things churn inside me. I shook off the hint of desire.

"Thanks for the heads-up on Jacqui," I said.

Mike curled his lip. "Guy's a jerk. I tried to tell him to get lost, but he didn't listen."

Seth glanced from Mike to me and back. "What'd I miss?"

"Nothing."

"Kinte Wells," Mike said at the same time.

Seth's brows rose. "Here?" Apparently, he hadn't known about the boy in Jacqui's bedroom.

"Yeah," Mike said. "I left them in the living room. They were watching something on TV."

I shook my head. "They were *in* Jacqui's bedroom, Mike."

A thundercloud crossed Seth's handsome features. "Jeesus! If I'd known—You need me to escort him out?"

I sighed. "Already done."

Seth frowned at Mike. "Why didn't you tell me?"

"They were just watching television," Mike defended himself. But he sounded younger and less certain of himself. "And mom said she'd be home in a few minutes."

The bottled-up anger I hadn't been able to completely lose wanted to lash out, but Jacqui wasn't Mike's responsibility. Neither was she Seth's. She was mine and I'd failed her. I bit down on the nasty things I wanted to say.

"You hungry?" Seth said wiping his hands on a rag. "I could fix you something."

Looking relieved that he was off the hook, Mike said, "There's some pizza leftover."

My stomach rumbled. "Thanks," I mumbled and turned back toward the stairs.

"I think we're done here for tonight, Mike," Seth said just before I reached the top of the stairs and entered the kitchen.

The pizza box sat on the counter with two slices inside. I grabbed one very cold piece and took a bite. Seth and Mike's footsteps sounded on the stairs and I swallowed before turning around. "Thanks for saving me some."

"You can pay me later." Mike pointed at the sales slip shoved under the saltshaker on the table. He was generous but also scraping hard to get his Mustang fixed.

Seth hesitated between the basement stairs and the outside door as if deciding whether to stay or leave. He reached for the doorknob. "It's getting late."

"Stay," Mike said. "Keep Mom company while she eats. I've got homework." He glanced at me, then winked at Seth and headed for his room.

Seth's hand remained on the doorknob. "Should I stay? Or . . ." He left the alternative unsaid.

"Anywhere else you might go would probably be more enjoyable. For you." I did want him to stay, but was afraid to admit it.

"Tough day?" Seth's warm brown gaze grew softer. "Anything to do with the investigation, or is it the issue with Jacqueline?"

"Everything," I replied as I scooped up the second slice of pizza and put it in the microwave. Hands braced on the edge of the counter, I debated if I should just tell him to leave or enjoy some understanding companionship while I downed the rest of the leftover pizza.

I jumped when Seth's hands closed over my shoulders. His thumbs began to massage the taught muscles in my neck and I couldn't stop the groan of pleasure they brought.

No point in asking him to leave now.

The clean masculine scent of his now familiar aftershave enveloped me. I really was uptight, but it wasn't the lack of nookie in my life so much as the constant drive to prove myself and cope with pressure. My mother's disapproval. The murder investigation and my guilt over Dan. And now Jacqui growing up way too fast.

I groaned again as Seth worked his way down my back. If only I could let myself enjoy this man's friendship and anything else he was willing to offer. I distrusted myself emotionally and no way was I hurting Seth the way I'd hurt Dan.

The microwave dinged, and Seth removed his hands. When I retrieved the pizza and turned around, he was seated at the far side of the small kitchen table.

"You want a beer or something?" I asked as I slid the pizza slice onto the table.

"Sounds good."

I grabbed two local brews from the fridge, popped the caps off and brought them to the table.

"I'm sorry. I had no idea he was even here. Mike didn't mention him when I came in."

"Not your fault," I said.

"I'll have a word with Kinte if you'd like. I know his father, too," Seth remarked after taking a swig.

"The whole boy-in-the-bedroom thing blows my mind." My baby wasn't even a teenager yet. What was I going to say to her? The idea of putting her on the pill was impossible to contemplate. She's just a baby.

"How far did it go? Or shouldn't I ask?"

I shook my head. "Just making out." He was half undressed, but thank God Jacqui hadn't been. Just knowing she'd been kissed by a boy distressed the hell out of me.

"Let me know if you change your mind." He leaned back and brought the bottle to his mouth again. That same something that had stirred in me at his smile in the garage hit me again as his lips caressed the rim of the beer bottle

In spite of my exhaustion and my dismay over Jacqui, I

wondered what his kiss would feel like. I ripped off another bite of pizza.

"With nothing on the news about an arrest, I'm guessing the investigation isn't going too well," he said.

I sat back at the change of subject. "I felt like the ball in a pin-ball machine today. Rafe and I bounced from one place to another, but at the end of the day we rolled into the slot with zero for a score."

"Any idea if the attempt on Hoffman is the same person?"

We had no idea at all, but I shouldn't discuss it. Not even with Seth.

"Upshaw must be breathing down your necks," he continued. I'm sure the fact that it's an election year makes a difference, but Upshaw's personality makes for a problem any time. Laney was his little girl. Now she's gone, he's sure to want vengeance." Seth brought the bottle to his mouth again, and I considered getting him another beer.

Seth might not know all the politics that went on down at the sheriff's office, but everyone knew Upshaw and his methods of intimidation.

I swallowed the last bit of pizza. "I can't really discuss an open investigation."

"I hope you know that if you ever need to vent, or just mull your thoughts over out loud, I'm a good listener, Quickdraw. I'm good at keeping secrets, too. It wouldn't go any further than here."

Mother would have admonished me if she'd seen my shrug, but she wasn't here. She wouldn't have approved of Seth's nickname either, since my hasty dash into gunfire early in my career was a story she did her best to forget. "I don't believe Dan killed his wife and we've no idea who tried to take Dan out.

But the only leads we had either alibied out or are in the wind. Praying tomorrow is more productive."

"Follow your gut," Seth said putting his empty bottle down and getting to his feet. "You were dead on about that rash of homeless deaths last month."

How did Seth know about my gut? Or my track record? Certainly not from Mike. I didn't discuss my work with my son. I stood and tossed the paper plate in the rubbish, then turned to face Seth who instead of moving toward the door had followed me and stood dangerously close. Dangerously tempting. If I just leaned forward a little bit, I could press my face into the middle of his broad chest and find some . . . some what? What did I think I wanted? Or needed?

I squared my shoulders. I didn't need anything.

One corner of Seth's mouth quirked up in a half smile as if he'd read my thoughts. Even the glimmer in his eyes seemed only half there, being pushed aside by something else. Something more suggestive. Then he touched my chin lightly with the crook of his finger and flashed his full smile.

"Go to bed. You'll think better with a few hours' sack time." He moved to the door and pulled it open. "Ciao."

I stood by the sink as Seth's casual comment mingled in my head with Rafe's suggestion that I get laid. Did all guys solve their issues with sex? Or was my mind in the gutter with Rafe's?

CHAPTER 9

CLOSING IN ON ELEVEN O'CLOCK and nearly two days with just a two-hour nap, I still faced an uncomfortable discussion about sex and boys with my daughter. The brief respite in Seth's supportive company over, I collected his empty beer bottle where he'd left it on the counter and dropped it with mine into the recycling bin under the sink. How had Jacqui gone from an eager pre-pubescent kid to a teenager with hormones overnight? Almost teenager, I corrected myself. Her birthday was still a month away.

I took Murphy out to do her thing and checked on my struggling tomato plants. I wasn't procrastinating. Just marshalling my thoughts.

"Sorry," I apologized to my wilted veggies. "I didn't forget you. I was just busy." I watered them, then watered a bit more. Was I just as negligent with my daughter? Was this all my fault? Where had she picked up this Kinte Wells kid anyway? I should have asked Mike.

Murphy moseyed her way across the lawn sniffing every interesting scent, finally arriving at my feet. She looked up at me with her tongue lolling.

I opened the door and she trotted off down the hall.

I followed with far less energy, and she'd disappeared into Mike's room before I reached the end of the hall. I squared my shoulders and knocked on Jacqui's closed door.

"I'm busy."

Not very welcoming. Not that I'd expected her to be eager to discuss the hormone-driven scene I'd interrupted.

She flipped her laptop shut at the sight of me, and slapped her hand down on top to emphasize no prying. Probably sending outraged emails to her grandmother. Or worse, to Kinte.

"We weren't doing anything," she began, her jaw set.

Not doing anything if you didn't count giving each other tonsil checks. The pink walls, ruffled curtains and shelf full of dolls were so at odds with my little girl's earlier activities.

But, I'd give her a chance before I laid into her. I crossed the room and sat on the edge of her bed. "You call what I saw not doing anything?"

"It was Kinte's idea."

Not the best defense. I didn't really care whose idea it was, only that my daughter thought it was okay. "And if Kinte thought it was a good idea to jump off the Bridge of Lions, would you jump?"

"You think I'm stupid?" Her tone flippant.

"No, I don't think you're stupid. Naïve yes. But not stupid. And being rude is not helping your cause."

She tossed her hair over her shoulder and lifted her nose a notch. "My cause?" Her eyes flashed. "We were just kissing."

"You're twelve years old—"

"Almost thirteen," Jacqui snapped back.

I ignored the interruption. "You think climbing into bed with a boy, one who is partially undressed, by the way, and making out with the door closed is something I'd approve of?" Heat flushed my skin. "You know better than that."

"I bring all my other friends to my room all the time." She gave me that haughty look her grandmother excelled at.

"All your other friends are not boys." My words were clipped, my head about to explode. I needed to calm down.

Jacqui studied me, her eyes half shut. "So, it's okay if I have boys in my room so long as I don't shut my door."

"No!" My denial came out like a gun shot, harsh even in my own ears. I tempered my voice. "It's not okay to bring a boy to your room. Door shut or open. Mike says—"

"Mike's not my boss," she sneered.

I wanted to slap the expression off her face. "Trust me, he has no desire to be your boss, but he seems to think there's good reason I wouldn't approve of Kinte Wells."

Jacqui *tsked*. A habit she clearly picked up from me. I wasn't sure if I should be pleased there was at least a little of me in her or dismayed because it sounded as rude as my mother suggested. "He's just jealous. Kinte is the most popular kid at school." Again that toss of the hair.

I stared at the lineup of stuffed animals on her bed, trying to cool my jets. Best to leave Mike out of the conversation. Just focus on Jacqui and her naïve ideas.

With a steadier breath, I got back to the issue at hand. "This isn't about your brother, or even about Kinte. It's about you and what's smart and what's not. You want to be all grown up, but you're not. You're still—"

"I'm not a baby any more, but you're treating me like one." She got up and flounced across the room to the window before facing me, her arms crossed tight over her chest.

"And I'll continue to treat you like one as long as you act like one."

"I want to live with Daddy."

That hurt more than having a two-year-old say I hate you for the first time. "Living with your father would not change the fact that you can't behave like a tramp and get away with it."

"You act like I was hooking up or something."

Hooking up? Holy crap! What was going on in that juvenile mind? "Kissing with your tongues down each other's throats is just the beginning. If I hadn't come home when I did, when were you planning to put a stop to it?"

"Mo-om."

"Don't Mo-om me. I know a lot more about boy-girl stuff than you do, and I don't want you to find out the hard way that getting a guy turned on is a whole lot easier than getting him turned off."

My tactical vest would not have saved me from her stare. I wanted to shake her until her teeth rattled, but I abhorred physical violence so I shot from the bed and lurched to the door.

"You're grounded. For a month."

My daughter probably would have slammed the door behind me in outrage at the longest discipline I'd ever dished out to her . . . but I beat her to it.

Morning came far too soon. Sleep hadn't come easy as my mind insisted on replaying my discussion with Jacqui, pointing out all the places I might have been more diplomatic. What if she did ask her father if she could live with him? We had joint custody, but living with Elliott had never been discussed. What kind of failure did that make me?

Jacqui already worshipped Elliott's new and fresh young girlfriend, Brandy Hope Lovejoy. Even the woman's name put my teeth on edge. Mother would say my daughter's defiance was all my fault. If I hadn't been so caught up in following my dad's footsteps into law enforcement, I'd have seen this coming, she'd say. I'd have been a better mother, she'd add.

I dragged myself into the shower. The cold water woke me up, but didn't cool me off.

Being Saturday, both kids still slept when I strapped on my service weapon and headed for work. I left a note on the table reminding Jacqui of her sentence and cash to pay Mike for the pizza. If I arrived at work ahead of everyone else, I'd put in a grocery order to be delivered. Nobody would say I didn't put food on the shelves for my kids.

Rafe's Jeep wasn't in the lot. Thankfully, neither was Lieutenant Ward's silver Lexus. I dropped my jacket over the back of my chair, sat and placed the grocery order, then sent a text to Mike to let him know when it would be delivered, and ask him to please put the refrigerator stuff away when it did. Mother duties accomplished, I began going over my notes for the Hoffman case and adding pertinent details to the whiteboard along with a photo of Kyle Wallace with a slash drawn through the question mark.

Corporal Dalton, Lieutenant Ward's new right-hand man, stuck his head in the doorway. "The boss wants to know if anyone has managed to catch up with Victor Moretti?"

I shook my head.

"Ward wants a complete update. In his office. In ten minutes. Broussard and Rafe, too." Dalton turned on his heel and strode down the hall.

Rafe appeared with his cell to his ear. He flipped the bird toward Dalton's retreating back.

The phone on my desk lit up and I grabbed for it. Dora from Comms. "A guy called earlier," she said. "Wouldn't leave a message. Just said he needed to talk to you."

I snatched my pen, ready to write. "Name? Number?"

"Moretti. A Virginia number."

In the wind and a long way from home!

My heart raced as I jotted down the number. "Thanks Dora."

Should I call him back immediately? Or wait until after the showdown with Ward?

Immediately. Maybe we'd have something worth reporting. I punched in the number on my cell instead of the landline. Lieutenant Ward could wait.

I grabbed Rafe's sleeve. "Moretti," I mouthed as I put the phone on speaker and set it on the desk. We both hunched over it as if shielding it from prying eyes and big ears.

"Hello?" The deep voice sounded wary.

"Is this Victor Moretti?"

"Ah, ya. And who is this?" Dripping with suspicion.

"Detective Jesse Quinn. You called me." No need to mention I'd been hunting for him for the last twenty-four hours.

"Dan Hoffman didn't kill his wife. But I might know who did."

My mouth went dry. "You got a name?"

"Not over the phone," he whispered. "We need to meet."

"Where are you?"

"Not saying. It's not safe. There are people following me."

"In Virginia?"

"I'm not in Virginia."

Rafe's eyebrows lifted as he glanced at me.

"Okay. Why don't you just come to the sheriff's office instead of all this cloak and dagger stuff? You'll be safe here."

"No!" His voice rose with a hint of panic.

I kept my voice calm in spite of my eagerness. "Who is following you?"

"Someone who wants to kill me. Three people are already dead because of what they knew."

Good God! How big was this thing? "Who besides Laney Hoffman?"

"Two guys we both knew in Afghanistan. I tried to warn her, but now I'm afraid maybe I led them right to her."

The picture on my phone, taken of the framed photo on Dan Hoffman's credenza leapt into my mind. "Who else besides Ms. Hoffman?" I repeated. My heart raced like a parent determined to grab the latest toy craze on Black Friday.

"Isaac Leitz and Dominic Garcia."

Two of the names on the Arlington list. If they'd been killed in this county wouldn't that have shown up in our search? Rafe jabbed at his tablet, not bothering to take his stylus out.

Moretti hadn't answered my initial question. "Who is after you?"

"Look, Detective. I'll tell you everything I know. But it's gotta be in person and not at the sheriff's office. I don't know who the guy's got in his pocket and I'm not taking chances he's got ears in that place, too. I've already talked too long."

If whoever Vic Moretti was afraid of had ears here, he'd taken a chance just leaving his name and phone number with communications. "Where?"

Nothing. Moretti had disconnected. Shit. I should have had someone pinging his phone.

Rafe looked up with a grimace of disgust. "Crap."

"My thought exact—" My cell buzzed.

"There's a big re-enactment going on at the fountain," Moretti said in a rush. "Lots of tourists, lots of costumes. I'll stay lost in the crowd unless you come alone."

I shook my head even though Moretti couldn't see me. "Not happening. I'd be crazy to come alone and you know it. You could be the killer. Where would that leave me? My partner comes with."

Another long pause made me think I'd lost him again.

Moretti's voice came at last. "Meet me behind the boat over by the watch tower. In half an hour."

The line went dead.

Great. Finally had a promising lead, and we were expected in Lieutenant Ward's office five minutes ago.

Rafe glanced at his watch. "What are we going to tell Ward?"

I shook my head. "We don't tell him. At least not until after we've got Moretti in custody."

Rafe frowned, "He finds out we knew where Moretti was and didn't keep him the loop he'll blow a gasket. Never mind what Sheriff Kennedy will say."

I wagged my head. "But what if whoever killed Laney does have someone in the sheriff's office? What if her death is connected to those other two and Moretti has a good reason to be worried?"

"Conspiracies like that only happen on television. The sheriff runs a tight ship here. And we know everyone," Rafe pointed out.

"Except Corporal Dalton." It suddenly hit me. "Who just happens to be from Virginia where Arlington Security is home-based. Kind of convenient, don't you think?"

Rafe dragged a hand over his fashionable scruff. "Okay. We tell Ward after, but we better get a move on before he sends his watchdog down here to get us."

As we hurried up the hall, questions swirled in my head. If Moretti was the killer, why had he called me instead of putting as much distance between himself and St. Johns County as possible? And if he hadn't killed Laney, how had his fingerprints ended up on the murder weapon? And who else might be involved that we didn't know about yet, and what had happened to Isaac Leitz and Dominic Garcia? And who was after all of them?

My cell vibrated. I lurched to a halt, checked caller ID and put it to my ear. "Quinn."

"Detective Quinn. Henry Dalton, here. Lieutenant Ward was called away on a family emergency. You're to report anything new to me. When you have something, that is." A supercilious scorn colored his words. He thought he was big shit just because he'd worked on a city department before ending up in our sheriff's office.

"Thank you, Dalton." Thank God, actually. We wouldn't have to run the risk of lying to Ward after all. He might still be pissed if anything went wrong and we hadn't appraised him of the meet, but at least it wasn't like standing in front of his desk lying outright.

"We're off the hook." I said, hanging up.

"So," Rafe wagged his eyebrows. "Do we get dressed out as Spanish colonists or go as detectives?"

CHAPTER 10

"MORETTI'S GOING TO SEE US before we see him," I told Rafe as we hurried toward my cruiser to head to the reenactment going on at the Fountain of Youth. If there'd been time, I might have detoured by the house and grabbed the gear I wore when I participated in these reenactments.

But no time. My Saturday cargo pants and department polo shirt would have to do. "Why you're wearing a suit coat in spite of the heat on a weekend shift, I've no idea, but in a sea of reenactors and tourists, you'll stick out like a peacock in a flock of seagulls," I commented.

Rafe snickered, shucked his jacket, jerked his tie free and unbuttoned his collar. He yanked his shirt out of his waistband to cover the sidearm on his hip. "Better?"

"Not even. Everyone at the Fountain will be wearing shorts and flipflops or garb appropriate to Spanish settlers in 1565. Besides, where's your vest?"

He shrugged. "In my locker."

"Get it."

"I'll be fine."

"Not if this guy is our killer." I wasn't adding shot partner to all the other baggage I carried around.

"Yes, mother." He scowled, but then winked and sprinted back into the sheriff's office complex. I popped the trunk and dug out my own vest.

A couple minutes later, Rafe returned wearing an oversized bright blue T-shirt with a gator on the front. Didn't hide the vest, but made it less obvious. Now I would be the recognizable LEO since my vest didn't fit under any shirt I owned.

"I brought you one, too." Rafe shoved a second t-shirt at me.

I held it up. *Happy as a Seagull with a French Fry* "Are you kidding me?"

Rafe belly laughed. "You mean you're not happy we're finally catching up with this guy?"

I snickered. Couldn't help it. "Close your eyes." The change wasn't easy in the front seat of my cruiser, but better than heading back inside and making us late.

THE PARKING LOT AT THE TOURIST attraction known as the Fountain of Youth was packed. To be expected with a reenactment going on. Tooting horns and frustrated drivers hunted for scarce spaces. I eased my cruiser through the jockeying mob to the employee lot. Hopefully whoever owned the rusty white Volvo wouldn't have to get out any time soon.

We flashed our badges at the ticket booth and hurried out onto the grounds where we threaded our way through knots of people, some dressed out in period costume and others laden with cameras and visitor maps. A giggling pair of twins nearly tripped me, but their father, with a stern rebuke, pulled them out of my way.

As we cleared the straggling line of visitors waiting for their sip of the fountain's supposedly youth restoring waters, Rafe pointed past the reconstructed chapel. "How about I circle around and come at the tower from the other side. That way he'll only spot one of us unless he's got eyes in the back of his head."

I nodded as I dialed Rafe's phone. "Let me know if you see anything hinky."

Rafe inserted his Bluetooth earpiece and headed off in the direction he'd indicated. I waited a beat, then began circling in the opposite direction.

What on earth had Moretti been thinking when he suggested a meet here? What was I thinking to have agreed? I'd been to these events. I'd participated in them. I knew about the milling visitors, excited kids, vendors selling period reproductions and reenactors with a schedule to keep in the midst of the chaos. If anything happened Ward would have our heads.

I cleared the last of the tourist throng and skirted a line of reenactors loading their matchlocks, preparing for a demonstration. As I made to go around them, one of the men stared, his eyes squinting to read the silly slogan printed on my shirt. I flashed my badge and he jerked his head back as if I'd slapped him.

I strode past.

Rafe appeared out of a thicket of trees about a hundred yards away, his phone up, snapping photos of anything even remotely like a Kodak moment.

His hushed voice came through my earpiece. "You see him?"

"Nada." The crudely built lookout tower perched at the edge of the swampy riverbank with a short length of stockade wall behind it. A Fountain employee, garbed in sailor slops and a loose shirt with his long blond hair tied at the base of his neck sat on a bench with a long gun across his lap.

Just beyond, between me and Rafe, the hull of a Spanish sailing vessel loomed on its cradle. Where was Moretti?

"I think I see him," Rafe whispered. He'd stopped at the edge of the Fountain property, munching on what looked like a drumstick from my vantage point. Where had he gotten that? "I think that's Moretti on the boardwalk that goes out over the marsh."

"Not seeing anything." Times like this I wished I was taller than five feet three.

"He's headed your way. I'll wait until he's on shore and has his back toward me, then close in. Take him by surprise." Rafe shoved his phone back in his pocket and tossed the drumstick into the weeds.

I made one last visual sweep of the grounds before ducking into the shadow of the boat.

A man in a garish Hawaiian print shirt, dark hair plastered with sweat, stepped off the boardwalk and approached. "Detective Quinn?" He frowned at my very unprofessional jersey.

I tapped the star on its lanyard hanging around my neck and rested my hand on my Glock. "Victor Moretti?" It wasn't really a question. The picture on my phone matched this man exactly not counting the longish hair and a few days growth of beard. "I'm here. Start talking." I'd cut the call keeping me in touch with Rafe and hit record. "Who's following you?"

"I don't know. I just know someone's out there. It's a feeling I get, and it's been going on for more than a month. He's not very good at it or else I'd never have noticed. But good enough not to let me catch him. Definitely not one of my crew. Someone he hired from outside, maybe."

"He who?" Moretti still hadn't answered my question. "Who wants you gone? Someone from Arlington? Someone you worked with in Afghanistan?"

Rafe closed in but didn't announce his presence. Apparently, he was better at it than whoever had been dogging Moretti.

Moretti hesitated as if trying to decide how much to reveal. "He's running for congress, and I know things that could sink his campaign. So did Laney. So she was silenced, like the other two."

A volley of matchlocks went off. Moretti hit the dirt and Rafe covered the last few yards, ignoring the roar of the period long guns.

"Hey, man. It's just black powder. You can get up now." Rafe bent to help Moretti up, but the man didn't move. Rafe grabbed his shoulder.

I gasped as Rafe rolled Moretti onto his back. A neat round hole punctuated his forehead.

I jerked around, looking for a shooter behind me, but saw only the line of reenactors, their matchlocks still butted into their shoulders with a cloud of smoke wreathing around their heads. All were aimed out over the river, and not toward us. A crowd of onlookers gathered behind them, no one looking in my direction.

"Call for backup," I said over my shoulder as I scanned the trees and landscape beyond the reenactors. The blond guy in slops still sat with his long gun across his lap watching the reenactors. The shelter called the boathouse appeared empty in spite of the crowd of tourists. No hurrying figures trying to disappear into the crowd. No one furtively trying to stay hidden in the onlookers.

No use calling for an ambulance. Moretti's sightless dark eyes would never identify who'd been following him and we'd been left with only a hint of a lead. Not much more than we'd had when we started the day. Shit.

The clutch of tourists who'd been watching the matchlock demonstration began to dissolve. Some toward the tower, some headed back across the green. Two sandy haired boys with wooden replicas of the guns just fired, a mother with a toddler clinging to the rail of his stroller, and a dad with a girl of about four or five on his shoulders remained, apparently studying their map of the Fountain grounds.

I stormed past them over the trampled grass to the line of men with their guns now resting butt down on the ground. They were beginning the process of cleaning out the barrel and reloading.

"Which one of you had a ball in your piece?"

They looked up in surprise. Glanced at each other, then back at me, heads jerking in a negative. "It's just black powder, ma'am." I knew many of the men and women in the local historical crews, but hadn't met any of these guys before. I looked at their replica matchlocks, then closed my eyes and pictured the neat round hole in Moretti's head. That shot had not come from these guns. But I was taking names anyway.

"Can I see some identification?"

They fumbled through layers of period clothing and produced their wallets. I snapped a photo of each, jotted down phone numbers and thanked them. Then left them still totally in the dark about the dead man only forty yards away.

I cursed in frustration. Even if backup arrived right this minute, there was no way to secure the scene before whoever took that shot had opportunity to disappear. Clusters of people milled about everywhere and no one would have heard anything over the sound of the matchlocks. Our only hope would be a sighting of someone running from the scene. But if the shooter was smart and they were toting a handgun, the most likely possibility given the projectile didn't exit Moretti's head, they could just drop the gun into a backpack and mosey along until they reached the parking lot.

Rafe appeared at my elbow. "I couldn't hear much. He tell you anything before someone took him out?"

I held up my phone. "I recorded the conversation. What there was of it. Something about a politician but no names."

Four deputies ran across the open green toward us.

"I guess we do our best to set up a perimeter and interview everyone leaving or about to leave. Not that it's likely to do us much good."

As the deputies loped to a stop, Rafe explained what had happened. "There's a low fence over there someone could easily climb over." Rafe pointed to the place he'd passed on his circuitous route to the tower. "Not sure what the building is on the other side, but check it out."

Two deputies took off running.

I pointed back to where Moretti lay out of sight. "You two, secure the scene behind the boat and don't trample on any evidence."

Two more uniforms showed up and I sent them back to guard the main entrance. Mac was one of them so I assigned him to keep track of who came and went. Low man on the totem pole always got the least interesting job. I apologized but Mac grinned in acknowledgement and headed back to the gate.

Three more deputies trotted up with Broussard on their heels. Two St Augustine PD uniforms weren't far behind.

"We're in the shit now," Rafe hissed in my ear.

Crap! Ward was storming our way, too.

CHAPTER 11

THE CHAOTIC SCENE AT ST AUGUSTINE'S famed Fountain of Youth with uniformed officers from two departments and gawkers trying to get a look at the crime scene, didn't deter Lieutenant Ward who apparently didn't care who overheard his rant.

"What part of 'Keep me in the loop' did you not understand, Detectives?"

Neither explanation nor argument would be listened to, so I kept my mouth shut. Let him say his piece and get it over with.

Planting his hands on his hips, Ward went on. "Dispatch says you got a call from the man we've all been hunting for."

The man Rafe and I've been sweating our asses off hunting for while you've been sitting in your office with the AC on. But I didn't say it.

Ward shook a finger at me, did a double-take at my choice of t-shirt. "You can't just go off half-cocked without a plan. And why the hell meet the guy here? This is the last place anyone should be conducting an interview. He wouldn't have gotten shot if he'd come into Central. And I'm betting Broussard didn't approve this insanity."

"I wasn't available," Sergeant Broussard said joining the group. "I'm sure there's a good explanation, but right now we've got better things to do than argue in front of the public." Good to know the sergeant had our back, although he'd probably chew us out eventually.

Ward sputtered, "If you don't catch this shooter fast, you can kiss your careers goodbye. And this time, keeping me in the loop means reporting in every hour." He turned to Broussard. "A word, if you will." Clearly, we weren't invited. The two men moved away.

Rafe blew a kiss at Ward's retreating back. "He never even mentioned my shirt. And I wore it just for him."

I couldn't stifle a guffaw. Rafe was a University of Florida Gator's fan, but Ward had graduated from their arch rival. "But he did notice mine. I'll probably get a lecture on appearance along with the rest."

By now a small army of green clad county deputies and a dozen or more city PD officers in blue had rounded up every group of visitors and reenactors present for today's program at the Fountain. Questioning could go on for hours.

The sun, without a single cloud to cast any shadows, beat down on the open space, baking everyone stuck out here. The only saving grace, a sea breeze had sprung up adding a bit of respite along with a salty tang.

Rafe mopped his brow with the hem of his oversized T-shirt. "The manager won't be a happy camper either with the day's events on hold. I wonder how many people we've managed to piss off?"

A short man with a shiny dome and shinier shoes strode up. "What's going on here?"

Speak of the devil. "You're the manager?" I didn't need to ask.

Baldy waved at the crowd. "I am, and I demand to know what's going on."

"A man has been shot." I glanced toward the boat that hid Moretti's body from sight.

The manager's eyes widened along with his mouth. He jerked around, glancing at the men with the matchlocks now being questioned by two men from the city police department. "One of them do it?"

I shook my head. "Not likely. We're really sorry for the inconvenience."

"Inconvenience!" The manager slapped his palms against his shiny dome, then threw them in the air. "You call this an inconvenience?" He swept an arm wide to take in the semi-orderly chaos reigning in his domain.

"We have plenty of officers here and we'll be able to let people move about or leave shortly." I pointed in the direction of the boathouse. "The only place that will have to be off limits for now is the area behind the boat itself and over there where we've marked with crime scene tape." Eventually we'd have to search the ground looking for spent casings and didn't need them trampled into the dirt by clueless gawkers looking for a bit of shade.

Baldy wasn't done. "But what about the reenactors?"

I gritted my teeth. How could anyone be so single-minded? "They're fine so long as they don't leave and don't cross the crime scene lines."

A peacock strutted boldly under the yellow tape as if to mock my warning. Just what we needed. Hopefully he wasn't attracted to shiny things on the ground.

The manager *harrumphed*. "Keep me informed. Please." He turned on his heel and marched off.

Rafe mimicked the manager's *harrumph*. "Think we should start a checklist of people we need to keep informed?"

The ME and one of our evidence techs passed the angry manager and headed our way.

"Where's the body this time?" Sandeep asked with a chuckle.

"This is not funny," I told the irrepressible ME.

Sandeep chuckled again. "So, I've got a warped sense of

humor. Wasn't one of those guns, I hope." He jerked his head in the direction of the shooters with the matchlocks.

"I doubt it. But you'll be able to tell me more. I think the bullet is still in the victim's head. This way." I turned expecting Sandeep and Molly to follow.

As we rounded the end of the boat, Sandeep grimaced. "I see what you mean."

Molly tapped me on the shoulder. "I'm going need your clothes."

I glanced down, for the first time noticing that I was wearing Moretti's blood. "Great!" I left the evidence tech and the ME doing what they did best. "Be right back," I told Rafe as I headed off to change.

I slithered my way through the crazy maze of parked cruisers with lights still strobing to my own where I had to stop and do a double-take. Another of the Fountain's peacocks spread his tail feathers and shook them in front of a late model pickup truck with shiny bumpers.

Takes all kinds. Dumb bird's making love to a truck. I snickered at the strange sight and unlocked my trunk, grabbed my go bag and headed to the rest room, where I peeled the sweat soaked and blood-spattered seagull shirt and khakis off and dropped them into evidence bags.

When I returned to the scene of Moretti's murder, Rafe had stationed two sentries to keep the gawkers away. He stood hands on hips watching the ME. "Broussard says the gun used on Dan Hoffman belonged to his wife," Rafe said when I stopped at his side.

I handed the evidence bag of shucked clothing to Molly's assistant. "So, what does the sergeant think that says about whoever tried make it look like Dan committed suicide?"

Rafe shrugged one shoulder. "Well, it's a sure thing Laney didn't use the piece, but had to be someone familiar with the couple. Someone who knew she owned a gun and maybe where she kept it."

When we'd been sleeping together Dan had always asked me to leave my weapon in the car. "Dan hated firearms. Never wanted them around, but I guess that was just one more thing he conceded to Laney."

My phone buzzed. A text from my daughter.

"What do they think grounded means?" I muttered out loud.

"Which kid got grounded? Rafe gave me a sideways glance.

"It's a long story." No time to explain last night to Rafe. "Just that I grounded Jacqui and now she thinks that couldn't possibly include tonight's football game."

Broussard whistled to get our attention.

I typed NO! and pocketed the phone.

"You're in charge," Broussard told us. "Along with Ken Rabb from the St Augustine department. They are deferring to the sheriff's office, but offer any assistance we need."

I checked the closest pair of city police. "One of them Rabb?"

"The red-head. Y'all should get along just fine." Broussard started to move away, then hesitated and looked back. "And please, call me with any updates. Before you call Ward, so I'll know what I'm dealing with before he does."

Rafe and I saluted in unison.

"I think I've met the guy," Rafe said nodding toward Officer Rabb. "Ex Special Forces. Walks with a limp due to a prothesis if it's the guy I'm thinking of." Rafe stopped and looked down at me. "You need to call home? I'll go make nice."

Like I needed the distraction right now. But I wouldn't

get home before Jacqui had a chance to ignore my warning. I considered my options. Mother, who would ignore my punishment. Or Elliott and his super cool girlfriend? I opted for Elliott.

He was fiercely protective of his daughter and would agree on my meting out the grounding. I tapped the number I knew without having to look it up.

"Hey Jessalyn. What's up?" I rarely called without serious need.

I replayed a condensed version of the scene the night before. "So, now she thinks this doesn't include the football game. I'm caught up in a murder investigation and can't get home to make sure she stays there. I thought maybe you could pick her up and keep her until Tuesday morning when you could drop her off at school."

"Who is this kid. I'll tear him apart," Elliott fumed.

"Get in line. Can you do it?"

"Sure. Brandy is away for the weekend." That was good news. "It'll give us a little father-daughter time. I'll call her and tell her I'll be by in half an hour. But why Tuesday?"

"Teacher workshops on Monday. Thanks Elliott. Appreciate it. And one other thing. Jacqui told me she was moving in with you when I sent the kid packing last night."

Elliott snorted. The last thing he wanted on a permanent basis was a pre-pubescent teenager cramping his love life with Miss Lovejoy. "You go do your sleuthing thing."

The line went quiet and I stared at the phone for a minute before shooting off a text to tell Mike that his father was on the way over to collect Jacqui. Mike'd probably disappear into the garage to work on his car and stay out of sight.

Time to go meet Ken Rabb and sort out who was doing

what. Broussard hadn't chewed us out yet, but he definitely would if we didn't come up with some answers soon. Especially after this morning's debacle.

Someone was going to have to make the death visit to Moretti's wife, too. Then we needed to start looking into this Arlington group and find out who was running for congress.

CHAPTER 12

WITH THE INTERVIEWS COMPLETED, notes shared, and the city cops and extra deputies returned to their patrols, we headed back to Central to change into suitable attire and make the death notification to Moretti's next of kin.

Our least favorite newshound accosted us as we emerged into the Fountain of Youth employee parking lot. I put my head down and escaped to my car without making eye contact. Rafe wasn't as fortunate.

"Hey Detective." Scotty Parker shoved a microphone into Rafe's face. "What can you tell us about today's killing?"

Rafe batted the microphone away. "Shove off. I've got nothing to say."

Not one to take no for an answer, Scotty thrust the microphone back into Rafe's face, hustling to keep up with his fast walk. "But this is hot news. A real killing at an annual reenactment event. Doesn't happen every day."

Rafe whirled on the reporter. Scotty almost slammed into him. "Call public affairs. You have the number."

Already in my cruiser, I shoved the passenger door open and Rafe tumbled in slamming it behind him. "Let's get out of here before he decides to block the driveway."

Having sat in the sun for hours, the cruiser was an oven, and we were both already soaked with sweat. I cranked the AC to high and pulled out onto tree-lined Magnolia Avenue.

Rafe mopped his brow with the tail of his soggy shirt. "Want me to check in with Broussard now, or wait until we get back to

Central?"

I joined the traffic on San Marco right behind a horse-drawn carriage full of tourists. "Figures," I muttered in frustration. No way to pass, and the horse only had two speeds. Slow and slower. "Yeah, go ahead and check in. Maybe Ward's gone for the day and we'll only have to talk to the sergeant."

Rafe placed the call and put the phone on speaker.

Broussard picked up after just one ring. "Anything new?"

"Wish I could tell you we caught the guy and were on our way in with him, Sarge, but that just isn't so." Rafe made a face Broussard couldn't see.

"Collect any brass?" Broussard asked.

"We did," Rafe said. "A lot further out than we expected. Nine millimeter. Rules out all of the reenactors' pieces." Rafe planted a palm on the dash as I slammed on the breaks to avoid hitting a pedestrian dashing between the carriage and me. The oldest city in the country was more crowded than usually with tourists in spite of the September heat.

I wanted to honk my horn, but refrained. No need to spook the horse. "I leaned toward the phone. "The evidence team has them."

"Them?"

"Two casings," I said. "Could be the same weapon. Maybe we'll get lucky and the gun will be in the system."

"Or not," Rafe added.

"Take this off speaker," Broussard ordered.

Rafe frowned, but did as asked and put the phone to his ear. His face registered first surprise, then a frown. "Okay," he said, after a beat. "See you back at Central." He tapped end and glanced at me, the frown still clouding his brow.

"What?" I said.

"Upshaw has no alibi for the time Hoffman was shot. The gun belonged to his daughter and he was very familiar with the Hoffman house." Rafe's jaw worked. A habit he had when processing unexpected information. "Broussard's on his way with Detective Oliver to question Upshaw again. Said he'd meet us back at Central after we make our visit to Mrs. Moretti."

"Jayzus!" I swallowed my surprise. "I knew he hated his son-in-law, but not enough to try killing the man." And when did Oliver get added to the mix? What was Ward up to?

Rafe rubbed his palm over his scruff. "Guess we weren't dealing with Hoffman fast enough for Upshaw."

I had no love for Upshaw, but I liked and admired Sheriff Kennedy and if Upshaw was guilty our sheriff would be devastated. Perhaps not politically, but Upshaw was a personal friend and a staunch supporter of law and order. What would this do to Kennedy's reelection campaign?

"Broussard think he did it?" I asked when Rafe didn't say more.

"He's not saying, but I think he's leaning that way."

"Why'd he suggest you take the phone off speaker?" Did Broussard think Rafe wouldn't turn right around and share whatever he'd said with his partner?

"Just wanted to make sure it didn't end up on the radio. Not everyone is in that loop. Yet."

"So, throw another detective at the mess. That ought to keep the lid on it." I muttered as I merged onto US 1 and sped up.

"You've got me." Rafe slid his lower teeth back and forth beneath the uppers – a habit he had when pondering things. "Broussard's been working his end alone and you wouldn't want him heading out there to question Upshaw with no one to watch his back."

He had a point. But why did it have to be Oliver? The only detective I didn't get along with. Not that it was my fault. Oliver clearly thought women didn't belong in law enforcement, or maybe me in particular, on the major crimes squad.

Rafe plucked at his damp shirt. "That shower is going to feel awesome. Straight up cold and not a drop of hot."

Couldn't disagree with that prescription. I might as well have spent the morning in a sauna fully dressed. We drove in silence until I claimed one of the few slots with any shade out behind our building.

Just before we split up, Rafe tugged me to a stop with a hand on my shoulder. "Today wasn't your fault. You know that, right?" Was he reading my mind? That self-condemning thought had been battling it out with the logic of Moretti's demand and our capitulation. I tended to think I was always in charge, and therefore responsible for everything that went wrong. A habit I was trying to overcome with little success.

"Feels like it." Everything about the last twenty four hours felt like a failure and today wasn't even half over. Death notices were even worse than autopsies. Getting chewed out by my mentor wouldn't be a picnic either, but Broussard couldn't blame me for anything I hadn't already blamed myself for.

And then there was Zack Oliver.

Rafe gave my shoulder a squeeze. "At least we've got a lead. We talk to Mrs. Moretti, take our lumps from Broussard, then we get busy following up on Arlington. And there's always tomorrow."

Rafe's cheerful optimism was a good foil for my tendency to expect the worst. "You have to be the most optimistic person I know."

"But you're glad to have me." He gave my shoulder another squeeze and loped off to the men's locker room.

I'd had some qualms when we were first partnered up. I tended to be a cowboy and Broussard had kept a rein on me. Rafe was a lot of things I wasn't, but we had that cowboy thing in common, and we tended to behave like a posse of two. But he kept me focused, and seemed to understand things I couldn't put into words. I *was* glad to have him.

One last chore before I hit the showers. I paused just inside our office door and hit Lieutenant Ward's extension.

"Ward."

"Checking in Lieutenant." I emptied my pockets as I spoke. "Everything at the Fountain is tied up. I have tons of notes from the various cops and deputies who took statements. Evidence has the brass and the ME has the body. Rafe and I are changing and headed out to make the death notice." Nothing new, of course, but he said to report every hour and it had actually been more like an hour and a half.

"Thank you, Detective," Ward replied as if he hadn't had a hissy fit at the Fountain. "I expect immediate notification if anything changes."

Really? No more hourly demand, especially with the Upshaw concern? At least I didn't feel like a teenager checking in on my every move.

Ward hadn't even said goodbye, but the line was dead. Good. Now, I needed to check in with my son. Before I could open the app to send him a text, my phone began to play the ringtone I'd assigned to Mike.

He rarely called, preferring to text "Hey, Mikey Mike. What's up?".

"Just getting ready to head out to the game. Dad came by

to pick up Jacqui. So, I was wondering if it would be okay if I stayed the night at Seth's?"

I glanced at my watch. Wondered how late I'd be and if the dog would be okay until I got home.

As if he knew my next concern, Mike added, "Seth said we can stop by after the game to take Murphy for a walk. In case you're really late. Actually, he suggested we pick Murphy up and take him with us, but I told him you don't like coming home to an empty house, so we'll just walk her, feed her and leave her to hold down the fort until you get home."

My child knew me well. "Tell him thanks, and have a good time. See you tomorrow sometime."

"Love you, Mom."

"Love you more." I clicked off, a warm spot around my heart. With all my faults and all the troubles we'd been through together, my son's support meant more than I could put into words. In spite of being a teenager, he was observant enough to remember how much I hated being alone in the house. I pocketed my phone and headed to the shower. With partners in life like Mike and Rafe, I couldn't complain.

FORTY-FIVE MINUTES LATER, Rafe and I stood once again on the Moretti porch, waiting for someone to answer our ring. After the third attempt, Rafe stepped back and sighed. "I'll check around back and take a peek in the garage."

I watched him disappear around the corner and pressed my finger against the doorbell a fourth time.

Just our luck she wouldn't be home. I really did not want to make this trip again today. It was hard gearing up to deliver the devastating news that a loved one is dead. Hard observing the grief, finding the right words and offering solace, but it was part of the job.

Rafe reappeared from the far side, having circled the house. "Garage is empty. Think she already knows?"

"Name wasn't released to the press." I joined him on the walk. "You'd think, having reported her husband missing, she'd be waiting at home for word."

"You'd think," Rafe agreed.

We climbed back in the cruiser, and I was pulling out of the driveway when my phone rang. I shifted the car back into park and answered it.

"You said to call if I heard anything." A familiar voice, though no name had come up on caller ID.

Rafe looked at me expectantly so I put the phone on speaker.

"May I ask who this is?"

"Irma Jean Moretti, and I'm calling to say you needn't come out to the house full of false sympathy to tell me Vic is gone. I already know."

Rafe's brows rose.

How the hell did she know already? "We're sorry for your loss, Mrs. Moretti. How did you—"

"Skip all the sorry shit and find out who shot him."

I started to reply, but she'd already hung up.

"Well," Rafe said pulling his face into a mock pout. "We're batting a thousand in the pissing people off category."

"What I want to know," I said, slamming the cruiser back into gear, "is who leaked the information we were working so hard to keep under the radar?"

CHAPTER 13

RUNNING LOW ON PATIENCE and carbs, Rafe and I made it back into town just in time to grab lunch at the Crave Food Truck on Riberia Street. Andrés greeted me like an old friend, took our orders with a smile and had two healthy veggie-wraps put together in just minutes. We rewarded ourselves by eating at the outdoor tables overlooking the river before diving back into the investigation.

A breeze off the river tugged at my damp clothing as I slid around the bench until the fluttering umbrella shaded my face from the late afternoon sun. The clink of halyards against aluminum masts made a musical backdrop to the alfresco dining area. This little place tucked outside of the hustle of the old city was one of my favorite places to grab a meal, and I didn't get to stop in often enough.

"How the hell did Moretti's wife find out?" Rafe had already scarfed down half his sandwich.

I *tsked*. The Fountain of Youth Archeological Park was a like a colander – full of holes for information to leak through. Too many people involved for one thing. "Could have been the manager eager to make lemonade out of lemons. Get a little free publicity chatting up the newshounds."

Rafe scooped up a chip full of humus, popped it in his mouth and swallowed. "Don't see how a modern-day murder does much to enhance the ambiance of a living history museum."

Might not do anything for historical ambiance, but there would always be gawkers avid to catch every gory detail. "Murder is everyday news in Jacksonville, but not so much here in St Augustine. We should've insisted on meeting somewhere else."

"He was pretty adamant, Jess. You can't control everything, and you've gotta stop thinking it's somehow your fault when shit happens."

"I don't blame myself . . . not all the time."

Rafe snorted. "Last month it was your fault you didn't catch on to who was taking down homeless guys before he killed that vet you befriended. The month before that, it was that old lady who refused to move out of a trailer that should have been condemned and ended up toasted to a crisp when an electric short burned the place down. Shit happens, Jess." He picked up another chip and hesitated with it poised over the tub of humus. "I bet you even blame yourself for Elliott cheating on you."

I lowered my head and took a large bite of my wrap. Rafe was five years younger than me with a whole lot less experience in life and relationships, but he was remarkably observant and surprisingly accurate. Or was I that easy to read?

Back then, I'd been too busy being a mother. Too tired when Elliott wanted to make love. Caught up in one of Mother's grand plans when my husband preferred me elsewhere. An understanding priest I'd gone to for confession helped me get my head out of my butt.

He helped me see the self-flagellation began long before Elliott. In my twelve-year-old mind, my father's death was all my fault because I'd been the one to tell him about a classmate whose father beat up on her mother. My deputy daddy had called on the wife to follow up . . . and was ambushed and murdered.

When I looked up again, Rafe gazed out over the sailboats bobbing in the San Sebastian River, chewing on his meal.

"Do you read minds all the time, or just mine?"

His eyes came back to me. "I don't read minds. It's the things you say that give you away."

"But I don't—" I'd never even mentioned Elliott as far as I could recall.

Rafe grinned. "And maybe your buddy Anna gave me a hint about this God complex you have."

"God complex!" I sputtered, almost choking on a chip.

Rafe sighed. "Those weren't Anna's words. Exactly. She only told me what a jerk Elliott was and I put two and two together. If I came up with five, I apologize, but in every case we've worked together you've found a way to make at least some piece of it your fault." He took another chip loaded with humus.

"Moretti's paranoia was the problem this morning. If we hadn't agreed to meet him on his terms he might have slipped into the wind or gotten shot somewhere else." He glanced at his watch, then at my half-eaten sandwich. "Eat up. We have work to do, and it *will* be your fault if we have nothing new to report next time we have to check in with Lieutenant Ward."

DESKS FACING EACH OTHER in our small office, Rafe and I tapped away at our computers tracking down facts. We'd shucked our jackets and Rafe had parked a row of bottled water between us.

It hadn't taken very long to put a name to the man running for congress. Glen Rhodes had been the commander of the six-man team Arlington had contracted to guard an Army base in Afghanistan, and he'd parleyed the contacts he'd made overseas into a campaign network.

"If Moretti's right about Rhodes, he's got someone doing his dirty work for him," I said scribbling notes in my little book.

Rafe looked up. "Guess that means he's got an alibi for this morning?"

I turned my monitor to face him and he leaned forward to study the image of would-be Senator Rhodes at a campaign rally earlier that day. In Virginia.

"Gotta wonder what happened when they were stationed in Afghanistan that Moretti thinks Rhodes wouldn't want known." I noted Rhodes' schedule for the next few days in my book in case we had to reach out to him.

"Humph." Rafe sat back and palmed his usually tidy scruff that two days in was getting more than a little scraggly. "Isaac Lietz went off the road driving home to Georgia from Virginia. Police deemed it a tired-driving accident. Happened at three am and he'd been on the road for hours."

"What about the other guy?" Victor Moretti had been convinced the deaths of two former teammates were related to whoever was following him and possibly to Laney's murder.

"I've got a call in to the coroner there. Obit doesn't give a cause of death. A news article only suggested suicide. Hadn't been confirmed when the paper went to press." Rafe surged to his feet and stretched. He reached for one of the bottles and downed half of it before wiping his mouth and screwing the cap back on.

If only we'd insisted on meeting Moretti somewhere besides the Fountain. I replayed his actual words in my head. *He's running for congress, and I know things that could sink his campaign. So, did Laney. So, she was silenced, like the other two.'*

I stared at the list of men in Moretti's private security group that had been stationed together when Laney Hoffman nee Upshaw had spent two months with the unit on a fact-finding mission. Glen Rhodes - running for the Senate, Isaac Lietz – dead in a car crash, Dominic Garcia – possible suicide,

Hank Pearson – still with Arlington, but now on a Navy ship somewhere in the South Pacific, Adam Hahn – also still with Arlington and currently in Iraq. And Victor Moretti, deceased as of this morning.

Something no doubt went down in Afghanistan. I'd asked Moretti that question but he hadn't had a chance to answer.

Frustrated, with all the dead ends, I looked up at Rafe. "Come up with any contact information for Hahn?"

Rafe plopped back into his chair. "I left a message with someone in his unit for him to call, but it's—" He looked at the clock on the wall. "It's almost eleven their time. He's probably in the sack already."

"Did you know it's hotter in Iraq than here, even in the middle of the night?"

"Like I give a crap what the temperature is in Baghdad."

Rafe was usually amused by my temperature trivia so his burst of bad temper surprised me. "Something else go wrong I don't know about?"

"I was supposed to pick Win up for some big fund-raiser she's involved with." He sighed. "Now she's pissed she has to go alone, and I won't hear the end of it for a week."

I sat back, thankful for a break from peering into my monitor. "Did you really want to go?"

He snorted. "Not really. But she'll nag me about it, and complain about the tux rental I never picked up, and she's paying for. Then I'll have to—"

His computer dinged and snared his attention. "Well, I'll be . . ." He motioned for me to join him.

I scooted around the corner of the desk to look, but the screen was blank. Then a moment later a man popped up. A dark-haired man, about thirty-five, dressed in a sweat-damp

T-shirt sat in a folding camp chair, one hand reaching toward us, apparently manning a computer mouse, the flutter of a tent wall behind him. "Adam Hahn, here. I got a message you wanted to Skype with me."

"Welcome to St Augustine, man," Rafe replied, his good humor restored. "We are very thankful you could get back to us. I'm Detective Rafe Morgan. This is my partner Detective Jesse Quinn. We're with the St. Johns County Sheriff's office."

"Florida, huh?" Hahn said, scratching at something on his cheek.

Rafe jumped in before I could. "I know it's late there so we'll try to keep this short, but we're investigating the deaths of Laney Hoffman, nee Upshaw, and Victor Moretti. We hope you can fill in a few holes Moretti didn't get a chance to tell us about."

Hahn sat back in his chair as if pushed. "Vic is dead? How?"

Nothing like delivering bad news when a man least expected it.

"Someone shot him before he could tell us who he thought was after him," I knelt beside Rafe's desk to be on eye level with the computer screen. "He thought Laney was killed by the same person who was after him."

"Jesus!" Hahn scratched at his cheek again. "Over here that kind of thing hangs over you every minute, but you get home, it's the last thing you expect."

I could tell from Hahn's reaction that even a man conditioned to sudden brutal death, could still be shocked when it happened to people he knew. "Mr. Moretti seemed to think he was being followed because of something that happened while y'all were stationed in Afghanistan together. Something that would put Glen Rhode's bid for the Senate in jeopardy, maybe? What can you tell us about the time you were all together at the base in Afghanistan?"

Hahn leaned forward again, his face filling the screen. "Nothing happened that would hurt Glen. Oh, I know Vic had this notion that Glen was responsible for the deaths of a family of civilians, but that's just not so. And Glen didn't know anything about the kids we smuggled into the states."

My turn to sit back as if pushed. Smuggled kids? Where was this investigation taking us?

"Moretti didn't mention any kids," Rafe said into the silence of my surprise, filled only by the rush of wind whipping around Hahn's tent.

"They were a pair of orphans. Came from the house where the civilians were killed, but Glen didn't have anything to do with that. He was in the house just before the mortar hit, but all he did was haul the kids out and take them back to the base hospital. Makes him a hero, if you ask me."

"Who was responsible for getting the kids into this country?" Rafe asked, ignoring the alleged facts of Glen Rhodes' heroics.

"Vic, Dominick Garcia, Hank Pearson and me. Issac Leitz knew about it, but he wasn't really involved. A Canadian priest got them out of Afghanistan and slipped them over the border into the US. Vic knew a couple in Georgia who desperately wanted kids but never had any and they were willing to adopt both kids. I only have a name. Don't know anything about how they got all that paperwork past the courts or even if they did, but Glen Rhodes was never involved in any of it."

Before either of us could ask for the adoptive family's name, a loud popping sound and static filled the screen which then went blank.

"I hope that's just a signal issue," Rafe said as we both stared, shocked, at the empty screen.

I slapped the desk in frustration and stood. "And once again, we didn't get any names."

Rafe's phone dinged.

He had a personal email. "Win probably emailing to take my head off for missing our date," he muttered as he opened the app. Then surprise colored his voice. "Well, well, well. Hahn's still among the living. Names are Matt and Lucy Springer of St. Mary's, Georgia."

CHAPTER 14

RAFE STUDIED ME ACROSS the span of our desks as he reached for another bottle of water. I grabbed one for myself. Caffeine would be better but the pot was empty. "What do you think the chances are Hahn would lie to cover his former commander's ass? They say war is even more intense than policework, and men form bonds that are nearly unbreakable."

"It's possible," Rafe said thoughtfully. "But I didn't sense that."

I sighed. Neither had I.

"But," Rafe said, holding his bottle up. "Rhodes is running on the Republican ticket. Right?" When I nodded, he went on. "If it even hinted like he'd been involved in smuggling a couple Muslim kids into the country, considering the current antagonistic attitude toward immigration, it could throw a monkey wrench into his campaign."

I glanced at the clock. "Too late to drive to St Mary's tonight. You up for a ride in the morning?"

"Can I drive?"

No way was I spending another day jounced around in his Jeep. "Only if we take my cruiser. When does yours come back from the shop, anyway?"

He tossed his empty bottle toward a recycle bin by the door. "They promised it by end of day Monday. What about your RAV4?"

"On official business?"

"It's fun to drive. Besides, we'd stick out less. It's not our jurisdiction."

A uniformed deputy stopped in the doorway. "Broussard's got Upshaw in interrogation. He asked you to join him." Then she was gone.

"Hell, yes," Rafe said launching to his feet. "His daughter's gun used to take out his hated son-in-law? I want to see how Upshaw wiggles out of this."

We hurried down the hall and stepped into the interrogation room. Broussard was explaining to Upshaw the situation, meaning he was not under arrest and therefore didn't require his Miranda rights to be read, but he was also under no obligation to answer anything with or without a lawyer present.

Lawrence Upshaw, dressed in crisply pressed slacks and a polo shirt bearing the logo of an exclusive golf course glanced at the clock and scowled. "I don't need a lawyer."

Broussard glanced over his shoulder and nodded at Rafe and me, then turned back to Upshaw. "It's no secret that you disliked your son-in-law, and you made it quite plain you blamed him for your daughter's murder," Broussard began.

"It's always the husband," Upshaw snapped back.

"Quite frequently, yes," Broussard agreed. "But with nothing proved yet, your assistance might be helpful in determining who did kill her. Also, who tried to stage Dan Hoffman's supposed suicide. Have you ever seen this gun before?"

Broussard slid a handgun in a plastic evidence bag across the table. Upshaw glanced at it, then back at Broussard.

I might be facing Dan's assassin, and my antipathy toward him ran deep. Upshaw appeared cool, as if this were nothing more serious than a city council meeting to discuss more parking meters. Broussard's body language showed a hunger to nail a suspect.

The room hummed with tension.

"Have you ever seen that weapon before?" Broussard repeated.

Upshaw frowned. "I might have."

"Didn't you gift this gun to your daughter at her request just a year ago?"

How had Broussard found that out? I studied the gun as if I expected to find *'to my precious daughter from her loving dad'* engraved on the barrel. Rafe just rubbed his fist over his growing stubble.

"I might have." Upshaw thrust his lower jaw out. "I mean, I gave her a handgun. I just don't know if that's the one."

Broussard pushed a sheet of paper across the table to join the gun. "But the dealer said you picked it out personally."

I bent to read the copied document. A sales receipt. Guess I knew what Broussard had been doing while Rafe and I made our abortive attempt at a death notification.

Upshaw swallowed, his jaw no longer so pugnacious. "I— Yeah, that's the gun I bought for Laney. But I haven't seen it since I gave it to her."

I still had a hard time believing Dan would have let his wife keep a gun in his house, but there appeared to be a number of things I thought I knew about Dan that had changed.

I moved closer and put a hand on the table to insert myself into the interrogation. "And you're saying that Laney kept this gun in her home? Dan hated guns. Didn't want them anywhere near him."

Upshaw's dark eyes flashed. "Dan was a wuss."

"But he didn't let Laney keep the gun at the house, did he?" I said.

With his gaze still on Upshaw, Broussard didn't stop me.

"She kept the gun at your house, didn't she?" I said.

A muscle in Upshaw's temple jumped. "Yes," he finally admitted, the muscle still spasming. "I installed a gun safe in her old room. But she came by to collect her weapon the day before she was killed. She said she was headed to the gun range for some practice. She didn't return the gun to the safe." He sat back as if this exonerated him.

That certainly made sense. If Moretti had come to warn Laney to watch her back, maybe she had come after her gun and headed to the range to practice up in case she needed to defend herself. But she hadn't shot Dan. So, who had? My vote remained on Upshaw.

"Kind of convenient." Broussard jumped back into the discussion. "Laney can't confirm or deny your account of how this gun left the safe in your home and ended up in Dan Hoffman's hotel room."

"You can call the Saltwater Shooting Club. They'll corroborate."

"Oh, you can be sure we will." Broussard jotted the name of the range down. "Now let's get back to where you were on Thursday night."

The jaw stood out again. "I was home."

"Can anyone verify that?" Broussard asked with calm patience, while I wanted to grab the man by his shirt collar and shake the truth out of him. Rafe took notes on his tablet.

Upshaw's expression morphed into one of grief. "My wife died. My daughter was killed. My son is overseas. I live alone." Poor me. What an act.

"And you did not have any company Thursday night. Perhaps a lady friend?" Broussard suggested.

"What kind of man do you think I am?" Upshaw demanded. "I don't bring lady friends into my home."

He played the grieving widower to the world. Maybe he paid for favors outside of his home? Not that it had any bearing on the matter of Dan being shot.

Broussard scribbled in his notebook, then looked up. "You're free to go Mr. Upshaw, but please don't leave town." He gestured toward the door.

Lawrence Upshaw looked startled, then scrambled to his feet and strode out without looking back.

Broussard rubbed his temples. "He's lying about something," he finally said. "I just don't know what."

Probably everything. Grieving over his wife who everyone knew he'd ignored in favor of his daughter. Not having seen Laney's gun at any time since he purchased it, and probably about being in his own home two nights ago.

CHAPTER 15

BROUSSARD AGREED THAT RAFE AND I should make the trip to St Mary's the following day to interview the adoptive parents. It seemed like a long-shot that two little kids smuggled into the country half a dozen years earlier would be reason enough to kill anyone, but we couldn't dismiss the possibility. Or any opportunity to learn more about what drove Vic Moretti. Then we called it a night and left the office, cutting the lights behind us.

With no one waiting on me at home but my puppy, I headed over to Flagler Hospital to sit awhile with Dan. We'd heard nothing more about his condition, and I worried about him. How long could doctors keep people in comas and still have them emerge without lasting damage?

People died and had medical emergencies at all times of day, in an ER especially, but a hospital at night held a strange ambiance of peace. Even the parking lot, bathed in yellow light, was mostly empty as I walked across the cooling tarmac to the hospital entrance.

The deputy on watch worked a crossword book on his knee, pencil poised. He greeted me with a nod and went back to his puzzle as I stepped past him into Dan's room. I scanned the array of monitors and drip lines, and moved to the bed then stopped abruptly . . . jolted by the sight of Dan's clear blue eyes, open.

"Dan!" My heart rate jumped. "You're awake."

How long had he been conscious?

His eyes roamed the room, his body unmoving. "Laney's gone," he whispered, his voice broken.

I scooped up his left hand and pressed it between both of mine. "I know, Dan. I'm so sorry."

"How long . . ." his voice trailed off, and he licked cracked lips.

I reached for the sweating plastic pitcher an arm's length away on a wheeled stand. I poured some of the cool water into a cup and put the straw between Dan's lips. He sipped, then let the straw fall away. "How long have I been here?"

"Two days." This dear man had endured so much. Lost his wife, been questioned as a suspect, then nearly killed. The questions I needed to ask would only add to the trauma, but they had to be asked. "Do you remember what happened?"

He started to move his head, but his face closed in, a flash of pain in his eyes.

I debated what to ask next. He knew Laney was gone, but how much of the rest of that day? "What's the last thing you remember, Dan?"

The crease between his brows furrowed deeper.

I reached for a folding chair someone had left leaning against the wall, popped it open and sat regaining Dan's hand. "Do you recall your lawyer taking you to the hotel?"

"Ahh." The furrow eased and he carefully turned his head to look more directly at me. "Marty ordered room service for me before he left, but . . ."

"But?" I prompted when he didn't finish the thought.

"I don't remember eating anything."

"Do you remember the food arriving?"

Dan bit his lip and the crease between his brows deepened as he strove to retrieve the illusive memory. "I think so."

I pictured the bent backside of a hotel employee dragging a dinner cart into the room. "Do you remember who brought your meal?"

Dan closed his eyes. Perhaps trying to form a similar picture in his mind. "A little."

"Can you describe this person?"

"Someone in a hotel uniform," he finally said. "But I wasn't really looking. I went for my wallet to tip him."

"You're sure it was a man?"

Again, Dan paused, frowning as he sorted through what was probably a kaleidoscope of memory fragments.

I hated to push, but we needed to know what he remembered. "Did you see a face? Was it anyone you recognized?"

Dan licked his lips again and I brought the straw to his mouth for another sip.

"Didn't get a chance," Dan said when he pushed the straw free. "He was behind me, shoving a gun against my cheek."

I reached out to touch the yellowish purple bruise running from his jaw to his temple.

I should have been recording this. I grabbed my phone and started. Better late than never. My mind raced with possibilities. Upshaw had a finger in so many pies he'd easily find out where Dan Hoffman spent the night with his home a crime scene.

"Did the person with the gun say anything?"

He frowned as if trying to fit the question into the context of what he remembered. "Told me . . . I shouldn't have come home early."

"The voice?" Dan would recognize Upshaw's voice, wouldn't he? "Did you know the voice?"

"Hoarse like a smoker." Dan's hand clenched into a fist within my grasp and a whimper escaped his lips. He was in pain.

I should go find a nurse to let them know he was conscious and in need of something for the pain. But not quite yet.

I uncurled his fingers and massaged them until they relaxed.

Upshaw could have been whispering. He didn't smoke. Or maybe he deliberately altered his voice, except why would he do that if his plan had been to kill Dan? For that matter, why be so careful to hide his face?

I continued to stroke Dan's hand. "And you don't remember anything else?"

His eyes were closed. The furrow gone.

A moment of panic hit me, but the monitor continued tracing a steady heartbeat. Relief. He'd only fallen asleep.

Gently laying his hand back on the fold of white sheet, I bent to whisper in his ear. "Stay strong, Dan." Then I stopped the recording and went out to the nurses' station to report Dan's moments of wakefulness.

BACK IN MY CAR, I brought up Broussard's contact.

"Quinn?" His voice sounded gruff as though woken.

"Dan's awake."

If Broussard had been sleeping when the phone rang, he was awake now.

"Did you talk to him?"

"I did. He didn't see who tried to kill him. He remembers a gun pressed against his cheek and a husky voice telling him he shouldn't have come home early."

"What else?"

"His lawyer ordered room service for Dan before he left and Dan remembers someone bringing it into the room, but he didn't get a chance to eat any of it."

"Humph!"

I pictured Broussard rubbing his temples, not happy with my answer. "He was in pain, Sarge. The nurse explained that one of the machines he's hooked to delivers a regular dose of pain meds, and it apparently put him back to sleep. Oh, and they started bringing him out of the coma this morning, but until tonight with me, he hadn't really come to."

Broussard didn't reply right away.

"Sarge?"

"Did you ask the deputy if he'd had any visitors?"

"Yes, and no he hasn't. Except for you, me and hospital staff. You still want Rafe and me to head up to Georgia in the morning?"

"Yeah. That's the next logical step in figuring out who followed Moretti. I'll get down to Flagler first thing and see if Hoffman remembers anything else. And I'll send Zack Oliver over to the hotel to question the staff and review their security tapes again. Stay in touch. G'night detective."

Still holding my phone, I gazed at the pond reflecting lights from the restaurants that were still open on the corner of US 1 and 312. Who other than Upshaw had a reason to take Dan out? All they had to do was slip into Dan's room when room service brought up his dinner, maybe even pretend to deliver it.

But why the subterfuge? Whoever had done it, would assume Dan would die, so no need to alter their voice. Dan might have been surprised to see his father-in-law, but he would've opened the door and invited him in.

Except that was not what Dan remembered.

Suddenly Upshaw wasn't so keen a suspect.

ST. MARY'S IS A PRETTY, coastal Georgia town of less than twenty thousand bordered by the St. Mary's River and the

Cumberland Island National Seashore. I'd been there once to take a boat out to Cumberland Island with Elliot before we were married and several years later with Mike and Jacqui to visit the Submarine Museum at Kings Bay. Happier times. Happier reasons to be here.

Rafe easily found the address for Matthew and Lucy Springer and pulled up before a two-story yellow clapboard home surrounded by a white picket fence just down the street from the First Presbyterian Church. A beat-up Chevy pickup truck sat in the driveway and two bicycles lay on their sides at the edge of the lawn.

Rafe turned the engine off and handed me the keys. "Think we can chat with these folks without pissing anyone off today?"

"Why, when we're so good at it?" I said, and climbed out. Rafe joined me on the sidewalk, I clicked the lock on the car fob, and we headed for the front door.

A middle-aged man in cargo shorts and a "Go Navy" T-shirt came around the corner of the house before we reached the porch. "Can I help you folks?"

I extended my hand. "Deputy Detective Jesse Quinn. And you must be Matthew Springer."

His mouth turned up into a welcoming smile as he accepted the grip. "I am. Are you collecting for something?"

Rafe laughed. "You can keep your wallet in your pocket Mr. Springer. I'm Detective Rafe Morgan. We're from St. Augustine."

"Beautiful city, St. Augustine. We keep meaning to take the kids down to check out the oldest city in the US, but with soccer and scouts and one thing and another . . . Well, I'm sure you didn't drive all the way up here to hear about my kids."

Actually, that was exactly what we'd driven up to talk about, but broaching the subject without dampening the welcoming smile might prove impossible. "It's your kids we came to ask about."

A wary expression pinched the man's features. "They're ours. Legally. We've been to court. It's all documented."

"I'm glad to hear it," I said and meant it, hoping there would be no reason to throw trouble his way. "Is there somewhere we can sit down to talk?"

Matthew Springer glanced at his house, then back at us, his expression still guarded. "Lucy and the kids are at church, so I guess it's okay." He headed for the house. We followed.

Inside, a pair of soccer cleats and an assortment of sneakers and flip flops flowed out over the foyer floor beneath a series of hooks holding jackets of different sizes. As we moved into the living room, we stepped over and around more evidence of kids living a happy active life. A project involving poster board and tempera paints occupied a folding table in the corner and two backpacks spewing books and other school paraphernalia sprawled open on the floor. The furniture was meant more for comfort and durability than fashion.

Mr. Springer gestured toward the chairs. "Can I get you officers something to drink?"

With an amiable smile, Rafe responded, "Water would be nice, Mr. Springer."

"Just call me Matt," the man said and disappeared down a short hallway that opened into a kitchen.

On his return, I accepted one of the bottles offered. "I understand you adopted the children through a priest from Canada?" No easy way to start this conversation.

Matt sighed as he lowered himself into a recliner. "Father Francis."

Rafe sat on the edge of the sofa. "It would be nice to see those documents, but we aren't really here to question your parental rights. Rather, we are wondering if you have noticed anything out of the ordinary lately. Anyone following or watching you or your children?"

Matt's eyes widened. "Are they in danger? Are we?"

I took the matching recliner and answered the man's concern. "Not that we are aware of, but I regret to tell you that one of the men responsible for getting your kids out of Afghanistan felt that he was being followed, and he's . . . not with us anymore."

Matt gasped and covered his mouth with his hand. "Was he back over there?"

Why does everyone assume bad things only happen in war zones? "He was in St. Augustine. We don't have anything concrete to suggest it's about the children. In fact, one of the men in his group suggested Mr. Moretti was paranoid for an entirely different reason, but we needed to follow up and make sure all was well here, and perhaps warn you to be extra careful. Lock your doors. Pay attention to where your kids are. And report anything you notice that worries you."

"We will." Matt Springer swallowed visibly. Probably trying to digest the warning or how serious it might be. "We surely will."

AS WE WERE LEAVING, Lucy Springer pulled into the driveway in a newish Honda Pilot and two kids jumped out, only halted in their dash for the house by their father's voice. We were introduced to eleven-year-old Hasan and Safia, nine, who greeted us in perfect English with impeccable manners. Jacqui could have taken a lesson from them. Lucy Springer was all smiles and cordiality. A friendliness that would probably take a serious hit the moment her husband passed along our warning.

Perhaps all adoptive parents harbored a lingering fear of losing children they've chosen to pour their hearts and souls into, but I was sure the Springers had different doubts, and now we'd added to them. I regretted having come, but it was probably better in person than over the phone.

On the road, Rafe driving again, I flipped through copies of the adoption papers and everything appeared to be valid. The children did not have original birth certificates but possessed valid social security numbers and had been deemed legal citizens of the US. Matt had dragged out photo albums depicting two young, confused children at the time of their arrival and documenting their growth to the happy, well-adjusted kids they appeared to be today. Holidays, first-days-of-school, beach outings, soccer games, learning to ride a bike. All the usual family milestones.

As Rafe accelerated to merge onto the highway, I said, "Maybe we should try to reach the last guy in that unit. The one on the ship. Can't be totally unreachable." I couldn't think of a single reason why anything we'd learned today would impact Rhodes' campaign negatively.

Rafe put the Toyota on cruise control. "And what? Get the same story Hahn told?".

"Maybe there's something Hahn didn't want us to know. There has to be a reason someone was following Moretti, and it's awfully coincidental that half of that squad is dead." Half the squad and Laney Hoffman. I couldn't rid myself of the thought that Victor Moretti might still be alive if he hadn't come out of wherever he'd been hiding to tell us what he knew.

Rafe drummed his thumbs on the top of the steering wheel, then asked, "And how does any of this tie into the attempt on Dan Hoffman?"

I *tsked*. "We just have to keep digging. We're missing something. The Hoffmans and Moretti have to be connected."

Rafe glanced my way. "But what if has nothing to do with Arlington?"

CHAPTER 16

RAFE'S QUESTION WAS VALID. What if we'd wasted an entire day and department dollars following yet another thread that probably had nothing to do with the deaths of Laney Hoffman or Vic Moretti?

We spent the rest of the drive back from St. Mary's discussing every detail we'd uncovered so far and spinning tales about how they might fit together. Some thoughts very out of the box, but in the end, we decided first thing Monday morning, we'd take another run at the less-than-helpful Mrs. Moretti. I dropped Rafe off at his apartment.

Since I'd been out of the house more than three days running and didn't feel like cooking, I stopped at Publix to pick up a rotisserie chicken and vegetables I could serve raw. When I don't have a list, things tend to end up in my basket that I don't need, like the Double Stuff Oreos I binge on when I'm frustrated, as I was now over the lack of progress on the investigation. Mentally promising to share them with Mike, I pocketed my receipt and headed for the car.

My day got a little brighter when I spied Seth's Dodge Ram in my driveway, and upon entering the kitchen, the aroma of something baking hit me. Glancing into the oven was an even bigger surprise. Mike liked to cook, but to my knowledge, he'd never tried sweet bread. Brownies were more his speed. From a box.

I opened the door to the basement garage, but the lights were off. No puppy. No one working on the Mustang. I would have Mike's head if he'd left the oven on and taken Murphy to the beach.

"Mike?"

"He's at football practice."

I whirled at the sound of Seth's voice. He looked good. He looked especially good standing there in shorts and a tank top, barefoot and tanned. Like he belonged in my house, baking sweetbread.

"Mike said you didn't like coming home to an empty house, so I thought I'd fill it up a little." Seth winked and things inside me went from pleasant surprise to something more. A mixture of excitement and doubt that boosted my heart rate.

His being here had nothing to do with Mike and everything to do with me, but how did he know I'd be coming home at all?

My mind had been so taken up with solving two murders and an attempted murder, I'd barely found time to make sure my kids were surviving. It took a moment to shift gears and take in the fact that I had an entirely free evening and some especially pleasant company to spend it with. Maybe I could share the Oreos with Seth instead.

"Is that zucchini bread I smell cooking?"

He strode toward me and my heart jumped into overdrive.

"It is. I figured you'd be hungry and there was a zucchini just waiting to be harvested on your back deck. When was the last time you actually sat down to a meal?"

He passed me to check the bread in the oven, and I fought a twinge of disappointment. What had I thought he was going to do? Kiss me hello? *Damn straight, Jess, but get a grip. You're not desperate.* But still, what kind of man lets himself into a woman's home and bakes bread just because she doesn't like coming home to an empty house?

The answer left me a little breathless.

He pulled the bread from the oven and set it on the counter. "Why don't you go shower and get into something comfy while I put the steaks on the grill?"

The chicken would be just as good cold. Before I could think too much about it and change my mind, I closed the short distance between us and gave him a hug.

"You are too much for words."

He returned the hug, then leaned back to peer down at me. "All good words, I hope."

"All good," I muttered turning away before his astute gaze could read me.

He'd stopped asking me out when I kept insisting that it wasn't appropriate for me to date my son's tutor, but he hadn't been Mike's tutor for a while now. And somehow, he just seemed to always be there when I needed a friend. Occasionally even a friend with desire in his eyes, but he hadn't acted on it. Yet.

I took my time in the shower, trying to sort out the intent behind the kindness, and what I wanted to happen next. In all honesty, if he'd stepped into the shower with me at that very moment, I'd have welcomed him. Maybe Rafe was right about what I needed in my life. That thought should have made me blush but didn't.

I shut the water off, toweled dry and found shorts and a flirty sleeveless top. I headed for the door, then made an abrupt turn back to the bathroom to dash on a tad of makeup. Might as well look my best.

Seth had set the table on the deck with the tiny patch of ocean view. There were even flowers on the table. Murphy slept curled up on a towel in a late afternoon shaft of sunlight. Her fur still damp, she slept the sleep of a well-exercised puppy.

"You took her to the beach?"

Seth set a salad bowl on the table along with two open bottles of beer, already sweating in the humid air. He rubbed his shoulder, with one hand. "Feels like I won't be able to lift my arm to write on the blackboard tomorrow. She sure loves chasing that tennis ball."

"I'd have warned you, if you asked." The conversation seemed very remote from the hum of something else that wasn't being said.

The moment stretched as we gazed at each other without speaking, then shattered at the sound of the kitchen door blasting open. Mike stood there grinning and smeared with dirt.

"I'm just in time." He stopped short seeing only two settings. He swallowed, his Adam's apple bobbing.

"Shower first," Seth said. "We'll wait, but make it fast."

Whatever the moment might have held for Seth and me alone was gone, replaced by easy camaraderie between the three of us as we devoured Seth's perfectly marinated and barbecued steak, moist, spicy zucchini bread and tossed salad.

Mike was full of details about the game I'd missed the night before. "You should have been there, Mom. I finally got to play for a change." Did I detect a note of censure in his voice? I swallowed my own disappointment and asked how he'd done.

"I caught a pass that turned into a touchdown. We won fourteen to ten. Coach said I could start the next game."

Now I felt doubly disappointed that I had not been there to watch my son in his first varsity game.

"Sammy and PJ have decided Mike's their new hero," Seth said. Obviously, Seth and his twins had attended Mike's game even if I hadn't.

"Where are the twins tonight?" I asked.

"I dropped them off at their grandparents for a birthday party for one of their cousins."

"Hey guys," Mike jumped to his feet and picked up his empty plate. "I've got a paper to finish. Super meal, Seth." On his way to the kitchen he paused long enough to give me a hug. "Love you, Mom."

His plate clattered into the sink, waking Murphy who trotted off to see if Mike had scraped any leftovers into his doggy dish.

After a companionable silence while we finished our beers, Seth and I cleared the table and moved into the kitchen. We cleaned up as if we'd been doing it together for years. Seth seemed to know where everything went without asking, but then, he'd spent a lot of time here with Mike over the spring and summer months.

I admired the competent way he worked the kitchen, and truth be told, drooled a bit over all six feet of trim, tanned muscles, wondering where this might go from here. Then my phone rang, rattling against the kitchen counter where I'd left it.

I snatched it up. "Quinn."

"Are you watching TV?" Rafe sounded breathless.

"No?"

"Go turn it on. Right now. You won't believe CNN."

Seth lifted his brows in question. I hurried to the family room and found the remote. Seth followed me.

With the phone still pressed to my ear I clicked over to CNN. Not a station I usually tuned in to.

"Does anyone know how it happened?" asked a voice off camera.

The reporter, garbed in a rain slicked jacket, hair tucked up under a soaked ball cap with the CNN logo stitched on the front and a finger pressed to one ear, apparently trying to block out competing noise, shook her head. "All we know at present is that the candidate's SUV slid off the road and through the guard rail right here." She turned to gesture behind her to a yawning gap in the safety rails that marked the perimeter of a sharp curve in the road.

Red and blue lights whirled, flashing off the wet pavement, and men in yellow raincoats milled about as a tow truck backed toward the damaged opening, adding flashes of yellow to the scene.

"The passenger is well known to everyone here in Virginia," the reporter went on. "Glen Rhodes is running for the senate, and was returning from a weekend of rallies. The driver was pronounced dead. Mr. Rhodes was taken to the hospital just twenty minutes ago. He's in serious condition but that is all we've learned."

The screen changed to show a news anchor seated behind a desk in a suit and tie with the image we'd just seen live, on a screen behind him. I stopped listening.

My phone had drifted away from my ear as I watched. I yanked it back. "If that was just an accident then I'm Miss America."

CHAPTER 17

WITH MY PHONE STILL PRESSED against my ear, I paced. Five hard steps toward my front door, then back to a spot in front of the television. Seth watched, his attention divided between me and the news anchor, his brows knit.

Rafe snorted on his end of the call. "I'd register you for a pageant, but I doubt the lieutenant would give you the time off."

"Knock it off, Rafe. I'm not in the mood for your humor."

The fourth member of an Arlington Security team had been airlifted to a hospital from the scene of an accident on a highway somewhere in Virginia. Three others were dead, along with Laney Hoffman, and I was very sure it had nothing to do with the children we met in Georgia just hours earlier. Unless there was more to the story of how those kids became orphans than Adam Hahn said.

Vic Moretti had hinted that Glen Rhodes was behind the elimination of witnesses to whatever had happened over there, but now Rhodes was the one fighting for his life. I wanted to swear, but refrained with Seth looking on.

That left only Adam Hahn in Iraq and Hank Pearson aboard a Navy ship somewhere in the Pacific. Maybe this was bigger than a six-man team once stationed in Afghanistan, because there was no way either Hahn or Pearson could have been up to no good in either Virginia or St Augustine.

"We need to contact whoever's handling the accident in Virginia," I said, thinking through our options.

Rafe snorted. "Probably highway patrol and they'll be out

there cleaning this up for a while. Nothing we can do until morning." Was that a giggle? Rafe hadn't wasted any time hunting down one of his women.

Amped up for action, pacing wasn't doing it for me, and sitting down to watch the television with Seth wasn't going to work either. My mind raced through a dozen scenarios. "I can't just sit here."

"Cool your jets, Miss America. By morning the initial findings on this accident will be in. We can talk to the troopers who handled it. We can tackle Mrs. Moretti again to see if she knows more than she's told us, or maybe more than she knows she knows if we ask the right questions. Spend your evening planning that interview and I'll see you first thing. Want me to pick you up?"

Visions of another day in Rafe's Jeep made me shudder. "I'll meet you at central."

"Go get some 'beauty' sleep." He laughed as he hung up. I'd probably never hear the end of my unfortunate remark about being Miss America.

While I spoke with Rafe, Seth had disappeared into the kitchen. He returned with two steaming mugs which he set on coasters before dropping onto the couch. "If you need to bounce ideas around out loud, I think I already mentioned I'm a good listener." He propped one foot on his other knee and reached for one of the mugs.

Still filled with energy that had no outlet, I continued pacing. "I can't discuss an ongoing investigation."

"In between flying jets and resigning my commission, I did a stint with JAG." He stopped and took a sip. "Made up my mind law was not the next step for me, but I had a knack for investigating. I'm good at puzzles too."

I looked at the man with new eyes. "I thought all you did in the Navy was fly planes."

He slowly winked one of those dark coffee colored eyes. "Well, that was my favorite part of being a sailor and if it hadn't been for my wife wanting me to stay ashore, I'd probably still be catapulting off aircraft carriers. Or maybe by now I'd be commanding my own ship."

Completely diverted from my own problems, I stopped to consider the choices this man had made on behalf of others, and the huge change that had brought about for himself. Something we had in common, this mid-life leap to an entirely new career. He from fighter jock to teacher and me from stay-at-home mom to cop. Except he'd made the leap for others. I'd chosen my path for me alone, with little thought as to how it would impact my kids. Something I was coming to terms with on a daily basis.

I dropped into my recliner. "Why did you end up leaving the Navy?"

"Trying to save my marriage."

"But it didn't help." I knew he was divorced, but nothing beyond that fact.

He shook his head. "Annette was done with *me*, apparently. Not just the Navy."

Annette was a jerk. "So, you turned your back on a career you loved, and it turned out to be not enough? Why did you stay in the area? Didn't you grow up in North Carolina?"

"My boys are here. Annette's parents live in Nocatee, and this is where she grew up. If I wanted to be a part of my twins' lives, I needed to stay here. So, I did the troops-to-teachers thing, and here I am."

I'd bet anything he was an amazing dad, considering his relationship with my son and how he'd turned things around for Mike without ever being heavy handed about it. I began to relax and settled back into my recliner. "They're lucky boys. I'd like to meet them some day." I'd seen a photo of them with Mike. Miniature versions of their dad and like two peas in a pod.

"I'd like that too." He set his mug down, fiddled around squaring it up on the coaster, then looked up at me, his gaze serious. "But right now, I'm guessing you need to concentrate on figuring out this business with Laney Hoffman, her injured husband and the guy who got shot at the Fountain. Anything you share with me goes no further. I hope you know that."

He wrinkled his forehead. "I know from my own stint with JAG that sometimes just talking it out, saying things out loud, trying to explain it to someone who hasn't been involved from the start often shakes things loose in your own brain, or puts a new spin on facts you've been trying to fit together without much luck."

It went against the grain for me to confide in anyone outside the force, but he was right about me spinning my wheels. Rafe and I had gone over everything on the way home from Georgia and come up with nothing new. Nothing reasonable, anyway. Then this evening's bombshell dropped into the mess and even the unreasonable ideas we'd come up with exploded.

"How much do you already know?" I finally picked up my mug and took a sip of what turned out not to be coffee, but tea. A surprisingly tasty cup of tea with a hint of vanilla. "This is good."

"It's the additives." Seth grinned.

I held the mug to my face and inhaled. The scent of almond hit my senses, along the vanilla. Not being a tea drinker, I'd never considered the idea of anything beyond plain old English Breakfast. "Thanks." I took another sip.

"So, how much do I know?" Seth held up one hand and began folding down his fingers as he ticked off the things he knew. "It began with Laney Hoffman. Her husband was likely the prime suspect until someone tried to do him in. Then a friend of hers got shot at the Fountain of Youth while you were talking to him. There are a couple of kids in Georgia you went to see today, but I've no idea how that connects. And now this accident in Virginia." He nodded toward the television, now muted, but still showing a reporter on the scene. Seth knew far more than I thought had been made public. Was he reading my mind, too?

I wrestled with the idea of discussing the investigation with him, then gave in.

"Well, here's what you don't know," I said, and then outlined the string of events surrounding the Arlington Security group. "Six guys on the team. One died from a car accident. One took his own life. At least that's how it was reported, but Vic Moretti was sure he was being followed and suspected it might not have gone down that way. He came to warn Laney to watch her back. A lot of good that did. She ended up dead, coshed over the head with a glass prism taken off her husband's desk. We're looking at Upshaw for the attempt on Dan, but don't really know if that's a separate issue or part of the other string of deaths. Moretti insisted on meeting away from the sheriff's office fearing someone in the department might be listening who shouldn't be, and that ended up being a disaster. And now this accident in Virginia. And what's confusing me is that this guy in Virginia is running for Congress and Moretti apparently thought there was something the whole group knew, including Laney Hoffman, that would cast a shadow over his campaign."

Seth's brow furrowed again. "Two dead, two in the hospital

and maybe two different investigations." He harrumphed. "What did Moretti say happened?"

My turn to snort. "He didn't say. That's just the problem. He insinuated. The kids living in Georgia were mentioned. A Canadian priest smuggled them out of Afghanistan and back to Canada, then into the US where they were adopted by the Georgia couple." I took another sip of the calming tea. "But frankly, I can't see how the kids' story could have a negative impact on Glen Rhodes' bid for a senate seat."

"Were they orphaned or stolen from their parents?"

Holy crap! That thought hadn't occurred to me at all. Were they part of trafficking ring, or was it an isolated event? We definitely needed to reach out to the guy on the ship. What was the possibility Hahn had already managed to connect with the guy and warn him to keep his mouth shut? But if we could talk to him, he might say something that clashed with Hahn's polished story, or at least left a seed of doubt.

Seth smiled, an expression that lit his whole face. I liked the way his eyes got into the act. I also liked the way it made me feel. All jittery with some kind of eager anticipation.

Seth dropped his foot to the floor and rested his elbows on his knees. "I can see from your expression that's a question you hadn't asked before. See what I meant about explaining it all out loud?"

I copied Seth's pose, leaning toward him like a co-conspirator. "We were already planning to visit the widow again tomorrow and see if she would be more forthcoming. Vic might have told his wife things that could help us. She might even know things she has no idea are connected. But thanks for helping me get my thoughts sorted, and finding a new spin to consider."

"My pleasure." Seth leaned toward me and put a hand on my

knee. "I'm going to take myself home now and hope you will take yourself to bed. You look beat, and you'll need to be on your toes tomorrow." He grabbed his mug off the coffee table and stood. "Remember, I'm just a phone call away."

He disappeared into the kitchen and a moment later, there came the sound of the mug being rinsed and placed in the dishwasher. Then the a door shut and his footsteps retreated down the outside stairs. The warmth from his hand on my knee lingered.

I was remarkably calmer than after ending my call with Rafe. A fresh plan was coming together in my head.

I tried to calculate what time it was in the South Pacific. Not that I knew exactly where in the South Pacific Hank Pearson was, but it was sometime tomorrow morning. I wanted to call him right that minute, but I didn't have the name of his ship. Wasn't even sure anyone was going to give us the name without a fight over turf.

But as Seth had boiled it down . . ., there were only two possibilities that made the children's involvement make any sense. Either the kids' parents had been murdered and they'd become orphans at an American's hand, or they'd been abducted from their parents. Either might be worth killing to cover up.

CHAPTER 18

BROUSSARD, ZACK OLIVER, Rafe and I convened over a platter of bagels and another round of coffee. The murder board had two new photos pinned to it and the investigation had become more tangled than a basket of yarn a litter of kittens had gotten into. Rafe had already outlined the events in Virginia from the evening before, or at least what we knew of them.

Glen Rhodes was conscious and the state trooper who'd been at the scene of the accident was headed to the hospital for a statement. At the moment, however, we had no proof that it was anything more than a highway accident, or that it was in any way connected to the murders of Laney Hoffman and Victor Moretti.

I went over the visit Rafe and I had with the adoptive father of the two children who were somehow mixed up in the Afghanistan events. For Zack's benefit, him being new to the team and in spite of my personal animosity, I explained Moretti's suspicions about being followed and his insinuations that Glen Rhodes was somehow involved in the deaths of four people, three Arlington men and Laney.

Zack leaned back in his chair and listened without comment, his long legs crossed at the ankles. In his late thirties, with longish blond hair and a deep tan, he looked more like a beach-loving lifeguard than a serious detective, but he was thorough, fair, and insightful on the job. And a pain in the ass with a superior attitude toward female deputies. We sparred more than I ever had with my brothers.

I glanced at Broussard, hoping he'd had better luck with Laney Hoffman's father the second time around.

"Zack and I didn't learn anything new from Upshaw," Broussard said, answering my unvoiced question. "We asked Upshaw if he knew anything about the children, if Laney had mentioned them at any time, but either she was not in the loop about the kids or she didn't share her knowledge with her father."

Rafe stopped tapping on his tablet. "Did Laney share *any* of what she experienced in Afghanistan with her father?"

"Her opinions," Zack drawled without abandoning his relaxed pose. "She appeared to have quite a bit to say about the politics of the US stationing troops in the country, but most of what she told her dad had already been reported to the Senate committee responsible for her being there in the first place. The unspoken goal apparently to come back with enough negative findings to force the President's hand and get us out of the country entirely."

I reviewed the timeline of Laney's involvement with the fact-finding mission, comparing that to the arrival of the children in Georgia and the details Matt Springer shared about their short stay in Canada. "Perhaps Laney knew nothing about the kids."

Rafe's head swiveled toward me. "How could she not know anything if Moretti made a point of going to her house to warn her to watch her back? Moretti seemed pretty certain the kids were part of the story."

Although Rhodes' accident seemed to rule him out, Seth's suggestion the night before inspired me to pursue the possibility that there might still be a sordid story underlying all the deaths. "Moretti was sure of a cover-up, but Hahn didn't think the kids were part of it. Actually, Hahn thought Moretti was paranoid about nothing. But we still haven't spoken to the last guy on the team."

Broussard sat with his elbows on the table kneading his temples with his fingertips. "Two orphaned kids are not a good reason for three, maybe four murders, and that's not counting the attempt on Dan Hoffman or Glen Rhodes' accident yesterday."

Not wanting to admit I'd discussed the case with Seth the night before, I offered his thought as my own. "What if it's not a simple matter of orphaned kids? What if they were kidnapped? Perhaps with the aim of funneling them into a child trafficking ring?"

All three men nodded as if that thought or one similar had already occurred to them.

Rafe spoke first. "Christ! Who would sell kids that young into anything?"

"How young were they?" Zack's relaxed manner disappeared.

I did the math in my head. "Around five and three when they came to the US. Hasan is eleven now and Safia nine."

"Well," Broussard said, rubbing his temples again. "If they were abducted that would be plenty of reason to want to cover it up, but then they were delivered by a priest for adoption into a decent-sounding family. They weren't sold to the Georgia couple, were they?"

I shook my head. The idea had made sense when Seth suggested it, but Matt Springer had seemed like a decent guy, not one to lie, and the kids had acted like normal happy American kids. "Other way around. According to the adoptive father, three of the guys on the team were sending him checks to help with expenses for the first couple years until the adoption was final and the Springers told them to stop sending money. But maybe someone on that security team was responsible for their Afghani parents' deaths."

Zack fiddled with a pencil, tapping the eraser end on the table while he considered this.

Rafe pushed away from the table. "It's way past time to reach out to Hank Pearson. We need the name of the ship he's on and a military switchboard to patch us through."

"And revisit Moretti's wife," I added. I didn't like the woman and she hadn't been helpful, but if we dug deeper she might spill something new to point us in the right direction.

Broussard gathered his pad of paper and notes. "Zack is still working that break-in case and I have two burglaries to follow up on besides this, so we'll stay here, and track down that ship. Someone might have to take a trip up to Virginia." He looked at Rafe, the only single deputy on the team.

"I might be able to get my brother to visit Mr. Rhodes." The idea had just popped into my head. "Brady is currently stationed at the Pentagon and since he's with NCIS, he could probably get access to the candidate and ask a few questions."

Broussard got to his feet. "Call him. See if he can help. Then you two head out to tackle Mrs. Moretti." Not expecting any argument, he turned and left the room.

Zach gathered up his notes and stood. "The man we need to connect with is Hank Pearson? Is that Henry, or just Hank? He's not military, right?"

"Right," Rafe confirmed. "Not sure about the name or nickname."

I handed Zach a copy of my list of the team from Arlington. "The only member of the Arlington team who spent a year in Afghanistan guarding a military base who's still living and not on the injured list except for Adam Hahn. We spoke to Hahn two days ago." What felt more like a week ago. "We just want to get Pearson' version of what the team experienced during that tour of duty. Focus on the time Laney Hoffman was embedded with the team, and be sure to ask how they came in contact with the kids, who smuggled them out and how. And who knew."

Zack took the list, glanced at it and smiled, a smile that didn't reach his eyes. Kidnapped kids wasn't a happy thought. "Will do."

Rafe stretched, clasped his hands above his head and pressed them back toward the wall behind him. "Well, time to get this show on the road and visit Moretti's wife again."

I held up a finger. "Hang for a minute while I catch Brady and see what he might be willing to do for us."

Rafe nodded and left me thumbing through my contacts for my brother's number.

Brady answered on the second ring. "Hey, Sherlock. How goes it in Florida?"

"Busy." And filled with doubt, guilt and mixed emotions. But it was good to hear my brother's voice.

"The kids okay?"

"They are, but—"

"You didn't call me in the middle of the day to chat about family. What can I do for you?" Brady was always quick to pick up on my moods.

I filled him in on the current string of deaths and suspicious accidents, along with the history of the Arlington team, what we knew of their activities in Afghanistan as well as the kids smuggled out to Canada.

"The thing is," I concluded, "that man shot at the Fountain two days ago was convinced that he was being followed. He thought Laney's death as well as an earlier reported suicide and auto crash were part of a cover-up effort, possibly connected to the commander of the unit who is running for Congress up there in Virginia. But last night the commander was run off the road and is recovering at Inova in Alexandria."

Brady snickered. "That's inconvenient."

"Very." My brother, ever with the humor. "So, I was wondering if you would be willing to pay Glen Rhodes a visit and see what you can find out about his time with the Arlington team in Afghanistan, and more specifically about what he knows about the deaths of Dominick Garcia and Isaac Leitz. Feel him out about the two kids smuggled in, although one of his team insisted Rhodes was kept out of the loop on the kids. The guy could have been lying to protect his commander, but we have no proof either way."

"That's all?" Brady snorted, then got serious. "I'll see what I can find out and get back to you. Anything else you need?"

Zack was already working on it, but in case he didn't get anywhere, I asked, "Yeah. Maybe. One of the Arlington guys we'd like to connect with is on a Navy ship somewhere in the Southwest Pacific. If you could find out what ship, that would be helpful. Name's Hank Pearson. Check both Hank and Henry."

"You don't want much, do you?" Brady chuckled.

I chuckled back. "You know you like a good mystery. Now you can be part of solving one."

"Love you, Sherlock. I'll call as soon as I have anything."

"Love you back."

The connection ended.

Okay! I headed to find Rafe. Time to track down Mrs. Irma Moretti.

A GREEN FORD FOCUS liberally spattered with mud sat in the Moretti driveway. Hoffman's nosy next-door neighbor had mentioned a small green car on her street that she hadn't recognized the day Laney was murdered, but some things really were coincidence. I rapped on the door as Rafe stepped up onto the stoop beside me. When no one answered, I knocked again with the heel of my hand.

A sullen teenager opened the door partway. "Yeah?"

I introduced myself and Rafe. "We would like to speak with Mrs. Moretti."

"Whatever." The youth finished opening the door and stepped back. "She's in the living room." He turned and took the adjacent flight of stairs three at a time leaving us to find our own way.

"Nice kid," Rafe muttered as we stepped inside.

I mimicked the kid's welcome. "Yeah?" I'd have Mike's hide if he was ever that rude to anyone at our door. Especially law enforcement.

The woman wearing a colorful mumu and nearly swallowed up by the recliner was not Vic's wife. Considering the resemblance to Vic and the fact that the rude teenager had said Mrs. Moretti was in the living room, I deduced this was Vic's mother,

White haired and wrinkled, she looked to be in her late seventies. Possibly even Vic's grandmother. She looked up as we entered, glanced past us, then at Rafe and me. She started to struggle out of the recliner, but Rafe hastened closer and patted her wrist.

"No need to get up, Ma'am. I'm Detective Rafe Morgan. And this is my partner, Detective Jesse Quinn. We're sorry for your loss."

The woman's faded blue eyes teared up as she nodded acceptance of Rafe's expression of sympathy.

I stepped closer. "May we ask you a few questions?"

Her brimming eyes turned my way. "I don't know why

anyone would want to hurt Victor. Everyone loved him."

What mother would claim different? But someone hadn't loved him. Or what he knew.

"You can't think of anyone who might have an ax to grind?" I'd give her age the benefit of doubt.

A vigorous shake of the white head.

"Maybe someone he once worked with at Arlington?"

Mrs. Moretti appeared to consider this question at length. "I don't think so. He didn't leave because of anyone he worked with, and he loved his job. He just wanted to be around more for his son. Gio's a good boy but he was getting a little wild. He needed Victor to stay home and teach him how to be a man. It was a good decision. Irma was putting ideas in his head that didn't belong there."

I eased down onto the chair closest to the older woman. "What kind of ideas?" Where this was going or what possible connection it might have with Vic's murder or Laney's was beyond me, but any new intel was good when all we'd been doing was chasing our tails.

The elder Mrs. Moretti narrowed her eyes. "She lies, you know. Always with the lies. She tried to poison Gio against his father. Didn't work, but she tried. She just wanted Gio to side with her so she told him things."

The possibility that the sullen teen might be a killer crossed my mind. "What lies did she tell her son about his father?"

"She told Gio his daddy was a liar and a cheat. Victor was never a liar and I'm sure he never cheated either. That's not the way I raised him."

I wanted to make the *tsking* sound my mother hated, but I refrained. Victor had almost certainly been cheating. More than once with more than one woman. "I'm sure you didn't," I said in my most neutral tone.

It wasn't hard to understand how being told his father had been unfaithful could turn a boy against his elder. All I had to do was look at my own son Mike who still was barely on speaking terms with Elliott, all because Elliott had been unfaithful to me. But I hadn't been the one to tell him about it. How Mike had found out, I was never sure, but my young man seemed to have known before I came to the realization, and his defense of me had been of heroic proportions. While I valued my son's support, I lamented the rift between he and his father, but apparently Irma Moretti had fostered the antipathy.

Rafe leaned forward, his elbows on his knees. "How did Gio respond to that?"

Mrs. Moretti pursed her lips and smiled. "Gio loved his daddy." Then she frowned and a tear slipped down her cheek. "But now his daddy's gone, and he only has his momma to listen to anymore." She blinked her eyes hard a few times before her faded gaze intensified on Rafe, then on me. "That woman told Gio his daddy died because the cops were careless. Why would she say something like that?"

CHAPTER 19

THE CLERK JAMMED BILLS into a paper sack with shaking hands. The robbers were white, their skin ghostlike in the depths of their black hoods, but their youthful features all too identifiable. What were the chances the kid with the gun would just walk out and leave the clerk alive to describe them? My heartbeat echoed in my ears. I swallowed back a moment of doubt and then stepped into the open.

"Sheriff's Department! Put the gun down."

The hooded kid whipped around to face me.

"Put it down," I ordered again.

He was just a boy. Just a scared kid. I didn't want to shoot a kid.

I repeated my command a third time, identifying myself along with the demand. I aimed, one handed, my gun as steady as I could make it, but the tip of the barrel jumped with every beat of my heart. I didn't want to kill a kid.

He took advantage of my hesitation. Pain screamed through my thigh. The clerk, too stupid to stay out of sight reappeared and the gunman swung his deadly black automatic back toward the clerk. From four feet away, he wouldn't miss.

I held my breath and squeezed the trigger of my service weapon.

The kid spun. Blood sprayed the register as he fell against a rack of tourist souvenirs, then toppled to the floor. Keychains and postcards rained down around him, and his gun spun away toward the door.

I JERKED TO A SITTING POSITION with bedclothes tangled around my body. My heart thundered. My throat so dry I could barely swallow. I blinked, trying to focus in the dim light of early dawn. Trying to get my bearings in the real world.

The nightmare of killing that kid hadn't haunted my sleep in a long time, but it was just as real and painful as it had ever been. I dragged myself out of bed, and straightened my pajamas that were skewed halfway around my waist. The cool blue light of my alarm clock read 5:05 am.

My heart rate had nearly returned to normal by the time I entered the kitchen and crossed the chilly tile in my bare feet to start a pot of coffee.

I'd lived with that horror for months after taking down the kid in the convenience store. I'd been cleared and put back on duty as soon as my wounded thigh had healed enough to allow it, but the nightmare continued. Ruining my sleep night after night. Hadn't mattered that it was him or the clerk. Or that he'd shot at me in the commission of a felony. It just mattered that he was dead, and I'd been the instrument of that death. And he'd only been sixteen. My rookie introduction into the world of split-second decisions I'd have to live with forever.

Before the coffee machine was even finished filling the pot, I shoved a mug under the stream, then carried it out to the front deck. I curled up on the swing, pulling my feet under me and hugged my mug. It would be another muggy September day in a few hours, but right at the moment, the pre-dawn air was cool. The sun hadn't come up yet. Wouldn't for another hour and a half, but the sky was beginning to lighten over the sliver of beach I could see from my deck.

Should put my sneakers on and go for a run. I needed the run, in more ways than one. After the coffee. Refusing to dwell on the troubling nightmare, I began reviewing my current case. I hadn't heard back from Brady yet, and we were scheduled to be patched through to the USS McCampbell at nine-thirty am our time which was one-thirty am their time. Tomorrow. Not just another time zone, but a whole different day. I wasn't holding my breath that talking to Hank Pearson would break our case for us, but just maybe something would pop.

Vic's son, Gio bothered me. His grandmother had blamed his surly temperament on his mother, but what reason could the woman have given the kid to make him believe that law enforcement was at fault in his father's death? She'd been just as surly, but I'd given her a pass since she was dealing with the loss of her husband. Grief can do strange things to a person's thinking. Perhaps it was grief we saw in Gio. Anger and hurt with nowhere to go, so blame whoever shows up.

I lifted the mug to my lips only to discover it empty. Time to run.

EVEN WITH A RUN THAT TOOK me all the way to Butler Beach and back, I was still showered, dressed and back at work before anyone else. I studied what had had been added to our murder board, then on a fresh pad of paper made a list of all the people we knew were involved in one way or another. I added notes of their comments and whereabouts at the time of Laney and Vic's deaths, then started asking myself what each of them had to gain from either death. I'd already done this a dozen times in my mind, but hoped a new day and a fresh mind might present new possibilities.

My phone buzzed in its holster and I pulled it free.

Brady. His smiling face felt like a hug even though I knew it was business.

"What did you find out?"

"Good morning to you, too, Sherlock."

"Sorry." Patience was not one of my virtues. *"Dia duit,"* I said, using one of my father's favorite Irish Gaelic greetings that literally meant God to you.

"That's better. I didn't wake you up, did I?"

I glanced at my watch. 8:30. "I've been up for a few hours, but it feels like twice that."

"Okay, here's what I learned."

I flipped the page on my pad of paper.

A rustling on the other end said Brady did the same. "Mr. Rhodes did not appear to know about the kids. He was not aware Victor Moretti was being followed but wasn't so sure it wasn't true in light of his own accident. He told me his car was run off the road deliberately. His driver is dead so even if the man got a good look at the plate or the other driver, we'll never know. The culprit's car was a black SUV. A Chevy Suburban, Rhodes thought but wasn't sure. He'd been reading through some papers when the other car slammed into them, and then sped off. Rhodes' car crashed through the guard rail and hurtled down a steep embankment, so Rhodes barely glimpsed the SUV."

I jotted the facts, but nothing I didn't already know per the Virginia State Police.

Brady kept talking. "I felt him out about events in Afghanistan, but he didn't think anything there could have triggered this apparent series of murders. He was pretty sure that Garcia did commit suicide. The man had been seeing a counselor and his marriage was falling apart. As for Isaac Lietz, someone offered him a couch to sleep on after a long meeting that broke up late, but he insisted on getting on the road. Bad decision."

I sighed in frustration. "Nothing about the kids, huh?"

"Nothing. Rhodes was injured in the bombing that left them orphans. He managed to dig the kids out alive and get them medical care. Rhodes thought they went from there to an orphanage. He did know the priest. Father Frank Devois had been something of a chaplain at the base and he was still there when the Arlington team left. Rhodes has no idea how to contact the cleric, though. Wasn't even sure where in Canada he came from. What didn't surprise him was that his men were willing to pony up monthly payments to help get them established with their new family. They were good men and had been as troubled about the kids and what happened to their parents as Rhodes was. They just apparently did something about it when Rhodes did not."

I *tsked*.

Brady chuckled. "Mother would not be pleased."

"Mother's not dealing with an investigation that appears to be going nowhere. But thanks for talking to Rhodes."

"Your other man Hank, and it is just Hank, not Henry, is aboard an Arleigh class destroyer, the USS McCampbell. You need me to grease the wheels to get in touch with him?"

"Thanks, but we've got that covered. Another detective managed to set up a call for this morning." I glanced at my watch. "In twenty minutes. But thanks again."

"Any time, Sherlock. You know I love you, right?"

The smile spreading across my face felt good. "I love you, too. When do you think you'll get home for a visit?"

"Thanksgiving. I promise."

"It'll be good to see you."

"*Slán abhaile*, Sherlock."

"Safe home to you, too, Brady."

Phone in my hand, and call ended, I imagined one of Brady's breath squeezing hugs. I missed him. Of all my siblings we were the closest. Liam, the eldest, took his position as first born very seriously and had taken over the job of man of the house when Daddy died making Liam seem far older. And my sister was the spoiled youngest. Very spoiled. I had nothing in common with her except our parents, and even that sometimes seemed slim. She was old enough when Daddy died to remember him but acted as if she didn't. Which left Brady and me, buddies, cohorts in mischief, watching each other's backs.

Rafe's face appeared at my level. "Earth to Jesse. Thinking good thoughts?" He plopped into a chair and dropped a small duffle onto the floor.

"Just talked to Brady." I repeated my brother's information.

Rafe ran a hand through his hair further disrupting his already messy head of curls. "I hope to God this Hank fellow has something new to share. I'm getting bruised running into nothing but dead ends."

Zach strode in and took the chair usually occupied by Broussard. His arrogance set my teeth on edge. As if he owned this investigation now. Just because he'd made the arrangements to contact Hank Pearson. Made me wish we'd gotten the info from Brady first so I wouldn't have to deal with Zach's smug condescension.

He'd been on vacation when the case began the week before but had apparently gone sucking up to the lieutenant to get himself added to the team, knowing it was high-profile and solving it would put a shine on his rising star. Or maybe I was just letting past experience color my attitude.

"Broussard sends his apologies. Those two burglaries have become three and they appear to be connected." He fiddled with the remote to turn on the flat screen bolted to the wall. "Sarge said to fill him in after we talk to Pearson."

The screen glowed dully.

"Got your questions ready?" Zach asked as if he was tutoring a pair of newbies. I ground my teeth rather than say something I'd regret.

An odd ring tone sounded followed by static and a brightening screen. Two voices speaking in some kind of military jargon must have been the military operator and whoever handled the call aboard the USS McCampbell. Then a lean, muscled man of about forty, wearing a plain white T-shirt and a ball cap with the Arlington logo on the front appeared.

"Hank Pearson?" Zack asked.

"The same. What can I do for you?"

I jumped in before Zack could completely dominate the interview. "Sorry for calling so late. I'm Detective Jesse Quinn with Detectives Rafe Morgan and Zach Oliver of the St. John's County, Florida Sheriff's Department . We are investigating the deaths of one of your former team members and a woman I believe you also knew."

"Whoa!" Pearson sat back in his chair, his face registering surprise. "Who?"

"Victor Moretti and Laney Hoffman, although you probably knew her as Upshaw."

"Jesus!" Pearson removed his cap revealing close-cut black hair marked with a scar that ran from mid-scalp to his left eyebrow. He scratched his head. "How did it happen?"

"Murder." I cut directly to the chase. "Ms. Hoffman's head was bashed in with a glass weight and Mr. Moretti was shot with a 9 mm handgun. Moretti was convinced he was being followed and thought there was some kind of cover up over civilian deaths in Afghanistan. Maybe involving kids smuggled out of the country. We're hoping you might be able to shed some light on those events or know more about whatever Moretti didn't get a chance to tell us."

Pearson rubbed at the scar, apparently clueless. "Who did Vic think was following him?"

"He didn't get a chance to tell us that either, but he thought it might have something to do with two dead civilians and two orphaned kids, and that your old commander might be behind it."

Pearson laughed with no humor in it. "Vic would think that. If he was being followed, that is."

"But you don't?" I asked.

"There's some animosity going on there. That Upshaw woman came here, all full of herself and the congressional oversight committee she was representing. Rhodes wasn't happy to have her in our midst poking into things in the first place. He especially wasn't happy with Vic for sleeping with her. They had words. Vic was told to end it or else."

I scribbled a few notes even though the whole conversation was being recorded. "Or else, what?"

"Else he could find himself another job." Pearson glanced at his hands then back at the screen. "Vic was a married man and Rhodes didn't approve of him cheating on his wife, never mind that the Upshaw woman was a pain the ass. I don't know if Rhodes was the reason he got canned when we got home or not, but Vic was sure the loss of his place on the team was the commander's fault. In any case, I haven't seen Vic or heard from him in years."

Rafe leaned forward. "What can you tell us about the kids? How did they become orphans?"

Pearson rubbed his scar again. "Commander Rhodes and I visited their house. Just to ask a few questions, but as we were leaving there was an explosion. I was knocked ass over end and took a few minutes to figure out what happened. Rhodes ran back to see if anyone had survived. The parents were dead. The kids were buried in the rubble. I got this—" He drew a finger over the scar. "Helping Rhodes dig them out."

Zack jumped into the questioning. "So, there was no cover-up of any kind?"

Pearson frowned. "Who said anything about a cover-up"

"Moretti implied it," I answered. "But what happened to the kids after that? Your commander seemed to think they'd gone to an orphanage."

"They should have, but there was this priest there who said he knew of a network of people in Canada and the States willing to adopt kids like that. Give them a better chance than they'd ever get in some run-down orphanage in Afghanistan. It cost money to get them out, and more money to get them funneled to the right place, but Vic and I felt we owed it to them since that interview most likely got their folks got killed. I think whoever did it wanted the parents made an example of and us dead. We should have been, but when the blast went off the Humvee we were driving was between us and the house. The kids only survived because they were playing outside the stone wall that surrounded the house in the back."

"How did your commander feel about all that?" I asked.

"We didn't involve Rhodes. Figured the less he knew, the better, but Vic and I helped finance the deal. Dominic ponied up money, too. I heard the kids ended up with a nice family in the Southeast somewhere. Georgia, I think."

Nothing seemed to point to a cover-up or even something worth covering up. The dead-end left me feeling as bruised as Rafe claimed he was.

I tried again. "So, you can't think of any reason someone

would be following Victor Moretti?"

"I'd look at his old lady. Man couldn't keep it in his pants."

Zach glanced at his watch, then stood. "Thank you for your time, Mr. Pearson. We appreciate it. If there's anything you think of that might give us a lead on who wanted to murder Laney Hoffman or Victor Moretti, you know where to find us."

I jumped in before Zack could disconnect the call. "One more thing, actually. Do you believe Dominic Garcia committed suicide?"

Pearson slumped back in his seat, his face suddenly looking drawn. "Yeah. Sadly, I do. We saw things over there that troubled him. Troubled all of us, but Dom more than most. Classic case of PTSD. His wife Erin tried to understand, but he just spiraled deeper. Nothing any of us said seemed to pull him back from the abyss. Sad . . ." he trailed off shaking his head.

With nothing else to dig after, Rafe thanked Mr. Pearson again and apologized for keeping him up into the middle of the night, then Zack ended the call.

I glanced at the page of scribbled notes in front of me feeling totally deflated. So, what now?

The news regularly featured nasty little events in a very nasty part of the world. I'd been certain Vic's suspicions had merit and solving his mystery would solve our murders, but of the three men remaining, none of them bought into the cover-up theory. Nothing to support the idea that they weren't telling us the whole truth as they knew it either. Which left us right back where we started that steamy night I'd entered Dan's home to investigate Laney Hoffman's death.

Right back to putting Dan Hoffman at the top of the suspect list.

<h1 style="text-align:center">CHAPTER 20</h1>

THE THREE OF US STOOD around the conference table digesting the information we'd gotten from Hank Pearson, not sure if we had more to discuss or where to go next.

"Well, that points us right back at Hoffman," Zack said with an irritating smirk.

My gut had screamed at me the moment Zack joined the team that his presence would inevitably turn negative. That time had come. "We ruled Hoffman out when he got shot and someone tried to make it look like a suicide."

Zack tipped his head back and looked at me down the length of his patrician nose. "You ruled him out. I didn't."

I itched to slap the man. "We. Ruled. Him. Out."

"Even Broussard agreed on that one, Zack," Rafe muttered.

Zack flicked a hand as if brushing away an annoying fly. "Ever occur to any of you Hoffman could just as easily have faked his suicide attempt to look like someone else did it to throw you off? He didn't die after all."

"He hates guns," I fired back.

Zack's eyebrows added to the look of arrogant superiority. "Or so you'd like to believe."

A string of seething replies leapt to my tongue. "I've known Dan for most of my life. He does *not* like guns and never has. He refused to go hunting with a bunch of guys from the high school football team even though they ribbed the heck out of him about it. I'm not even sure he's ever held a gun. Besides, what about that last print we got that didn't belong to either Vic or Dan? What about the maid?"

Zack shook his head like a severely disappointed teacher. "Broussard sent a deputy out to get her prints which haven't been processed yet, but she's got an alibi. She was cleaning someone else's house at the time Mrs. Hoffman was murdered."

Still punching, I gestured toward the dark screen on the wall. "What about Pearson's suggestion?"

Rafe nodded as if he knew where my thoughts had gone.

I repeated the Arlington man's words "I'd look at the wife." I didn't like the woman and hadn't from day one. Not that I thought she killed Laney, but she hadn't been very forthcoming with details about her husband and his whereabouts. And then there was the poisoning of her son's mind against law enforcement.

Zack turned toward the door. "Hoffman still has no alibi and everything we've learned since that initial interview gives him motive. I think it's time I questioned the man myself."

Just what Dan didn't need. Another detective running him through the wringer. This one determined to put him away.

I took a deep breath, then unclenched my fists. "What we need to do is take a hard look at Irma Moretti. I think she knows a lot more than she's telling us."

Zack jabbed a thumb over his shoulder toward the wall. "Based on what? That guy's snipe at a fellow operator's wife?"

Zack's overbearing attitude was getting to me. "Based on her behavior." My voice rose to a near shout. "Her non-answers to our previous inquiries. And because we really have hit a dead end with the previous line of investigation. Besides." I straightened my jacket and gathered my gear. "Dan Hoffman isn't going anywhere. Irma Moretti just might."

For a moment Zack stared at me as if working on just the

right put-down, but then his phone buzzed and he glanced away as he put it to his ear. "Shit!" he said. "I thought Upshaw was the bigger problem." He frowned as whoever was on the other end of the line replied. "Yeah. I'll meet you there."

Zack shoved his phone back into its holster. "Good luck with the Moretti woman," he said. "I've gotta meet Broussard out at Blue Water Jewelers. Another break-in, this time with injuries. The manager was found unconscious by an employee coming into work a half hour ago. But you better have something more to go on when I finish there or I'm pushing to get an indictment on Hoffman."

Rafe watched Zack disappear. "You want me to go talk to Dan so Zack won't when he gets back in the game, or visit the Moretti woman again with you?"

If Irma Moretti was a suspect, perhaps going alone wouldn't be prudent. On the other hand, if it was just me, would she be more likely to say something she wouldn't say with Rafe present? And then there was Gio. Maybe we should divide and conquer. Like I told Zack. Dan wasn't going anywhere.

"Go with. We can visit Dan together on our way back."

As Rafe and I piled into my cruiser, he glanced over at me. "Maybe we should have been looking at her as soon as Vic got knocked off."

I buckled my seatbelt. "Maybe. But we were focused on a conspiracy that didn't include her. At least not directly."

"You think she's likely?"

I shook my head. "I don't know. That was a pretty neat shot. Not the kind a pissed off wife would be likely to make. More like a practiced shooter. Maybe even a sniper."

"My thoughts exactly," Rafe replied. "So, what are we looking for today?"

"Dig deeper into Vic's extracurricular activities. She didn't give us much more than a friend and an employer and a local hangout to check out before."

Rafe wagged his head. "Right. Like gambling, or maybe dabbling in drugs. Maybe beer wasn't his drug of choice."

When traffic got heavy closer to downtown, conjectures gave way to concentration on my driving. As we cleared the bridge and headed north, I formulated a new line of questioning in my head.

THE DRIVEWAY AT THE MORETTI home overflowed with cars. The bumper of Vic's blue SUV, found at the Fountain of Youth, processed and then returned by the sheriff's department, almost touched the garage doors. The little green Ford Focus in front of that. A Chevy pick-up truck hooked to a utility trailer took up the rest of the driveway. Several other cars were parked along both sides of the street. I pulled my county ride across the end of the driveway behind the trailer. No one was leaving until I was ready to let them go.

As we approached the house, the front door opened and two young men, about the same age as Vic's son stepped out, leapt down the stairs in one bound and headed for the street.

I moved into their path. "Can we talk for a minute?"

The taller of the two glanced at my cruiser. "I ain't done nothing."

"Didn't say you have. Just wanted to ask if you were friends of Gio Moretti."

Broad shoulders and dreads hanging into his eyes, he looked like a punk. "Yeah. So what? He ain't done nothing either." The kid shared a bad attitude toward law enforcement with Gio.

"Do you happen to know where Gio was on Saturday?"

Dreads just glared at me. His companion answered. "At football practice. With us. Why?"

"All day?"

The kid shrugged. "Actually, yeah. It was a workshop day. They had a bunch of players from UNF doing workshops on stuff. Different defensive plays, kicking, tackling, that kind of stuff. We were there all day. Until maybe 3:30 or so."

"Thanks. That's helpful. What's your name?"

Dreads pressed his lips together as if getting ready to refuse. The other youth answered.

"Chip Henkerson, Ma'am. And this is Jeff Gorush."

I thanked them again, and they loped off toward a red Kia.

"Well, that rules Gio out," Rafe said as we turned toward the house again. "At least for his father's murder."

"Not that we were really looking at him in the first place," I said.

Chip and Jeff had left the front door ajar. A jumble of voices sounded inside, drowning out my knock. I tried again and when no one came, invited myself in.

The living room overflowed with teenagers, as busy a crush as the driveway outside. Likely teammates, they were dressed soberly in slacks and button shirts, clustered in knots chatting. Several arrangements of flowers graced the tables and mantle. A card table with finger food and cans of soda crammed into one corner. Apparently, we'd interrupted a reception of sorts.

The body hadn't been released from the medical examiner's office yet, but perhaps they hadn't wanted to wait to start honoring their lost loved one. I looked around for a familiar face and didn't find one.

Rafe nodded in the direction of a short hallway. "Kitchen?"

I moved in that direction.

The scene was a repeat – clusters of teenagers stuffing their faces with finger foods and chatting in small groups shouting over each other.

Then a young man in the center of one group turned, his mouth flattening into a disapproving line. His face flushed and words slightly slurred. "What're you doin' here?"

I stepped past three girls who turned my way at Gio's question. "I might ask you the same. Isn't it a school day?"

Gio had his father's coloring, and from the short time I'd spent with Vic, his mannerisms. And he'd definitely been drinking. Had his mother approved? "Is a teacher's workshop day, not that it's any of your b-business. My friends're paying respects to my dad who you won' even let us bury."

Having forgotten today was a school holiday, I assumed a more placating voice. "I'm sorry for your loss, Gio. We'll release your dad's body soon and I'm sure your mom will plan the funeral then."

The young jaw clenched. "What'd'you care? You're the reason he's dead."

Everything was the cops' fault these days. Live with it, I reminded myself. "I don't know what you've been told, but we are not the reason your father's dead."

Gio flung a hand in the air, then pointed at my chest. "If he hadn' been hidin' behind some freaking boat talkin' to you, it never would've happened."

"Gio," I said, "this isn't the time or the place to discuss this. Is your mother around?"

"She doesn' know anything she hasn' already t-told you. It was your job to find my dad but you got him shot instead."

A husky kid built like a linebacker moved to Gio's side. "You don't have to talk to them, Gio. Tell them to take a hike. You didn't invite them in and that means they're trespassing."

I ignored Gio's defender. "Where is your mother?"

Gio glared daggers at me. "You got no right to bother her."

"We just need to clarify a couple things. The sooner we talk to her, the sooner we'll be gone."

The boy's eyes darted around the kitchen as if instructions on how to deal with persistent cops was written on a sticky note somewhere.

"Tell them to get lost, Gio," the friend repeated. "And leave your mom alone."

Gio sighed as if accepting the fact that resistance wouldn't get rid of us. However much he'd had to drink, he at least was aware enough to realize I wasn't going away easily. He nodded in the direction of a door leading out to the back of the house. "She's on the porch." His lower jaw came out. "And don' harass her."

His dad was dead and we wanted to question his mother. How might Mike handle a similar situation? Probably not as much grief as there should be over Elliot, but he'd be worried about me for sure. My heart softened toward the kid.

"Thanks," I said, and left him to the solace of his friends.

Irma Jean Moretti and two other women about her age sat in a mis-matched set of wicker chairs with floral padding. The only other furnishings on the screened in porch were a pair of folding tables, both overflowing with plants and a cat bed. Unless we asked the women to leave, there'd be no sitting down to talk.

Irma Jean shot to her feet when she spotted us. "What do you want now?"

The other two ladies' eyes widened and their mouths fell into disbelieving Os. Without a word, they rose and brushed past us into the house.

"Sorry to intrude again," Rafe began in a conciliatory tone. "Can we sit?"

"Don't get comfortable. You ain't staying." Irma plopped back into her chair.

"Where were you on Saturday morning?" I hadn't meant to jump right into suggesting she had anything to do with her husband's death, but the woman pushed all my buttons. It was a wonder steam wasn't hissing out of my ears.

"Right here!" Mrs. Moretti pointed at the floor. "Where else would I be?"

I sat in the chair opposite her and Rafe took the remaining chair. "Anyone who can verify that?"

Irma Moretti glared at me. "Vic's mother. She was here all day, too."

We'd have to check with the elder Mrs. Moretti, who I had not seen so far today.

Rafe leaned forward, crowding her space. "Before, you gave us the names of a few of your husband's friends and his employer, but what we really need now are possible enemies. Anyone he might have had a beef with."

Irma Jean gazed at Rafe with a crease between her eyes. "Enemies? Vic didn't have any enemies." Then her gaze sharpened. "He was a friend to the whole world. Good old Vic. Give you the shirt off his back."

Sounded like a lot of anger behind those words.

"Like the kids in Georgia?" I asked, thinking of the money Vic and his teammates had been sending for their support.

Irma Jean scowled. "Yeah. Like the kids in Georgia. Like Vic had any obligation to them. It wasn't his fault they were orphans. He could have been putting that money away for Gio's college, but what does that have to do with someone shooting him?" She stuck her jaw out as if daring me to make some kind of connection between Vic's death and his largess.

"He never got into any disagreements with anyone?" I pushed. "Even little things, like neighbors not pulling their trash barrels in as soon as they're collected, or letting their dog crap on your lawn?"

Irma threw up her hands and flung herself back into her chair. "Hah! He'd never even notice."

"So, you have no idea if anyone ever had a beef with your husband?" Rafe asked again.

Irma turned on him. "Ain't that what I just said?"

I tried another tack. "Has your husband ever had a problem with gambling? Or has he ever done drugs?"

Irma Jean's face hardened. "No! And no! I think it's time you left."

"We're just trying to figure out why anyone would want your husband dead, Mrs. Moretti." I settled into my seat, making it clear I wasn't done yet. The only thing we hadn't covered was Vic's philandering. "How about angry husbands?"

Irma Jean's jaw dropped, but she just as quickly closed her mouth again. "There were no—"

"I know it's not a comfortable thing to talk about, Mrs. Moretti," I cut her off. "But we already know from several sources that your husband had at least one affair, possibly more. If any were recent, there could be an angry husband out to get justice."

She opened and closed her mouth like a fish out of water. "I—"

"Do you know if he was seeing anyone recently?" Rafe asked gently.

"I—" Her face flushed. "No." Her eyes shifted, giving away the lie.

She knew about his cheating. And maybe even about Laney Hoffman. Although, considering Laney's little pink journal, I doubted that affair had been recent. Laney had been into Kyle Wallace since her marriage and even Laney was unlikely to have continued seeing Vic while Dan was courting her. But that didn't mean Vic hadn't found someone else a lot sweeter and more fun to spend time with than his wife.

"I'm sorry we had to bother you at a time like this," Rafe said, rising.

Mrs. Moretti shot to her feet, clearly eager to be rid of us.

I stood too. "Is your mother-in-law here?"

"She went out with friends." Irma Jean pointed toward the door. "I think you need to leave. Gio and I have our friends here and this isn't a good time."

Back in the cruiser, Rafe imitated my *tsking* displeasure.

I drummed my fingers on the steering wheel and muttered words my mother would have washed my mouth out with soap for.

I started the car. "What is that woman hiding?"

CHAPTER 21

ON THE RIDE BACK INTO TOWN as we headed to visit Dan in hopes that he'd begun to remember more details from the day of his wife's death, Rafe and I lapsed into silence until we parked outside Flagler Hospital. We found Dan seated in a chair beside a freshly-made hospital bed in a regular private room with a snack of Jello and juice on the little bedside table.

My heart lightened at the obvious signs of steady improvement, and had I been alone, I'd probably have hugged him. "Dan. You're looking so much better. Any idea when they'll release you?" I settled into the visitor's chair.

"They said maybe a couple more days," Dan answered. "Will I be able to go home or do I have to go back to the hotel?"

He remembered. He sounded almost normal. "You're allowed back in your house whenever they spring you from this place." Unless Zack Oliver got his way. That thought took away some of the pleasure at seeing my friend on the road to recovery. "Rafe here," I turned to indicate my partner, "managed to contact your housekeeper and she's been busy getting the place cleaned up for you."

Dan had to tip his head at an angle because of the bandage covering the side of his neck and scalp to give Rafe a hesitant smile. "Thank you. Not sure how you figured out who does the cleaning, but I appreciate it."

"Detective Rafe Morgan." Rafe stuck his hand out. "Your neighbor gave us a clue."

"You've met Jennie Harker, I guess," Dan said.

Rafe nodded, then backed into the hall. A moment later he returned with a folding chair and planted it next to mine. "Mind if we walk you through what you remember of the last few days?"

"There are still a lot of holes in my memory," Dan warned with a grimace. "Do I need to call my attorney?"

Folding my hands into my lap where they couldn't reach out to offer him any false personal encouragement, I replied, "Not unless you want to call him. We can wait if you do."

Dan seemed to consider this, his eyes sharp as he studied my face. He suddenly seemed a lot more focused. More like Dan the lawyer than Dan my one-time lover and high school friend. But then he shrugged. "Go ahead. Ask your questions."

"I know this will be difficult, but we want to back up to the day you came home and found Laney's body in your study." I kept my voice as neutral as I could. I didn't want to encourage him to incriminate himself, but neither did I want him to feel threatened.

Dan sucked his lower lip in and bit down until the skin turned white. He nodded, his hands curled into fists on his knees. "Okay."

Rafe pulled out his tablet and brought up his notes. "You left work a little early, but then stopped at the cleaner on the way home. Do you recall telling us that earlier?"

"Yes."

"And you made another stop at the florist?"

"It was our eleven-month anniversary," Dan replied. "I wanted . . . to surprise . . ."

I leaned toward Dan. "We're sorry for your loss. We've been doing everything we can to find out who did this." I hurried on before his grief got in the way of remembering details. "What else do you remember from that afternoon? Anything before you actually went into the house?"

Dan stared at me as if his mind had gone completely blank.

"Close your eyes, Dan." I waited until he obeyed. "Picture yourself pulling into your garage. What did you do then?"

He thought for several long moments before opening his eyes. "I parked in the driveway because the battery in my garage opener was dead."

"Okay." That was a detail that hadn't come up earlier. Probably unimportant, but still, it might lead to others. "You got out of the car. Close your eyes," I urged him again. "What did you do next? Perhaps reach into the back seat for your cleaning? Or the flowers?"

Dan nodded, his lids dropping obediently.

"What door did you head for?"

"The front door. I could see that it was open. At least the inside door was."

"Was that unusual?"

Dan shook his head and opened his eyes. "No. But there was this woman coming down the walk. She said she was soliciting funds for a search for some missing fishermen but no one answered the door when she knocked."

Whoa! Dan had seen a woman coming away from his house? I jumped on that thought. "Did you recognize her?"

"No. Never saw her before."

"What did you do then?"

"I fumbled a bit. Had to put my cleaning under my arm and juggle the flowers so I could get my wallet out." He juggled his limbs to imitate his actions. "I gave her a couple twenties. She thanked me and left."

Another witness who might have seen someone leaving the

scene? "Do you recall what she looked like?"

Dan seemed ready to shrug a denial, then stopped. "Brunette, I think. She was wearing a hat with NRA on the front and a jersey with a big green D on it. Like a university logo or something. And she was tallish. Southern accent. Georgia, maybe. Sorry, that's all I recall."

Rafe spoke up. "Did you see what she was driving?"

Dan glanced at Rafe. Another shake of the head. "No. She walked up the street, but I didn't see where she went. I was going into the house by then."

We could go back to the possible wit, but there were other questions that needed asking. "What did you do when you entered the house?"

"I called Laney's name." A frown clouded Dan's face. "When she didn't answer, I put the flowers on the table in the hall and went upstairs to change. I thought she might have gone up for a nap, but she wasn't upstairs either so I ran back down and started going through the house. That's when I found her. I—" He looked away, gazing out the window, a glassy sheen to his eyes.

We already knew what happened after he found his wife and called 911. That was documented in Broussard's initial interview. The only new piece was the strange woman.

I'd almost forgotten Rafe was there until he spoke. "After you left Central your lawyer took you to a hotel where you were later found seriously wounded from an apparent suicide attempt. What do you recall—"

Dan's eyes flew wide. "I would never—you can't believe I—" He broke off, his mouth opening and closing like a fish gasping for air.

I grabbed his hand, Rafe be damned. "We know you didn't

do it, Dan, but you were attacked and it was made to look as if you tried to end your own life. Can you remember anything that happened that night?"

Dan's gaze jerked from me to Rafe and back. I squeezed his hand in reassurance and he appeared to relax. He took a deep breath, then, "Not much. I just remember checking in. Marty came in placed an order for room service, but he didn't stay to share it with me because his wife called."

Still gripping his hand, I said, "Close your eyes again and imagine the room. Imagine the events you've just outlined and describe them to us."

Dan's eyelids slid closed as he turned his head toward the ceiling. "Marty put my overnight bag on the bed. He called down to order dinner. Then he left. Said he'd be back in the morning and we'd go over what we knew."

"What did you do after Marty left?"

"I hung up my jacket. Then I heard a knock and someone called out 'Room Service', so I told them to come on in." He stopped talking again.

"Did you see who brought the meal?" Rafe asked in a hushed voice, as if trying not to erase the picture Dan painted in his mind. Or remind him of the accusation he'd just thrown at him moments before.

Dan shook his head. "I wasn't looking. I was poking through my bag, looking for a clean shirt. Laney's blood was still—was still on my clothes. But then I reached for my wallet to get the man a tip. Next thing I knew there was a gun pressed against my cheek and a husky voice telling me I shouldn't have come home early. Seemed like a strange thing to say. But—" Dan grimaced. "I don't remember anything after that until a couple days ago when I woke up here in the hospital."

"We're sorry for your loss," Rafe put a hand on Dan's shoulder. "Just one more question. Do you recognize this woman?" He held up his tablet with the DMV image of Irma Jean Moretti, enlarged and not very clear, but recognizable.

Dan studied the image, his eyes crinkling at the corners. "Maybe. I don't know. Should I?" He glanced from Rafe to me, frowning.

"No reason you should. I just wondered." Rafe took his tablet back.

"No, I—" Dan shook his head. "I don't recognize her."

A nurse came in pushing a stand with equipment. "How are we doing this afternoon, Mr. Hoffman?" She busied herself putting the cuff on Dan's arm and shoved a thermometer in his mouth. "Sorry. I'll only be a minute."

"It's okay. We were leaving," Rafe assured her as he stood and folded his chair.

I patted Dan's hand where it rested on his knee. "See you soon. At home, next time. With news to report, I hope." Dan's eyes bored into mine, his mouth clamped around the thermometer. He nodded and I turned away.

Rafe waited outside.

I pushed past him and hurried down the hall. "You thinking what I'm thinking?"

He quickened his pace to keep up. "If you're thinking we need to get back to the Hoffman neighborhood and find out who was collecting funds for the fishermen, then yes."

"There's that. But why did you show Dan a photo of Irma Jean Moretti?"

CHAPTER 22

I HANDED RAFE THE KEYS so I could think without the distraction of driving and jot notes to connect the dots. The scattered and previously misleading details seemed to be falling together, but still too damned many holes. As if we'd been making a jigsaw puzzle that had been put away in the wrong box and we'd been looking at the pieces for a very different picture.

The entire Afghanistan-Arlington Security thing had been a distraction. No idea who had run Glen Rhodes' car off the road, but that was a problem for the Virginia State Police.

If someone *had* been following Vic Moretti maybe it was more to do with his philandering. Either Irma Jean Moretti hoping to catch Vic with another woman, or she'd hired someone to dog his footsteps for her with a big divorce settlement in mind. I leaned toward the PI. A man trained as an operator in a hostile country, would have developed a sixth sense about being observed.

And if she or the hired gumshoe had followed Vic when he went to warn Laney about some conspiracy involving dead operators and orphaned kids, then Irma Jean knew about Laney, and thought she knew who Vic was cheating on her with.

Usually talkative while driving, Rafe stared ahead, markedly silent. I hadn't paid any attention to where we were going until he pulled into a nearly empty parking lot that would have been crammed with vehicles on a weekend or when the waves were good for surfing.

A stop not on our agenda. "What—"

He shut the engine and turned to face me. "We've been barking up the wrong tree for days."

"Woof."

Rafe held up a fist, then extended one finger. "The little green car Mrs. Harker reported could be the one belonging to the mother-in-law, and Irma Jean borrowed it because Vic and his SUV were missing." Another finger went up. "A strange woman comes soliciting donations and none of the neighbors were approached?" He paused, then, "Besides, I don't like her attitude. She made out like she was worried, but managed to lead us on a merry goose chase."

I leaned across the space between us and pushed another finger into line. "Laney Hoffman was killed by someone who was very angry, and Irma Jean strikes me as an angry woman."

Rafe frowned. "But why take it out on Laney instead of her cheating hubby?"

I *tsked*. "My guess is that she thought she'd confront Laney and tell her to leave Vic alone, but Laney, being the spoiled, arrogant woman everyone has described her to be, probably laughed in her face."

Rafe snorted. "That would do it. And once she had her down, she had to make sure Laney couldn't nail her for assault. Must have been a lot of rage, though, to go after Vic once Laney was gone."

My turn to snort. "A woman scorned and humiliated? Maybe Laney told Irma she wasn't the only one."

I pulled my phone from its holster. "Calling Santos to see if she can dig up any connections to a gun club for Irma Jean. That shot at the Fountain of Youth was dead on and from a fair distance. If she didn't hire someone to do her dirty work for her, which has a lot of risk, she'd have to practice somewhere pretty regularly."

Before I could punch in the number, the phone rang. Lt. Ward. What now? "Quinn." I wasn't in the mood for a check-in right now.

"Where are you?"

"On our way out to collect Mrs. Moretti. We have a new theory." I wasn't ready to lay it all out for the lieutenant, yet.

"Well, we have a new theory, too. Get your asses back here, now." The line went dead.

Rafe cranked the engine. "What the hell was that all about?"

I fumed. "We have to check into the mother ship to find out."

Rafe turned the cruiser around and headed back toward Central, our quest to dig up details on Irma Jean were on hold for now.

Just to make sure Rafe was on the same page, I ran down the list of tasks still on our plate. "We have to revisit the Moretti household for another chat with Vic's mother to confirm or discredit Irma Jean's alibi. Then we need to figure out how Irma Jean managed to take out her husband, if it turned out she could have been Laney's killer. Perhaps Dan was a loose end she felt she had to silence. That would explain his near-death experience at the hand of someone who didn't know he was a southpaw."

Rafe nodded without adding anything.

I pinched my lower lip, thinking. "I wonder how the hell she knew he would be meeting with us at the Fountain of Youth, though. She told us he went missing before Laney was killed. Do you suppose she was lying about that too and overheard him talking to us, then followed him?"

"Possible, but that's a lot of ifs. And how would she have time to set up for that kind of shot?"

I tipped my head, acknowledging his doubts. "I'm sure we're on the right track with this. As soon as we hear Ward out, we'll get back on it."

OLIVER AND BROUSSARD were seated in the conference room with the lieutenant when we walked in.

"New evidence implicates Dan Hoffman," Lieutenant Ward announced. "I'll let Oliver share the information, but I'm turning this case over to him since you've had four days with no arrest. We don't pay our detectives to chase conspiracy theories that have no substance."

Is he fucking kidding? "But," I blurted. "But we—"

"No buts." Ward stood. "Oliver is lead. If he wants to share his info he can. If he's interested in your new theory, he can ask." With that the lieutenant left the room.

Broussard shook his head, his eyes sending me a warning.

My jaw tightened with rebellion, my throat tight with outrage.

Zack balanced one ankle on his other knee and stretched back in his chair, hands clasped behind his head. "Dan Hoffman is our man. We'll bring him in as soon as the doctors release him. Care to know how we cornered the rat?"

I slapped the table so hard my palm stung. "He's not a rat! And he's not guilty."

Zack pursed his lips. "Hoffman was overheard talking to a client, and the discussion was not to his credit."

"That's confidential information," I shouted. "Attorney client privilege."

The sergeant narrowed his eyes at me. "You promised you wouldn't let your prior friendship with Mr. Hoffman get in the way of investigating with an open mind."

I almost shouted back, remembering just in time, who I was

talking to. "And I didn't. But I sure would like to know who this client was and why Zack is so sure their words implicate Dan." I needed to poke a hole in this line of thinking before Dan got hung out to dry.

Broussard's heavy sigh expressed disappointment. "You are off this case, Detective. I believe Lieutenant Ward has a different project for you to work on." Turning to Rafe, Broussard went on. "I'm not sure where you stand on this so you are free to remain and explain your new theory to Zack if you wish."

I stood there sputtering, wanting to lash out at someone. Namely Zack Oliver who'd come up with some overheard discussion that was probably just what I'd labeled it, 'privileged client information' that might sound incriminating but just as likely had nothing to do with our case. The only reason he'd gotten it to fly was that this was an election year. Something I'd been ignoring. Lawrence Upshaw was a force to be reckoned with and the sheriff's biggest campaign contributor. And Upshaw wanted Dan behind bars.

Broussard glanced at me, then pointed at the door.

I left the room fuming. Now my jaw really ached. Further protest would just make things worse, but we were on the verge of solving the case. Please, God, let Rafe make them take the time to check out Irma Jean before charging Dan.

In the hall I ran into Henry Dalton, Ward's toadie. He thrust a stack of files into my hands. "Cold cases from the Lieutenant." And they were going to get a lot colder if Ward thought I was putting Dan's future into Zack's hands.

CHAPTER 23

BACK AT MY DESK I shoved the cold case files to the side. It was no longer just a matter of clearing Dan, but nailing the bitch who was responsible for the mayhem that possessed me. Every crime deserved justice, but at the moment I didn't have time to care about the ones that had just been dumped on me when I knew a friend of mine was in the crosshairs of a detective too hungry for a check in the win column.

Rafe stuck his head in the door. "Hey. I've only got a minute. Zack's meeting me in the parking lot. Just wanted you to know I—"

"This is my case," I spat.

"Keep your shirt on, Jess. You know it and I know it, but right at the moment just sit tight and let me follow up on your hunch."

"I should be going out there with you," I insisted.

Rafe burrowed his fingers through his curls. Something he usually did when either Ms. Ambition or Barbie Doll vexed him.

I gestured to the murder board with photos and notes on the Moretti and Hoffman cases. "I know I got sidetracked with Vic Moretti's conspiracy theory, but we're on the right track, Rafe. We have to follow it up." Frustration added to the sick feeling in my stomach.

"And that's what Zack and I are doing." Rafe glanced down the hall behind him, then stepped further into our small space. "I convinced him we at least needed to tie up loose ends before arresting Dan Hoffman. And if it turns out the Moretti woman is responsible, we'll nail her."

I swallowed my impatience and displeasure. I just wanted Dan exonerated. It shouldn't matter if I did it myself or Rafe got the collar.

Rafe came close enough to lower his voice to a near whisper. "It's all political shit, Jess. Zack is doing his best to walk over your back to get a leg up with Ward and with the sheriff. Trust me. I'm not going to let that happen to my partner."

Before I could respond, the devil himself appeared in the doorway. "Let's get this over with Morgan." Not a word to me. Just a look of contempt mixed with triumph aimed at me down the length of that damn patrician nose of his.

Rafe squeezed my shoulder and followed Zack out.

I reached for the file on the top of the pile I'd shoved aside and opened it.

A wife gone missing after several domestic disturbance calls. No body was ever found, and the husband had been out of town at the time of the disappearance. Out of the country, actually. There had been no leads that hadn't ended in a dead end. What did Ward expect me to do with this now, twelve years after the fact?

The next file held photos of a boy about sixteen or seventeen whose murder appeared to be totally random. The kid looked a lot like Gio. My mind returned to Rafe and Zack and what might be happening at the Moretti home.

I dumped the missing wife file back on the pile and turned to my computer, but instead of looking up the missing kid, I typed in Irma Jean Moretti and firearms. It took only moments to find out that the woman was a life-time member of the local gun club and the NRA, and that she had reached the top of the ladder in marksmanship and won several awards for it. A few more clicks turned up ownership of several guns that included a rifle more suited to snipers than target shooting and the same handgun carried by most of the deputies. The same caliber that had taken Victor Moretti out.

What if Rafe and Zack were walking into trouble they wouldn't see coming?

I grabbed my phone, then hesitated. I'd been told to stay off the case. But Rafe was my partner. I tapped his name on my speed dial list. The call went to voicemail. That was odd.

I tapped in a hasty text. *Watch your back.*

No reply.

She's a sharpshooter.

Still no reply. Where was Rafe? What was he doing that he couldn't respond?

Concern ramped to unease. Maybe he figured it wouldn't be good to be caught talking to me with Zack listening in.

I looked up Zack's number and tapped it. Same result. Two detectives not answering their phone? My mouth suddenly dry, I grabbed the mug with the dregs of this morning's coffee and gulped it down cold.

I looked up the number for the Moretti house and tried that. That one just rang and rang. No answering machine, no answer.

Rafe and Zack were in trouble. My heart raced.

I slapped the file shut on the teenage boy, pulled my weapon out of the drawer I'd stowed it in only thirty minutes earlier and holstered it.

I nearly ran into Dalton on my way out. He carried more files which he held up to indicate were for me.

I jerked my head back toward my office. "Put 'em on the desk. I'll get to them as soon as I can." Without waiting for a reply, I hustled down the hall, slammed the release bar on the door and exited into the steaming parking lot.

I had to get to Rafe.

I broke every speed limit on the way back out to Vilano. Twice more I hit Rafe's number and twice more it went to voice mail. Same for Zack. Worry blossomed into gut wrenching fear.

All the pieces were falling into place. Irma Jean Moretti had followed her husband, caught him hugging Laney the day Mrs. Harker had seen him on the Hoffman front porch. She'd returned to have it out with Laney and ended up killing her. She must have thought Dan could identify her and somehow figured out where he was so she could shut him up, as well.

Then she decided to finish the job by taking out her cheating husband. The only thing I didn't know was how she'd known Vic would be at the Fountain. They didn't check backpacks there, although that might change after this, so anyone could walk in with a gun secreted in a purse or backpack, scout out the best place to shoot from and wait. But how had she known Vic picked the Fountain for a meet with me?

Just to add another layer to the misdirection, Irma Jean told her son we were the ones who got his daddy killed and gotten him all fired up against us.

My phone buzzed and Rafe's photo appeared on the screen.

I remembered to breath. "Rafe? Where the hell are you? What's going on? Are you okay?"

Dead air. He'd called me, but he wasn't there? "Rafe?"

Then I heard Rafe's voice, but he wasn't talking to me.

"Put the gun down, Gio. I know you're just trying to protect your mom."

My mouth went dry again.

Words even more distant that I couldn't make out. How come Gio hadn't heard me hollering into my end of the phone?

Rafe went on as if nothing bad was going down. "You've done nothing that can't be fixed, Gio. Just put the gun down and let me call for an ambulance. Deputy Oliver needs medical care. ASAP."

Jesus! Had Zack had been shot? By Gio?

I flipped on my lights, grabbed the radio off the dash and called dispatch.

The vision of a hooded teenager with a gun pointed at me flitted into my brain. I shoved it aside. Not another kid. Please God, not another kid with a gun.

Dispatch replied to my call.

"Officer down at . . ." I reeled off the address I knew by heart. "Send back up and an ambulance. I'm five minutes away."

As soon as dispatch acknowledged, I dropped the handset and concentrated on my driving.

Dispatch returned, patching a call through from Lieutenant Ward. I didn't have time for this.

"What in hell do you think you're doing Quinn? You're supposed to be at your desk and –"

"Rafe and Zack are in trouble, Lieutenant. I'll explain later and take my lumps, but right now I've got to go." I dropped the handset again and swerved around a truck and onto the street leading to the Moretti home.

I turned off the lights and siren. No need to announce my arrival. Please God, don't make me shoot another kid.

Sliding to a sand and pebble crunching halt out front of the way too familiar house, I grabbed my Bluetooth earpiece so I could continue monitoring Rafe's end of the conversation. I shoved my phone into its holster on my belt, and bolted from the cruiser. Rafe was still trying to talk Gio off whatever ledge he'd gotten himself out on. Calmly, but urgently. Still requesting he be allowed to call for an ambulance and calling out to Zack without any response I could hear.

Damn it all to hell. However much bad blood there was between me and Zack, I didn't want him hurt, or worse, dead. I also didn't want to have to take out Gio to save Rafe, but I would.

Give me some idea where you are, Rafe. I tried to telegraph the message without words.

"Think about this, Gio. Think about what this will do to your future. Just hand over the gun and I can just skip this little scene in my report. I'll just tell them we were talking on the porch when my fellow officer got shot." Rafe, reading my mind again. "Which is the truth. We both know your mom shot Deputy Oliver even if we didn't see her do it. You weren't involved."

They were on the porch at the rear of the house. Which, I recalled from earlier that day had a door on two sides, opening to both the garage and to the patio directly opposite. Gio could not have eyes on both doors even if he was watching for someone. Gun already in hand, I slipped closer to the house and crept to the back corner. A lightning peek revealed a glimpse of Gio, two hands on what looked like a small shotgun facing partially in my direction.

I ran back the way I'd come, along the front of the house and into the side yard. I hadn't seen Rafe, but his voice, still calm, continued. He must have been sitting on the floor out of my line of sight.

I crept around the corner, flattening myself against the house. Visible through the screen, Gio paced nervously. *Maybe I should just take him out now before his itchy finger has a chance to squeeze the trigger.*

Rafe faced my way and must have seen me, but managed not

to make any move that would give me away. "Put the gun down, Gio," he said with the same patience he'd used for the last tense twenty minutes.

"My mom didn't shoot my dad," Gio said with a quaver suggesting maybe he didn't believe that.

"If that's true, why have I got a target painted on me now?" Rafe asked.

I inched closer to the apron of the stone patio. Where was Irma Jean? Or Zack for that matter? Whatever had gone down between them, it probably hadn't been out here on the porch. She could still be inside the house, but if so, wouldn't Rafe have found a way to alert me to that possibility?

I edged my way across the patio, gun aimed, center mass, on Gio's back. Maybe I should deflect to wound and disable? I readjusted the sights to the kid's right shoulder.

"I don't want her to go to jail," Gio cried. I couldn't see his face or if there were tears to go with the distress in his voice, but he was desperate, alone and doing his best to hold it together for his mom. Whatever else she'd done, her son loved her and was willing to commit a felony to protect her.

Rafe, seated on the floor, leaned against the same chair he'd occupied that morning. His forearms rested on his drawn-up knees, and no one would ever have guessed a half-crazed teenager had a shotgun pointed at his face.

"Mind if I get up? My butt's getting sore," Rafe asked.

Gio waved the gun. In that split second, I had no idea if he meant it was okay for Rafe to get up or if his finger was tightening on the trigger. I fired my weapon.

The shot would have taken the boy out if Rafe hadn't launched himself off the floor, pushing Gio out of my line of fire. Now I couldn't fire again without the chance of hitting my partner as they tussled on the floor.

Gio bounced to his feet, and smashed through the screen before Rafe scrambled off the floor. A second later, the boy disappeared around the corner of the garage.

Rafe hesitated. Half a head taller than me and all legs, he'd been a track star. "Get him. I'll check on Zack," I shouted. "Where's the woman?"

"Gone," Rafe answered as he pushed through the ruined door after the fleeing boy. That's when I noticed his service weapon just inside the kitchen door. Rafe was unarmed going after a kid with a shotgun. Zack would have to make it a few more minutes on his own.

I took off after the pair. The alley leading between two garages was empty. At the end, a fence blocked my path. Gio and Rafe must have vaulted over it, but I'd never make it. I dashed back the way I'd come, around the far side of the garage, and forced my way through a hedge. Gio ran toward me, head swiveled to the rear toward his pursuer. I launched myself at him and we went down hard.

The shotgun flew several yards ahead before skittering to a stop. Gio wriggled beneath me as I struggled to grab an arm and crank it up behind his back. He continued to thrash until I planted a knee in his back and reached for my cuffs. Gio was skinny, but strong and I thanked God for the mountain of a man at the academy who'd taught me how to subdue a perp twice my size.

"Thought you were checking on Zack," Rafe said as he helped me up, then bent to jerk Gio to his feet.

Panting hard and still hyped on adrenaline, I whirled back toward the Moretti house. "You didn't have a weapon, and I'm supposed to have your back," I yelled.

The first faint sounds of a siren wailed as I vaulted onto the porch and into the house.

Sprawled on his back and unmoving, Zack's face was an awful shade of gray. I dropped to my knees and felt for a pulse. *Thank God.* "Zack."

He opened his eyes, but they were unfocused.

"Zack? Can you hear me?"

Sirens screeched to a halt out front and a moment later feet pounded through the front door and into the room.

"Did she . . . get . . . away?" Zack's voice, barely above a whisper.

Rafe appeared at my side. "Half an hour ago in Vic's SUV."

"Shit!" Zack groaned.

An EMT replaced Rafe, and I sat back on my heels. With practiced hands, the guy located Zack's wound and packed it. By the time he'd inserted an IV, two more EMTs squatted beside the fallen deputy and began easing him onto a backboard. "Hang in there," the first man said. "You're going to be okay."

Then I remembered Irma Jean was still on the loose and Ward was after my head.

CHAPTER 24

AS THE THREE EMTS WORKED to stabilize Zack and ready him for transport, I sagged back against the couch. My hands shook and I forced myself to take deep breaths. Irma Jean Moretti was on the run and we had to find her. Fast. She was a fugitive now. A fugitive with a weapon, well-trained on how to use itl, and with one officer down already, she wouldn't hesitate to take out the next one who got in her way.

Regret weighed me down like an anchor. We didn't catch her earlier because we'd been so focused on the Arlington group, but we didn't have time for recriminations right now.

I glanced sideways at Rafe, who, like me, did his best to pull himself together. "How did you manage to stay so calm?"

He stuck a finger under his tie and pulled it free. "I was faking it."

I stopped the deep breathing and pushed myself to my feet. "You could moonlight as an actor."

Rafe popped to his feet. "Did I thank you for coming?"

I glanced at him. "I couple times." Rafe might be dead if I hadn't disobeyed orders. I deserved a rip but it was worth it.

"If Ward gives you any grief, send him to me."

"He already started on me while I was careening through traffic to get here." I glanced down at the hole torn in the knee of my suit. My best suit. Dammit.

Rafe shoved his tie into his pocket. "I put out a BOLO. Along with an armed and dangerous warning."

"Which way do you think she'll go?" I checked my weapon,

but hesitated before shoving it back into its holster. I'd discharged it, but hadn't hit anyone. Who knew where my bullet ended up, but there wasn't time for that now. "Your ride or mine?"

"Neither," Ward boomed as he strode into the room. "You were told to stand down, Quinn. This time, I'm ordering you to go home, and I want you in my office at eight am sharp tomorrow to discuss your future."

Crap! Where did he come from? I pulled my service weapon out and handed it over. "It's been fired sir. Didn't hit anyone, and the bullet can probably be found dug into the woodwork on the back porch."

Ward's eyebrows shot up as he took the gun. "Figures!" He handed it over to one of the deputies who'd followed him in. "Find the slug," he told the guy. Then to me, "See the armorer for a replacement on your way home."

Right! The asshole was probably following protocol just so he could demand my weapon along with my badge in the morning . . . and gloat.

The lieutenant jerked his head toward the door. "Morgan. Outside." Then he disappeared without another word to either of us, or anyone else in the room.

Rafe shot me an apologetic look, then followed the lieutenant.

Thanks for saving your partner's life and helping arrest a kid with a gun and a grudge . . . NOT. Looked like Ward wasn't going to cut me any slack. If steam really did seep from a person's ears, I'd look like the Little Engine that Could.

A patrol deputy I'd worked with before muttered something under his breath and flipped the departing lieutenant the bird. I squared my shoulders and exited like a queen, not in the mood for the sympathetic glances from the deputy or the woman packing up the last of the medical gear.

The ambulance techs were preparing to load Zack into

the back of the ambulance as I stepped back into the steamy afternoon sunshine. Zack likely had the same opinion on any sympathy from me, but I hurried across the lawn to the gurney and laid my hand over his for a moment. "I'm looking forward to the day you're back at work and giving me a hard time."

"I'll . . . do my . . . best," he muttered weakly. For the first time since I'd known the man, there was no condescension in his words and a faint smile tugged at his mouth.

The EMTs folded the wheels and shoved the gurney into the vehicle. One climbed in after it and the other hurried to the driver's door. A moment later, the last medic joined the crew and they pealed out, siren blaring and lights strobing.

With one last look at the house, now swarming with deputies, I climbed into my car and buckled up. I prayed all the way to the armorer for Zack's recovery and a speedy end to the hunt for Irma Moretti. This needed to be over before she hurt anyone else.

After picking up a replacement for the service weapon I'd turned over to the lieutenant, I considered stopping at my desk, but decided against. The only thing now in my purview was a stack of cold cases, and I hadn't seen my kids for more than a few minutes here and there in days. Besides I was too angry to concentrate on anything but the apprehension of Irma Jean. And I'd been ordered to go home. Not that an order had stopped me before.

As I drove, a scramble of thoughts jostled in my head: What would I tell Mike when I returned to the house earlier than expected? That his mother was likely going to be fired for disobeying a direct order? Like that was a good example to set for my son. But then again, it might make points with my daughter seeing that she disliked authority figures so much.

An image of Daddy flitted through my head and for the first time since I was twelve, I was glad he wouldn't be around to see me get canned. All I'd ever wanted to be was a cop like him and now Ward's ominous summons to discuss my future hung over my head like a guillotine.

But, I'd made the right choice . . . one I could live with. I'd put my partner's life over my career and stopped what could have become a nightmare for a lot of people. Daddy would have agreed with that. He'd done the same thing himself according to stories I'd heard since joining the Sheriff's department.

Would Broussard go to bat for me? Did I even want him to? Maybe not. I wanted to succeed on my own, not on someone else's coattails, but having friends wasn't always a bad thing either.

I almost missed the figure staggering along the shoulder of the road. Dressed in jeans and a dress shirt with the sleeves rolled up to the elbows, the man limped, swaying like a drunk. Not a good street for anyone to be wandering down, especially not someone in his condition.

He appeared not to notice my unmarked with the blue lights flashing in the grill as I pulled in behind his meandering path. I exited my vehicle, hand on the butt of my weapon and the holster unsnapped.

I approached cautiously. "Sir? Are you okay?"

He whirled, the swift movement almost making him fall. I put a hand under his elbow to steady him. He shut his eyes for a moment, then opened them again and focused on me. They were the bluest eyes I'd ever seen. Went along with fine blonde hair so pale it almost looked white, except he couldn't have been more than twenty-something. Five ten. A hundred and forty pounds. Not particularly muscular. He looked like a college kid.

"My car was stolen and . . ." He reached up and touched the side of his head. His fingers came away bloody.

Jesus! "You're anything but okay. Come with me." I re-snapped the holster and tightened my grip on his elbow, guiding him toward my waiting cruiser.

"What's your name?" I drew him around to the passenger side of the cruiser, opened the door and invited him to take a seat. He slumped so abruptly that if I'd been any slower to react, he'd have smacked the back of his head on the roof.

I reached across and grabbed the radio, called dispatch and asked for another ambulance pick up. A trend for the day. Nothing like adding to my already colorful reputation.

The man pressed his palms against his forehead, moaning softly. I squatted beside the open door and pulled out my phone, hit record and asked him his name again.

"Jens. Jenson Bielke." He looked up, his eyes meeting mine. "I'm an Uber driver. I got a call to pick someone up at the Publix in Vilano. She wanted a ride to the bus station. Then—"

"What happened next?"

He frowned a moment, then his face cleared. "I had to stop at the corner on Ballard Ave. Weren't any other cars around, but still . . . Next thing I know I wake up in the gutter and my car is gone."

I asked for a description and when he gave it, I quickly brought up a photo of Irma Jean Moretti. "Was this your rider?"

Jens nodded, then winced as if the movement hurt. Probably did. "That's her."

"What kind of car do you drive? Know the plate number?"

"A Chevy. Impala," he added. "Dark blue, 2015."

"Plate number?" I asked again.

He frowned. Then rattled off a number. "It's equipped with

OnStar."

I relayed the information to dispatch. The Moretti woman was no longer driving Vic's SUV. She was now in the possession of a Chevy Impala. Smart move with a BOLO out on her.

As I squatted beside the injured man waiting on the EMTs, I punched in Rafe's number. He answered on the second ring. I repeated the information.

"Don't go after her alone," I warned him.

"Not to worry, Jess. I'm riding shotgun with Broussard now."

That relieved me a little, but very little. Irma Jean Moretti was a dangerous woman.

Then Broussard's voice came over the line. "I thought you were on the way home, detective."

"I was, but I came across an Uber driver, kid named Jensen Bielke, who'd been clocked and his car stolen. He identified his rider as Irma Jean. I thought you should know what the woman was driving now."

If I'd been sitting across his desk from the man, he'd likely have been rubbing his temples with his fingertips. "Thanks for the heads-up. Do I have to repeat the lieutenant's order?"

"No, Sir. But one more thing."

"Yes?" he sounded vexed."

"Bielke said she originally asked for a ride to the bus station. Not sure if she's still headed there, but thought you should know."

"Thank you. Get yourself home." Then the line went dead. I pocketed my phone just as the sound of sirens announced the ambulance's approach.

Sure that the head injury would keep Jensen Bielke in the hospital overnight, I told him I'd see him the following morning to have a formal statement written up and signed. Then I watched yet another ambulance pull away leaving me standing beside my cruiser.

I climbed back in, heaved a sigh and pulled back into traffic.

The bus station was almost on my route home. Well, a block off, but close enough. Might as well check it out on my way.

CHAPTER 25

THE BUS STOP WAS ONLY a block off San Marco. Couldn't hurt to check it out and report back to Rafe if there was any sign of Irma Jean Moretti or Bielke's stolen vehicle. I wasn't sure how fast OnStar would get back to Rafe and Broussard.

A bus with the image of a road runner on the side was just pulling into the stop as I rounded the corner. The new express run to Jacksonville appeared empty except for the driver. No sign of Irma Jean, but if she knew about the OnStar maybe she was smart enough to ditch the car and take the bus after all?

I pulled up to the parking garage ticket booth and flashed my badge. The attendant gestured for me to go on in. I cruised the first level, then the second. Nothing on the third either. The open-air fourth floor was about half full, but I spied a dark blue sedan wedged between two pickup trucks near the end of the first row. I approached cautiously but the Impala matching Jens' description was empty. No sign of Irma Jean.

Descending four levels quickly, eyes shifting on the hunt for a fleeing figure, I emerged just in time to see a woman who could have been Irma Jean climb onto the Road Runner bus.

Wearing jeans in spite of the heat and a bright red sweatshirt along with a camouflage ball hat pulled down backwards over her hair. I grimaced at the NRA logo, prominent even from this distance.

Shit! The bus was nearly full. If I abandoned my cruiser and boarded the bus to apprehend her one of two bad things could happen. Irma Jean might grab a hostage. Or she might just start shooting with a dozen innocents caught in the crossfire. Neither was acceptable. And I'd been told to stand down. I wouldn't live through another debacle for the day.

I punched the speed dial number for Rafe.

"Where are you?" I said as soon as he answered.

"Headed toward downtown. OnStar located the Impala."

"Yeah, so did I."

"What do you mean, so did you?" Broussard's voice boomed over the line.

Shit! Speaker!

"I thought you were going home," Broussard scolded.

I scanned the seated passengers trying to locate the NRA hat. "I was, but Bielke said the Moretti woman originally asked for a ride to the bus stop, like I told you, and it was on my way. I found the Impala on the top level of the parking garage and I just saw a woman that looks an awful lot like Irma Jean boarding the Road Runner to Jax."

"Don't do anything," Broussard directed. "We're on our way."

But they'd be too late. The bus was already pulling out. "Okay, but the bus is leaving right now. I'll just follow to make sure she's still on it when you catch up."

"Don't do a damn thing but that, you hear?" Broussard growled.

"Stay on the line." Rafe's voice again.

"Roger that," I replied as I settled my phone into the dash-mounted cradle. As the bus pulled past me, I surveyed the heads in the windows. None were wearing the ball hat or a red sweatshirt. She must have found a seat on the other side of the bus.

I hugged the bus as it made its way down West Castillo

Drive toward US 1. The light turned green before we got to the intersection, and it turned onto Rt 1 headed north. "We're on Rt 1 going now," I reported as I made the turn in the bus's wake.

"I've contacted the sheriff's department in Jacksonville," Broussard said. "They'll meet us at the station. Sending SWAT along with deputies."

Just what we needed! I gritted my teeth. I could just picture the scenario in my mind. The bus pulls into the terminal and Moretti sees a dozen guys geared up ready to board and she starts shooting innocent people or taking hostages. "Better send the hostage negotiator while they're at it, because I doubt she'll go easy."

"Not your problem, detective," Broussard replied. "You will be at home fixing dinner for the kids."

I shut my mouth before I could argue and get myself in deeper hot water. All the men who'd meet that bus had experience and knew what they were doing. But it galled me that after spending five days ignoring my kids and keeping my nose to the grindstone, someone else would take Irma Jean Moretti down.

"At the CVS, turning onto 16," I reported, then cursed as the light turned red and an eager driver coming the other way gunned it to cut me off. I could have turned on my lights and followed, but that would have caught the fugitive's attention. I drummed my fingers on the steering wheel, waiting for the lights to cycle through, then nearly peeled rubber when the arrow flashed green.

I'd counted seven cars and a dump truck turning onto 16. I had to get past at least the first four and the truck to keep the bus in sight. Damn.

I did a doubletake when I spied the bus pulled over in front of the Catholic church.

"The bus stopped at San Sebastian Catholic Church," I said, keeping Rafe and Broussard updated. "Don't see anyone getting off."

Rafe cussed. "Hope she hasn't got a gun to the driver's head."

Same thought had crossed my mind.

But then the bus pulled back into traffic cutting off the dump truck, disappearing from my line of sight again.

I slowed as I came abreast of the church. The lot was empty and nothing moved. Then, a fleeting glimpse of red showed on the far side of the retention pond at the entrance to an upscale housing development. Crap. Moretti'd been wearing a red sweatshirt. No obvious reason that bus would have pulled over in front of that church unless someone had demanded to be let off. Another diversion: buy a ticket to Jacksonville, but get off before the bus gets even close to its destination.

I tapped my phone to make sure the connection to Rafe remained. "Bus just pulled back onto its route. I didn't see anyone get off, but caught a flash of someone that could have been her disappearing into the Villages of Seloy. Since you've got the arrival of this bus in Jacksonville covered, I'm going to drive through the villages. Just in case it was her."

"Roger that," Rafe replied.

Broussard's voice came next. "Don't do anything stupid."

I swallowed the inelegant snort that rose in my throat. "Yes, sir." Beau Broussard was not a prick like Ward. He was genuinely concerned about my safety, and I'd already given him plenty to worry about.

As I passed the field-stone pillars guarding the entrance to the villages, there was no one in sight. Maybe that flash of red had been a figment of my imagination. I'd wanted it to be her so damned bad. I kept driving.

The Seloy Drive curved through carefully manicured palm trees. No sight of her. Or anyone at all, for that matter. I followed the road to the right where a large clubhouse appeared behind a curved drive. No cars. No people. To the left around the far side of the little circle, an as yet unpaved street barren of homes promised future construction. I continued on through another stone gate into what the sign on the gate declared was Coquina. The first homes came into sight, but nothing moving. Almost as if this were a model community with no residents as yet.

Then another flash of red caught my eye. Another disappearing act as the hint of red evaporated as soon as it caught my attention.

Rafe interrupted my thoughts. "Any sight of her?"

"Maybe," I replied slowing my unmarked cruiser and pulling over to the curb.

"Where are you?" Broussard demanded.

"Seloy Drive, just past the clubhouse at the second house on the left. I'm going on foot." I jumped out of the car before Broussard could warn me to stay put.

Passing the house where I thought I'd seen a glimpse of red, I hurried down the driveway and stumbled over a row of small rocks just as a shot whistled through the air over my head. I dropped to the ground.

The rocks I'd tripped over weren't nearly big enough to hide behind but tripping over them probably saved my life. I was a sitting duck for a sharpshooter, but to my astonishment, another shot did not come my way.

Scrambling over behind a row of trees, I scanned one hundred and eighty. Had to be Irma Jean. Who else had reason to shoot at me? My heartbeat thundered in my ears as I considered my situation.

Where were Rafe and Broussard?

In all this sea of dun colored homes and green shrubbery, a red sweatshirt should stand out like a beacon. Unless she'd forced her way into one of the homes. Damn.

Staying behind the trees, I crept backward to the far side of the house and prayed no residents would see me lurking suspiciously and come out to investigate.

As I eased through the shrubbery along the front of the house, I spotted her.

Less than eight feet away, her back toward me, she swung the handgun left, then right, obviously waiting for me to reappear somewhere near where she'd last seen me. She'd changed her location as well. No way that first shot had come from this corner of the house. I'd gotten lucky. Very lucky.

I took the last four strides fast and used my kickboxing skills to slam a foot into the hand holding the gun. Just as quickly I brought my other foot around the back of her knees. She went down hard.

I scooped up her dropped weapon and thrust it into my waistband, but before I could turn to subdue her, she grabbed my ankle. I went down, smacking the back of my head on the pavement.

My head exploded as pain radiated down my neck. I rolled away before she leapt, obviously planning to land on top of me. She did a face plant on pavement instead which gave me time to scramble to my feet.

Dizzy and fighting to stand stable, I stomped down hard on her outstretched hand. Then I dropped both knees onto her back with all the weight I had.

Irma Jean gasped for breath as I slapped a second pair

of cuffs on for the afternoon. I was batting a thousand. Two Morettis down. No civilians injured. No police shootings to be investigated. Just my splitting head and the dizzying stars dancing across my vision.

But I still had to get her back to my cruiser.

"Get up," I commanded backing out of reach and aiming my weapon at her chest.

She didn't move.

I knew she was alive and conscious because dead people don't curse. "Get up," I repeated. "Unless you'd like me to save the county the cost of a trial."

She hesitated long enough to make me wonder if I would have to make good on my threat, but then struggled to stand. Not an easy task with her hands cuffed behind her back. She could still run, and probably faster than I could, even if my head wasn't spinning. I prayed she wouldn't take it into her head to try an escape.

"I'm going to sue," she hissed.

"I've heard that before, now march." I jerked my head toward the street. A big mistake. The whirl of stars almost took me down.

Dimly amazed that not a single person had appeared to gawk, I followed at a safe distance. It would have been nice to have someone to call for backup.

Then she started running.

CHAPTER 26

IRMA JEAN MORETTI BOLTED for the street. Just like her son had a few hours earlier, she fled with her eyes turned back toward her pursuer, and ran headlong into the front fender of Sergeant Broussard's unmarked cruiser as he bucked to a stop in the middle of the street.

With her hands manacled behind her, she had nothing to break her fall as she slid across the hood and tumbled off on the far side.

Out of the cruiser almost before it stopped moving, Rafe bent to check on her.

I approached the road, slipping my newly issued sidearm back into its holster. Broussard gave me a brief glance with a sad shake of his head before he rounded the cruiser and joined Rafe.

I was in trouble, but I didn't care. We got our man. Or woman as it turned out. Even Ward would have to cut me some slack over the insubordination given the outcome.

The first resident of the area appeared. Took him long enough, but as it turned out, for the best because no innocent civilians had been sucked into the drama or hurt.

The man strode purposefully toward the street. "I called an ambulance. I saw what happened and it wasn't your fault." He directed this to Sergeant Broussard as he closed in on the scene beside the cruiser.

When I showed the man my badge, he jerked back a step. "Sorry, Officer. I didn't realize…"

I knew better than to shake my head again. "Not a problem."

"Heard the gun shot and saw you fighting and but I didn't know—"

"Please go back to your home, sir. Thank you for your concern." I turned away to shut down further discussion. Broussard or Rafe, or perhaps even a patrol deputy would have to take his statement.

The man stepped back onto his front lawn, but didn't return to his house. Rafe and Broussard helped Irma Jean to her feet still cursing, and the venom in her eyes could have killed the meanest rattler.

"The woman's slippery," Rafe muttered as he urged her toward the back seat of Broussard's cruiser. "And apparently indestructible."

Broussard nodded toward the civilian just out of earshot. "He see anything? Besides her crashing into my ride?"

"He says he heard the gunshot—"

Broussard cut me off, his eyes signaling concern. "Who took a shot?"

"She did. I'd probably be dead if I hadn't tripped over someone's idea of decorative border stones." Just how close I'd come to being dead finally hit me. I'd been running on adrenalin, instinct and training and hadn't considered how fortunate I was to still be among the living. A river of ice sluiced down my back, adding to the ache in my head.

At that moment, a patrol car appeared lights strobing, an ambulance right behind it. Two deputies sprang from the patrol car and headed our way. The EMT riding shotgun joined them.

Broussard pointed at the ground I stood on. "Stay here."

After a brief check on Irma Moretti, the EMT returned to his truck, the driver backed around and they left. Broussard spoke to the two deputies who fanned out and headed toward the closest houses, presumably to start a canvas of who had seen what.

After folding Irma Jean into the back seat of Broussard's cruiser, Rafe stood with his forearms resting on the roof, apparently waiting further instructions.

Broussard approached the man still loitering on his lawn and pulled a small recorder from his pocket, clicked a few buttons and began speaking. The man responded, looking at the recorder as if it might bite, but then appeared to get into his recitation of what he'd seen and heard. A lot of gesturing and pointing. First at me, then at the woman seated in the back of the cruiser, then back at me. He finished with a flourish that looked like a demonstration of Irma Jean flipping over the hood of the car.

Broussard nodded and put his recorder back into his pocket. He handed the man a business card and strode back toward me.

"Follow us back to Central," he ordered. Not waiting for a response, he gestured for Rafe to drive.

"I should ride back with my partner," Rafe objected, squinting at me as if asking a question.

Broussard shrugged and climbed into his cruiser and pulled out. A minute later, Rafe and I followed leaving the patrol deputies to their assigned task.

RAFE OFFERED TO DRIVE and I handed over the keys because the pounding in my head had begun to sound like God and all his angels were lobbing bowling balls.

"What happened before we showed up?" Rafe asked after we'd turned back onto Route 16.

In between the throbbing and the jostle of the moving car, I replayed the action from the time I'd exited my vehicle to the arrival of theirs. Even talking hurt and I had a feeling my tale was a bit disjointed but Rafe didn't interrupt.

When we arrived at Central he climbed out and narrowed his eyes at me again. "You okay?"

"Of course," I responded quickly. Nausea threatened, but I wasn't about to miss the showdown with Irma Jean by admitting I'd smashed my head and might be suffering from a concussion.

Broussard took Irma Jean directly to an interview room, then stopped me outside.

"It's best if you stay out here," Broussard said, clearly an order, not a suggestion. "Rafe filled me in on what went down at the Moretti home. If you think of anything we're missing, text me." Then he stepped into the room and shut the door.

Camped at the observation window, frustration didn't begin to sum up my emotions. This was my case. My collar even. I deserved to be in that room nailing her coffin shut. I zoned out, fuming, as the sergeant went through the routine of repeating the Miranda warning, and then summarizing the facts of the past few days.

Irma Moretti's lower jaw thrust out, her eyes still spitting venom. "I wasn't there when your deputy got shot."

That snagged my attention. Why wasn't Broussard challenging the lie?

Apparently Rafe had the same thought. His brow furrowed, but Broussard held up a warning finger.

"Where were you when your son was holding my deputy hostage at gun point?" Broussard asked.

"I don't know anything about holding a deputy hostage and I don't believe my son would do such a thing."

"Believe what you want. Where were you?"

The woman shrugged and made a face as if the question was

irrelevant.

"So, Gio took it on himself to threaten the life of a law enforcement officer. I'm wondering why he would do that?" Broussard's tone was almost conversational.

"If he did it, he was probably afraid for his life. You cops think you can get away with anything." She spit in Rafe's direction, but he didn't react.

Broussard picked up a different thread. "Why did you feel it necessary to injure an Uber driver and steal his car when he was already taking you to the bus station as you requested?"

Irma Jean's eyes narrowed. "I don't know anything about an Uber driver. I took Vic's SUV to the station."

"Which leaves me with another question." Broussard didn't challenge that lie either. "Why take a bus at all, when you had a car you could have driven to Jacksonville? And why were you going to Jacksonville?"

To get the hell out of St. Johns County was my bet. And put as much distance between herself and our departmental reach as possible while trying to throw us off her trail.

Irma Jean half turned in her chair as if dismissing Broussard's questions.

Rafe snickered. "Maybe she hit her head falling over the cruiser, Sarge. She seems to be having some trouble with her memory."

Broussard paused as if considering this possibility, but then returned to his questions. "Were you planning to skip town to avoid arrest and leave your son to face the music?"

Irma Jean Moretti slammed her cuffed hands on the table. "I think I want that lawyer."

Crap! Broussard had chosen the wrong tack, and now she was lawyering up. The hell with this!

I burst into the room.

"We got him booked, Sarge," I said purposely avoiding eye contact with Irma Jean. "Gio admitted he shot Deputy Oliver."

Irma Jean surged to her feet. "He didn't do it."

Broussard turned back to Irma Jean. "But you weren't there. How would you know?"

"Gio didn't do it," Irma Jean repeated falling back into her chair, shoulders slumping. "I did."

My instinct had been right. Irma would do anything to protect her son even if it meant confessing to assaulting a law enforcement officer. I advanced toward the table and Broussard didn't get in my way.

I crowded her space. "So, what happened at the Hoffman house, Irma Jean? Laney Hoffman give you lip and you couldn't stand it?"

Irma glared back at me, her lips pressed into a thin line.

I ignored the crescendo of cymbals in my head. "You went to warn her to back off your husband and she laughed at you. Am I right? And you just lost it. You grabbed the closest thing and smashed her head in."

Still no response. She had asked for a lawyer. Maybe I should take the confession for shooting Oliver and back off.

Not a chance.

"You were the woman scorned and you couldn't stand it." I tsked loudly.

"She pulled a gun on me," Irma Jean blurted. "It was self-defense."

I pounced. "A dozen times? Knocking her out would have been enough keep her from shooting you, but you didn't stop there. You just kept smashing her over the head even after she was down. You were furious."

"She was a bitch," Irma Jean spat.

Strike one, Irma Jean. On a roll, I continued. "What I don't get is your strategy at the hotel. I mean, why try to make it look like a suicide?"

Irma Jean had just told me how she came into possession of Laney's gun. And it made sense. Vic had come to warn Laney about his supposed conspiracy and told her to watch her back. Laney had retrieved her gun from her father's house, taken it to the range for a little practice and it must have been handy when a foaming, angry, cheated-on wife came calling. But for some reason Laney hadn't pulled the trigger.

Anger for the pain this woman had caused my friend almost choked me. "Dan Hoffman caught you coming out of his house and you had to be sure he couldn't identify you. Am I right?" I leaned in, removing more of her personal space. "Were you thinking suicide would make Dan look guilty of his wife's murder so no one would come looking for you?" That had been Zack's line of thought. And Lawrence Upshaw. They'd both been wrong.

Irma Jean glared, her mouth still firmly shut.

Maybe an attack on her family would get her talking. "And why Victor? He had no idea who killed his lover."

Irma Jean ground her teeth. At least she wasn't demanding that lawyer. And Broussard let me run with this.

"I'm thinking it was you who was having him followed."

The veins in Irma Jean's temples pulsed as she stared me down without answering.

My voice rose a notch. "You suspected he was cheating and decided to catch him at it."

"I knew he was cheating," Irma Jean exploded. "It wasn't just a suspicion. The fucking asshole bled our savings dry and put money on a house with another woman's name on the deed."

Whoa! That was new information. "Laney was a married woman. Married to a very successful and wealthy man. Why would your husband buy her a house?"

"He bought it for some slut he met at the Black Parrot. I found the paperwork in the suitcase the asshole was packing. He was planning to leave. He didn't give a shit about Gio or me or what would happen to us."

I couldn't believe she was laying it all out for us. "How did you know he planned to meet us at the Fountain of Youth on Founders Day?"

"I overhead him talking. I thought he was planning to meet that woman there." Irma Jean slit her eyes at me. "If I could have gotten off two shots, you'd be dead too. I thought you were the slut he was shacking up with. You've got red hair and you're about the right size."

She planted her face in her cuffed hands and shuddered. "I shoulda shot you when I had the chance."

Perhaps Rafe's sudden appearance around the end of that boat had given her pause, just long enough to hold that second shot. I'd probably never know.

I turned to Broussard. "That's all on tape, right, Sargent?"

He nodded, then spoke to Rafe. "Call a deputy to take her over to processing and call the public defender's office. Unless—" He looked down at a totally deflated Irma Jean. "Unless you have an attorney you'd rather we call?

She shook her head. "Like I can afford a lawyer. That no-good, two-timing jerk spent all my money."

Rafe went to the door and disappeared for a moment, then returned with a female deputy who put a hand under Irma Jean's elbow and urged her to her feet. She guided Irma Jean to the door and out.

Broussard sighed and turned to me. "Well, Quinn. I think you might have bought yourself a little wiggle room with Ward. In spite of everything, you managed pull a confession to two murders, and two attempts. One on an officer of the law. Plus the missing motive. Good work."

Memory of the frightened face of Irma Jean's son reminded me there were other victims in this sorry mess. "What happens to Gio?" Sure the kid had held a gun to Rafe's head, but Gio had thought he was protecting his mother. I doubted Mike would have gone that far, but he had come to my defense against his father and my mother, both formidable forces, more than once.

Broussard looked down at his hands and winced. "It's sad. He'll have to pay for it, but maybe, considering the circumstances we can make it as light as possible. I'll talk to the DA, but Morgan had the gun to his head. A man doesn't forgive that too easily."

I turned to Rafe, trying to focus on his face to get a read. The room spun and I reached for the doorjamb as the cymbals resumed their crashing assault inside my head.

"Quinn?" Broussard grabbed my elbow. "Are you okay?"

"I—"

"Quinn," he said again, his voice a zillion miles away and fading.

CHAPTER 27

THE ROOM NARROWED TO A TUNNEL focused on a light switch by the door. I struggled against a wave of dizziness, struggled to stay with the conversation.

Sergeant Broussard and my partner were talking like I wasn't in the room. Hey, guys. I'm right here. You can talk to me. At least that's what I wanted to say, but for some reason my tongue wouldn't cooperate.

"I think she might have a concussion," Rafe's voice sounded even more distant than Broussard's.

"A concussion?" Broussard's tone sharpened.

"She smacked her head on a cement driveway in the scuffle with Moretti," Rafe explained.

"Christ! Why didn't you say something when the EMTs were on the scene?" Apparently, this outburst was aimed at Rafe, but a moment later, Broussard pushed me into a chair and squatted in front of me. "You need to get checked out, Quinn." He pulled a tiny flashlight from his pocket and waved it in my eyes.

My eyes slammed shut at the stabbing pain.

"You should have told me," Broussard said, removing the light.

I had other things on my mind at the time.

Broussard stood. "She needs to see a doctor."

I finally managed to get my mouth working. "I'm not leaving here in an ambulance,"

Rafe put a hand on my shoulder. "I'll take her over to Flagler to get checked out if you can finish up the paperwork, Sarge."

He let go of my shoulder to fish my phone out of my pocket and hand it to Broussard. "She recorded stuff out at the house. And if anyone asks, I'm not pressing charges against the kid."

Broussard dropped my phone into his pocket. "No one's asking, Morgan. But I'll see what I can do about getting him released. Just don't know into whose care."

"I'm fine," I insisted trying to get to my feet.

Broussard shook a finger at me. "You are not fine, Quinn. Let your partner help you out for once."

Clearly, I was not going to win this argument. At least I wouldn't be leaving the sheriff's office in the back of an ambulance. With my luck Scotty Parker would have chased it, hoping for a sensational feature for the evening news.

Once outside, Rafe aimed me toward his cruiser with one hand clamped on my elbow as if he feared I'd make a break for it. "Why did you have to mention concussion?" I said.

He opened the passenger door. "Because you aren't fine. You just don't know when to quit." He placed a hand on top of my head like he would a detainee and guided me into the seat. "Buckle up, Buttercup."

"It's just a little knock on the head," I muttered as he climbed in and buckled his own seatbelt. I reached up to explore the back of my head and winced as my fingers came in contact with a lump the size of a golf ball. "Holy crap!"

Rafe grinned and started the car.

He enjoyed this far too much. I'm the senior officer, but for once, he was calling the shots. I decided to let him have his moment in the sun and sank back into the seat, careful to turn my head so that golf ball didn't come into contact with the headrest.

The waiting room in the Flagler ER was busy as usual, and I

refused to be taken out of order just because I was a deputy. I told Rafe he could take off, but he ignored my offer and distracted me with amusing stories about his mother's dachshunds as if he had nowhere else to be and all the time in the world to get there. Finally, an aide called me to go in for a cat scan.

Rafe crossed one ankle across his other knee, gave me a thumbs up and began flipping through a month-old issue of People.

"I can get an Uber home," I told him. "If I really do have a concussion, they'll keep me for a while."

He lifted one shoulder and gave me a half smile. "I'm good."

Oh, my God! My kids! For the first time in hours, their existence popped into my reeling brain. They have no idea where I am, and I can't call them because Broussard still had my phone. "Do me a favor?"

He tossed the magazine aside. "Sure thing,"

The aide tapped his foot.

"Call Mike. Don't tell him I'm in the ER. Just . . . just tell him to order pizza or something and I'll call when I can."

"Stop stressing. I'll call." Then he nodded toward the aide. "You gotta go." He pulled his cell from its holster and held it until I turned to follow the aide through the doors and down the hall.

THE VERDICT WAS A MILD CONCUSSION. The golf ball was more alarming than the actual damage to my skull. Good to know, but brushing my hair would be touchy for a week or two. They handed me a tablet to tame the pain. I didn't ask what it was, just tossed it back with a gulp of water, eager to get out of there and get home before my kids started freaking out.

After signing enough documents to fill a whole file drawer, I was free to leave. Under my own power, thank you very much. I refused to get into the wheelchair a young man in blue scrubs offered. The pill was already doing its job. Now to find Rafe and get out of here.

But Rafe wasn't where I'd left him. In his place, Seth Cameron sat, in almost the same pose I'd left Rafe in except his eyes were on the television.

"Rafe called, I see," I said as I approached.

Seth leaped to his feet. "You okay?" He peered at me, his eyes wide and worried.

His concern warmed me in spite of my determination to make light of my injury. "I will be. In a day or twelve." Instead of the intense pain I'd come in with, the exhaustion of five long days and very short nights had caught up with me. "I'm just . . . tired," I admitted.

"How's the head?" He started to reach out but stopped. "Not as bad as Rafe portrayed it, I hope."

Seth offered his arm as if preparing a grand entrance on a red carpet. "I didn't tell Mike or Jacqui anything except that you needed a ride home and made sure they were settled with supper and homework."

Truth be told, the pill made me happy for the support. I tucked my hand into his elbow. "Thanks for coming. And for not worrying my kids."

As he helped me up into the cab of his truck, I realized I'd never ridden in it before. Big compared to my Rav 4 and surprisingly luxurious. As he settled into his own seat, a frown of concern still coloring his face, my insides warmed. What would it be like to give in to the comfort and attention this man offered on an every-day basis?

A WEEK BEFORE ELECTION DAY, I stood at attention in front of Lieutenant Ward's desk.

He leaned back in his chair. "What have you got to say for yourself?"

I didn't argue. No point, since I'd done everything he'd outlined. Disobeyed orders twice. Once when I could have sent someone else to watch Rafe and Zack's backs. Once by chance when I spied our suspect boarding a bus with Broussard and Rafe too far away to catch her.

"At least we caught the right person," I said.

Apparently, Ward was never made aware that Broussard had ordered me to stay outside the interview room. He also didn't know about my charging in with the lie about Gio when the interview started falling apart and Irma Jean was ready to lawyer up.

Ward tipped back even further. "That's all that's saving you from a suspension. But you will get a rip in your file and spend the next two weeks delving into that stack of cold case files."

"Thank you, sir. I—"

"Dismissed."

I backed out of his office before he could change his mind.

I felt fully recovered and ready to be back on the road, but those files awaited me. It was good to be back to work and away from my son's hovering.

Mike had woken me every hour that first night, and continued to hover for the days I remained at home. Maybe I should count my blessings that the following days were school days and I was allowed to fend for myself with only Murphy and the cat to disturb my peace for at least part of the time.

Even Seth had left me to my lone recovery, only calling during the day while Mike was in school to check on me. I hadn't seen him since he picked me up at the hospital and truth be told, I felt a little let down by that.

I opened the first file, but my mind wandered back to Irma Jean, being held without bail and even the sleaziest lawyer unlikely to get her off with anything less than life. Gio, thanks to Rafe's intervention had been released into his grandmother's care. He'd landed in a diversion program with probation and community service. Glen Rhodes had recovered and the disgruntled voter who'd run him off the road languished in jail awaiting trial on manslaughter charges. Even Zack Oliver was back to work on a limited basis, and back to being a snot. All was right with my world. For now.

Rafe snickered, pulling my mind back to the here and now. I turned as Seth Cameron strode into the room.

He set a vase of flowers on the corner of my desk. "Happy Anniversary."

I gaped him, then shut my mouth. What anniversary did I share with Seth?

I leaned over to sniff the tasteful arrangement of calla lilies and blue hydrangia. How had he known these were my favorites?

My heart rate picked up at the unknown. "What anniversary are we celebrating?"

He pressed a hand to his heart. "I'm crushed." Then he slid into a chair and leaned closer. "It's the anniversary of the day my life changed forever." He grinned. That charming grin that caused his dimples to show and my heart to race.

I tried to remember some eventful day a year earlier. But I hadn't even known him a year ago.

Seth's grin faded.

Then I remembered. Six months ago, maybe six months

ago today, this man had walked into my life, sent by the school principle as part of the agreement I'd made to get my son's grades up before the end of the school year so he could stay with his peers and not repeat his sophomore year of high school.

After years of acting out after his father abandoned us all for a much younger woman, Mike had fallen to the bottom of his class. But this man had not only refocused Mike's attention, he'd become a mentor and friend. And he'd begun his pursuit of me.

I swallowed the lump forming in my throat. "You worked wonders with Mike, but I hardly see how that changed your life all that much. You have hundreds of students and two boys of your own." I focused on anything but the relationship Seth was trying to establish with me. My racing heart didn't get the memo.

"I thought we'd celebrate by going out to dinner tonight," Seth refused to be side-tracked. His dark eyes sparkled with humor and something a whole lot more exciting.

He reached out and covered my hand with his. The humor and sparkle disappeared. "I waited until I wasn't Mike's tutor since that seemed to be a sticking point for you. I'd like a chance to prove I could be something good in your life, too." He hesitated then added, "Please?"

Something in my gut stirred with undefined need. Not sexual, although that sure stirred in me, too. His earnestness reached me. Like he needed something, too. Something I didn't even know I had to offer.

I glanced down at our hands, his still covering mine, big and warm and inviting.

Before I could pull my hand away, he lifted it to his lips and placed a kiss on my knuckles. "Please?" He repeated.

"Okay." My voice sounded breathless. I felt breathless.

His smile returned. "Wear something . . . special."

Then he let go and planted a kiss on my unsuspecting lips before turning and walking away, high-fiving Rafe on his way out.

My lips still tingling, I watched him disappear.

Rafe snickered again.

I turned a suspicious eye toward Rafe. "Were you in on this?"

He raised his brows. Like butter wouldn't melt in his mouth.

"Did you tell him I liked calla lilies?"

Now he really did look innocent. "How would I know what kind of flowers you like?"

Mike? No way. He didn't know one kind of flower from another. I sniffed the arrangement again, the puzzle not solved.

"It's about time you gave that man a little encouragement and stopped playing hard to get," Rafe said scooping up a new file.

"I wasn't playing hard to get. I wasn't playing anything," I protested. "I just wasn't . . . ready." I buried my face in the flowers as heat flooded into my cheeks.

"And now?" The unusual softness in Rafe's voice brought my head up again. "You deserve a good man in your life, Jess. Don't let him get away."

A dress hanging in the back of my closet, one I'd never worn and had been saving for something special came to mind. Maybe it had been waiting for someone special.

If you enjoyed this book, consider leaving a review on Amazon,
B&N, or Goodreads.

Acknowledgements

Striking out into an entirely new genre was made possible by so many helpful people. I couldn't have done it without you.

There were two wonderful deputies with my local sheriff's department who allowed me to go for a ride-along. Thanks to Tony Clark and Nicole Burrell and her K-9 Ryker, for taking responsibility for my safety and showing me what a patrol officer's job is really like. Thanks also to the entire staff of The Citizens Law Enforcement Academy who shared their knowledge and experiences in classes covering all aspects of police work, including a few four-footed deputies. And a very special thanks to Detective Samantha English of the St. John's County Major Crimes Squad, who's been there at the other end of every text I sent with questions that came up while I was working on this book.

I also owe a huge debt of gratitude to C. Hope Clark, author of two very successful mystery series who helped me make that leap from romance to mystery with constructive and time-consuming critique. Thanks also to my Sandy Scribbler buddies for your ongoing encouragement, and excellent brainstorming sessions.

The history of the bullseye:

For those of my readers who are curious about the murder weapon featured on the cover. Sometimes called the bullseye, this heavy glass prism was originally the last bit of glass left over when windows were spun by hand in the 18th and 19th centuries. Some enterprising soul realized that the unique shape and material could be set into the decks of ships to allow light to penetrate to the lower decks, not just in a straight column as a flat piece of glass would allow, but refracted by the prism's shape to spread out into the far corners. This was before the age of electricity and all lighting would have been candles and lanterns, all a serious hazard on a ship built of wood. Today, replicas can be found in maritime museum gift shops. Dan Hoffman had just such a replica used as a paperweight on his desk within easy reach of our angry villain.

Skye Taylor, mother, grandmother and returned Peace Corps Volunteer, loves adventure and lives in St Augustine Florida where she enjoys the history of America's oldest city and walking on its beautiful beaches. She posts a sometimes weekly blog and sends out a monthly newsletter, volunteers with the USO, and is currently working the next book in this series. Her published work includes: Bullseye, The Candidate, Falling for Zoe, Loving Meg, Trusting Will, Healing a Hero, Keeping His Promise, Worry Stone and Iain's Plaid. Visit her website: www. Skye-writer.com to read her short stories and essays about her time spent in the South Pacific with the Peace Corps. She is a member of Sisters in Crime, Florida Writer's Association, and Women's Fiction Writer's Association. She loves hearing from her readers at Skye@Skye-writer.com

www.ingramcontent.com/pod-product-compliance
Lightning Source LLC
Chambersburg PA
CBHW050859130726
47900CB00013B/429